BIG CITY KISSING

"Anyone special in your life?" she asked.

"No. No one at all."

This time, he really did lean toward her, just a little, and he was not smiling. He was concentrating on her face, examining her eyes, her hair, her mouth.

A confusion of feelings was slithering all through her. She took another bite of her hot dog.

He was closer.

"You know I want to kiss you, don't you?" he said.

"I'm all garlicky."

"So am I."

"You look so serious," she said.

"You have the prettiest hair." His eyes were locked on hers. His finger lifted a strand away from her forehead. "It's the color of butterscotch."

"That sounds sticky."

"I know. But still . . ."

. . . and closer . . .

And then he did kiss her.

And she closed her eyes.

And it was the motorcycle ride all over again . . .

Books by J. M. Bronston

A PURRFECT ROMANCE

HER WINNING WAYS

Published by Kensington Publishing Corporation

Her Winning Ways

J. M. Bronston

LYRICAL SHINE
Kensington Publishing Corp.
www.kensingtonbooks.com

LYRICAL SHINE BOOKS are published by

Kensington Publishing Corp.
119 West 40th Street
New York, NY 10018

All Kensington titles, imprints, and distributed lines are available at special quantity discounts for bulk purchases for sales promotion, premiums, fund-raising, educational, or institutional use.

Special book excerpts or customized printings can also be created to fit specific needs. For details, write or phone the office of the Kensington Sales Manager: Kensington Publishing Corp., 119 West 40th Street, New York, NY 10018. Attn. Sales Department. Phone: 1-800-221-2647.

Lyrical Shine and the Lyrical Shine logo are trademarks of Kensington Publishing Corp.

First Electronic Edition: December 2015
eISBN-13: 978-1-60183-267-2
eISBN-10: 1-60183-267-2

First Print Edition: December 2015
ISBN-13: 978-1-60183-268-9
ISBN-10: 1-60183-268-0

Printed in the United States of America

For Annie, Mary, and Margaret

Prologue

Marge Webster pushed the stack marked "short-listed" to one side and removed the top packet from the pile. She looked around the conference table for confirmation and got a nod from each of her editors.

"So we're agreed," she said. "We're going with this one."

Matt Gerson, from the legal department, made an entry on the laptop in front of him and said, "I liked her essay. Simple, to the point, honest. Very appealing."

The features editor, Dinah Featherington, agreed. "Girl from Wyoming, grew up on a ranch—it'll make a great story."

And the beauty editor, Annelie Magano, added, "And good-looking, too. We shouldn't gussie her up too much. Feature the simple, western angle."

"Yes, she is good-looking." Marge picked up the photo in front of her, adjusted her glasses, and studied the picture one last time. "Naturally good-looking. She has a nice open face. Kind of childlike, like she's just waiting for something good to happen. Almost angelic, with those big hazel eyes and the long blond hair. And a nice figure, too. Not too skinny. I like her. Good choice, everyone." She put the papers together and handed them to her assistant, Jerry, who was standing behind her. "Okay, then. That's it. We're done here. Thank you, everyone."

The life of an editor-in-chief is high energy and no wasted time. Marge Webster always had other places to be, other decisions to make, other fires to put out. And now she was up and out the door, on to other meetings, in a swirl of pale silk, feathery soft wool, and a subtle Cartier perfume. The door closed behind her.

There was silence for about four seconds.

And then there was a general pushing back of chairs, a gathering up of notes and paper coffee cups, the checking of iPhones and BlackBerries—and a flurry of sociable commentary on the results of the meeting.

Eugenie Shaw, assistant to the features editor, walked out with Annelie Magano. "I saw in her bio, her mom's maiden name was Annemarie Wikstrom. She's from the original Swedish settlers in the area." Eugenie held the door as Annelie went through. "I'll bet that hair is naturally blond," she said.

"I noticed that. We may want to leave it untouched."

And right behind them, Helen Fiore, marketing director, said to Dinah Featherington, "I love that she lives on a cattle ranch—and that she won rodeo medals in high school. With that face and that background, she's such an interesting combination. It will make a great feature. So very American."

"Yes, it will play well with our European readers," added Sylvie Pilard, the Paris editor. "And the Galliard people have approved, too."

Chapter One

Surprise!

Liz's shriek came through the phone, loud as the sudden squeal of a new-branded calf. Startled students looked up from their books.

"Annie! Omigod, Annie! You won it! You won it! They picked you!"

"Stop yelling at me, Liz." Annie spoke sharply into her phone. "This is a *library*, you know." She pointed at the "Quiet, Please" sign on her desk, as though her sister, ten miles away, could see it. "What are you talking about?"

"The contest!" Liz's voice remained at top volume, her excitement spilling out uncontrollably. "Don't you remember?"

"Liz, please. People can hear you." Annie covered the phone with her hand and dropped her voice to a whisper, as though that would tone Liz down a few decibels. "No, I don't remember. What are you talking about? What contest?"

"That new department store! In New York City! Galliard's! Remember?"

"In some magazine, wasn't it?" Annie said. Slowly, it was coming back to her. "Way back in February?"

"Yes! Yes! In *Lady Fair*!"

Dimly, Annie recalled a night many weeks ago. The winds had been blowing hard across the valley, pushing the snow up in big drifts around the house. The dinner dishes had been cleared away, the kids had been put down for the night, and Liz's husband, Craig, had gone out to check on a sick calf. She'd been busy filling out registrations for the ranch's new quarter horses, and Liz, killing a few idle minutes by leafing through *Lady Fair*, had found the announcement of the contest. Just for fun, they'd each filled out an entry.

Now, digging through all the masses of data in her memory bank, what Annie really remembered about that night was not the essay she'd written or the prize that was offered. What she remembered was her fantasy of a glitzy, nighttime New York City transplanted out onto Wyoming's open spaces—the bright, edgy, big-city lights sparkling like fireworks up against the silent, star-filled sky that arched above the family's ranch. And a fancy French department store set incongruously on their wind-swept, mountain-rimmed, high plateau country. It had been an amusing fantasy.

That's the part she remembered.

"Galliard's?" she repeated, trying to focus her attention. "Was that the name of the store?"

"That's the one! That's the one!" Liz was still screeching, and the annoyed students were shifting in their seats, registering their irritation. "Listen. I'll read it to you." She took a deep breath and, as calmly as she could, read into the phone:

Dear Ms. Cornell,

On behalf of Lady Fair and the Sweeps-Spree Selection Committee of Galliard International, I am pleased to inform you that your entry has been selected as the first-place winner in Galliard's Jubilee Contest celebrating the grand opening of an exciting new store on New York's fabulous Fifth Avenue.

Liz paused. She was fanning herself with the letter. "Omigod, Annie. I can't believe this. Listen to what you get." She went on, reading out bits of the letter:

"'... a fifty-thousand dollar shopping spree ... five days ... all expenses paid ... for two. ...' For *two*, Annie!" she interrupted herself. "And there's more—'red carpet press coverage ... national celebrities and local dignitaries ... the mayor of the City of New York—'"

She broke off her reading.

"Five days, all expenses paid! For two! For *two*, Annie! That means I get to go, too, doesn't it? You wouldn't dare take anyone else, would you? Omigod, fifty thousand dollars! Oh, say I can go with you. Aunt Velma will take care of the kids, I know she will. And

Craig won't mind. He wouldn't *dare* mind. He can do without me for a few days. Oh, just think, Annie. Bags. And shoes. And Hermès scarves. I've never been to New York. *You've* never been to New York. It's like a dream."

Liz's chatter bubbled past Annie who by now had collapsed dumbly into the chair at her desk. All thoughts of student research papers, grant proposals, and new library acquisitions vanished from her thoughts.

Bags? Shoes? Scarves? And New York City?

Her large hazel eyes stared blankly out through the big library windows, over the bent heads of the students working at the library tables, past the trees that were in their full springtime bloom all over the campus, and beyond to the mountains, their peaks draped with the shining remains of winter's snow. In times of confusion, she always looked to the quiet majesty of those mountains to anchor her.

"Oh, yes, Liz. Wonderful clothes. I can't even imagine—"

New York City. Fifty thousand dollars. Celebrities. At last. An adventure!

"Annie? Are you there?"

New York City!

Annie breathed the magic words to herself.

Since I was a kid, wishing for a real adventure. Something I could tell my children about.

"Annie? Annie? Are you there?"

Liz—always at me to settle down, pick someone, for goodness' sake, have kids, make a home.

But I want to have an adventure first—with maybe just a little danger mixed in—she smiled to herself as she added a romantic twist to her fantasy—*and maybe there'll be someone tall and cute who'll ride to my rescue—and he'll sweep me off my feet —and —and then —*

She brought herself quickly back to the real world.

"Oh, yes, Liz. I'm here. And yes, we really are going to New York. You and me."

Chapter Two

Welcome?

Sunday

The plane banked left, and the island of Manhattan swam into view thousands of feet below. The throbbing vibration of the big jet engines matched the excited *thump-thump* of Annie's heart as the plane made its descent. She turned and poked at her sister, sound asleep next to her.

"Honestly, Liz. How can you sleep at a time like this?"

"Huh?" Liz looked around blearily, blinking, straightening up in her seat. "Where are we?"

"New York, Liz! It's New York! We'll be landing soon."

"I'm completely fuzzy." Liz dragged a hand through her hair.

"It must be the Dramamine you took. You conked out somewhere over Kansas. I haven't seen you sleep like that since we were kids. Your mouth was open."

"Well, thanks a bunch." Liz made a face at her little sister. She rummaged around in her bag, looking for a comb and a lipstick. "You could have poked me or something. Anyway, I wasn't really asleep."

"I did poke you. You were snoring."

"I was not. And so what if I was. Better that than being awake and scared. Thirty thousand feet up in the sky makes no sense to me. I prefer ground beneath my feet, like on the ranch." She'd found her mirror and was checking the damage. "Omigod! I look a mess!"

"No you don't. You look fine. Just fine. No one in New York will ever know you're an old lady of thirty-three with two kids, good

Wyoming dirt under your fingernails, and a couple of hundred head of cattle waiting for you to get back home."

"There ain't no dirt under *my* nails, ma'am." Liz put on a heavy cowhand drawl, holding up a perfectly serviceable hand in front of her sister's face. "And anyway, no one's going to be looking at me. You're the star of this trip and all the cameras will be on you. And what they'll see is the luckiest college librarian in all Wyoming. No," she corrected herself, "in the whole world." Liz finished repairing her makeup and dropped her lipstick into her bag. "And the giddiest. I swear, Annie, you've been revved up like a cowboy on Friday night. It's a good thing I came along. You're going to need someone to keep an eye on you, see you don't get into trouble."

Annie didn't answer her sister. She just turned her head back to the window, rested her forehead against the small glass panel and silently watched the buildings below grow bigger and the cars and taxis and trucks get closer as the plane descended over a dizzying network of highways. Soon the ground was rushing up at them. They'd be touching down in a moment and Liz's words were echoing in her head.

... see you don't get into trouble ...

There was a skiddy sort of screechy bump and then a head-filling, chest-whumping roar as the plane's brakes took hold and brought the big jet to a deafening stop. The flight attendant's voice told them to remain seated until they reached the gate. Passengers pulled out their cell phones, business as usual being quickly resumed. Annie was impatient to unbuckle her seat belt, so eager to get going.

Maybe just a little trouble? Not too much. Just enough to be interesting. Something that would make people fuss over me. Reporters interviewing me. My face on television.

Sailing along again, on the flow of her daydreams.

Lady Fair's rep was waiting for them at the baggage carousel. She was an astonishingly young woman and New York chic in stiletto pumps and slim skirt, with a clipboard clutched to her bosom. Her brown-and-ash-streaked hair was caught up in an untidy twist at the back of her head, from which flyaway strands escaped engagingly, and the scent of something expensive floated around her. Young as she was, she already had a well-practiced smile and a crackling enthusiasm.

"I'm Soraya Abbandando-Steinberg," she said. "I'm here to welcome you on behalf of *Lady Fair* and Galliard's International. Call me Mitzi." She waved a busy hand at them as though it held a magic wand. "*Love* your outfit."

Annie glanced down at her jeans and leather jacket.

My outfit?

Just ordinary clothes, comfortable for traveling. The soft leather jacket, made from the hide of a deer her grandpa shot years ago. And her everyday boots and jeans and the big silver buckle—her good luck buckle—that she'd won in high school in a local barrel race. How had they been suddenly promoted to an "outfit"?

But Mitzi was rushing on at warp speed before Annie could get out a word.

"We're just so terrifically thrilled to welcome you to New York." Mitzi gathered them up as though they were runaway chicks. "All of us at *Lady Fair*. Good flight, I hope. Weather's been terrific, thank God. New York's so great this time of the year. I have a car waiting for you outside. Give me your claim tickets." She gestured at an assistant hovering a few steps behind her. "Lester will pick up your baggage for you." And she was off in a rush toward the exit, with the two sisters hopping to keep up with her.

The terminal doors opened for them and they were out into an alarming crush of traffic that twisted with what seemed to be a hair-raising, split-second timing through a tangle of roadways. Liz was still groggy from the Dramamine and bewildered by the racket around her. But Annie instantly fell in love with the dizzying frenzy. It was everything she wanted it to be. It took her breath away. More cabs than she'd ever imagined, they performed an urban gavotte as passengers peeled off into the arriving stream, drivers hauled suitcases into the cabs' trunks, and away they went, replaced immediately by the next arriving cab, the next waiting passenger. The mass of cars and buses and vans and sleek black town cars, the skycaps wheeling carts of luggage, the blur of multihued, multinational images, the unimaginable variety of costumes and languages, the noise and flash and international variety—like countless others newly arrived in the big city, Annie felt a rush of energy, an intense focus of her attention, a delicious sense of her whole system shifting up into a new gear.

Her adventure was on its way!

* * *

At the hotel, Mitzi breezed ahead of them through the living room of their suite, being sure they noted the courtesy bucket of Champagne, the iced dish of caviar, the flowers, the enormous cellophane-wrapped basket of fruit (all provided by *Lady Fair*, of course), the view from the tall windows, the East River sparkling up at them from forty-four floors below. She showed them the two bedrooms, one for Annie and one for Liz, and next to each bed, a silver plate of chocolates. On Annie's pillow were a congratulatory greeting from the hotel management next to a *Lady Fair* packet of papers, welcoming the prize-winner to New York and laying out her schedule, beginning with a reception that very evening at The Green Parrot, a meeting with *Lady Fair* staff in the morning, to be followed by makeup and hair and photos. On Tuesday the ribbon-cutting ceremony, and then—and then!—the actual sweep through the store to gather up fashion goodies worth $50,000! With *Lady Fair* staffers to follow her everywhere to record everything and TV cameras to bring it all to local viewers, followed by three days of events, including a tour of the city, an evening at the theater—and even some time for them to explore on their own.

But Annie could hardly pay attention as Mitzi explained the details.

How could she? Exciting noises were coming up from the street, forty-four floors below, construction noises—jack-hammers clattering—and an impatient blare of horns honking at a stalled car, the siren of an emergency vehicle wailing down a nearby avenue as it crawled helplessly through the jammed-up traffic, the heavy-duty engines of buses and trucks, growling loudly through their gears as they started and stopped and started again. It seemed to Annie like an urban symphony, orchestrated just for her, a melody as natural to this place as were the familiar cricket sounds of her Wyoming nighttimes.

It was hard to be patient with Mitzi's high-energy chatter when all of New York was waiting for her.

Fortunately, Mitzi had arrived at the end of her spiel.

"So that's it, ladies," she said as she made some check marks on her clipboard and put her BlackBerry away. "The reception tonight is at five thirty so I'll have the car service here at five. And I'm back again in the morning at nine fifteen to take you to *Lady Fair*." She was already on her way to the door. "See you gals tonight. Till then, take a rest. Room service will bring you whatever you want. Call me if you have any problems. Have fun. Ciao!"

She placed her card on the table near the door and, with another airy wave of her hand, she was gone.

"Will you look at this place?" Annie was doing a quick tour, room to room. "I think they've given us the royal suite."

"Talk about royal. Come in here, Annie. You have to see this bathroom."

The word "bathroom" was too mundane for the peach-and-cream fantasy of baroque opulence in which Annie joined her sister. Imagine a bathroom with a full-sized gas log fireplace! Imagine filmy pale curtains drawn back to reveal a marble tub set flush into the floor, with a broad ledge all around on which a full supply of bath accessories, lotions, soaps, salts, and creams were arrayed. Imagine a small side table holding a cut crystal vase containing a bouquet of fresh hothouse flowers, and above the room's center a chandelier of brass and crystal with teardrop prisms and bulbs designed to flicker like candlelight. A long counter with two basins set into it ran the length of one wall, and mounted on the wall's length was an enormous mirror framed in ornate gilt and rosewood.

Annie stood behind her sister, and together, wide-eyed and silent, they looked back at their reflections in the beautiful mirror. Two young women, recognizably related, both with fine, naturally blond hair, past shoulder length and worn always in simple styles—today, loose and center parted—and bright hazel eyes (Annie's a little larger, with darker lashes and set a trifle deeper), and healthy complexions (Liz's a shade more tan, the result of ranch work outdoors each day). But Liz, who was older by seven years, was noticeably more mature, for marriage and motherhood had made their changes.

Annie, on the other hand, had about her a gloss of young innocence, a simple eagerness for life to unfold its special demands, its twists and its surprises. There was something almost angelic about Annie's face, something so open and sweet and straightforward that a stranger would be surprised to discover what those close to her all knew: Annie Cornell had the strong backbone of her pioneer ancestors. She could be stubborn as a mule once she'd set a course, and there'd be no use trying to make her change. But her stubbornness combined with a strong intelligence, and together these two had worked well for her—together with an unreasonable amount of good luck. Her reflection in the mirror smiled at her. It was the good luck that had brought her to this once-in-a-lifetime fantasy. It was certainly her intelligence that told her how very lucky she was. And she would rely on her stubbornness to not let anything spoil a moment of this great adventure.

She felt bubbly, as though she'd been filled with soda pop, as though the whole wide world was just waiting for her to explore its delights, and nothing in the whole wide world could possibly go wrong.

"And look at my hair," she said. She fluffed at it happily. "It must be the humidity. "Sudden body! It's wonderful. Oh, I just *love* New York. I can't wait to get outside."

"Not me," Liz said. "I'm really tired. I just want to take a long, relaxing bath in that fabulous tub, with all these mirrors and the bubble lotion. Watch a little TV. Maybe take a nap."

"Good idea," Annie said. She went into her bedroom. "In the meantime, I'm going to change out of these clothes and go take a little walk. I want to see the neighborhood." She'd already shed the jacket and was unbuckling her belt.

"Don't you go getting yourself into any trouble," Liz called to her. "You *hear* me, Annie!"

"You're being bossy again, big sister." Annie pulled off her boots, stepped out of her jeans and tossed her shirt onto the bed.

"Well, someone has to keep an eye on you. The city can be dangerous, and you're a stranger here."

"Oh, I'll be fine." She pulled a little sundress out of her suitcase and slipped it on. "It's broad daylight, I won't go far, and I didn't come all this way just to sit in a hotel room." She stepped into her sandals, grabbed her bag, and headed down the carpeted hallway. "What could happen in the middle of the afternoon? Honestly, Liz!"

Liz called after her. "You just be careful, Annie. I mean it. I don't want you getting into any trouble. Are you *listening* to me?"

"Sure. Sure," Annie murmured as she rang for the elevator. "I won't get into any trouble."

As she dropped breathlessly down forty-four floors, she checked out her reflection in the mirrored wall of the elevator and smiled approvingly. She flipped her fingers through her hair and decided that New York was already being kind to her. Nothing bad could happen to her here.

She adjusted the strap of the white straw bag on her shoulder.

But remember to hang on to your bag.

There had been warnings galore from all her Wyoming well-wishers about the dangers of the city streets.

Keep your eyes open, they'd said. *But don't make eye contact with anyone. Remember, anything left untended is a donation to the public. Be careful of the traffic. If anyone tries to steal your money, let them.*

She laughed at all the warnings, made one last quick inspection in the mirror and gave an approving nod to the summery look of her cotton dress. Even her hair—usually a palest shade of blond—had turned platinum under the elevator's bright, overhead lighting. She liked how she looked.

The elevator arrived at the lobby floor. She winked brightly at her reflection and stepped out. In a moment, she had crossed the busy lobby and was out on the street.

Like any good tourist, Annie's gaze was turned upward as she walked through the tall canyons of glass and steel skyscrapers that glinted in the afternoon sun. With one hand shading her eyes against the glare, her attention was focused skyward. Maybe that's why she didn't notice what was happening right around her until she turned a corner and someone tromped on her sandaled foot—*hard!*

"Hey! Watch it!" she yelped. "That's my foot!"

She was hopping about, rubbing the offended toe while glaring at the back of a big, lumbering fellow who had pushed her out of his way. But he'd already hurried on to join a crowd that was forming down the street. Even as she stood there, awkwardly poised on one foot, she was bumped again and she practically fell on her face. Her attention came down quickly from the skies above and focused on the events around her.

"What's going on?" she asked aloud.

She got no answer. No one was listening to her. She'd been overtaken by a throng of noisy, hurrying men, all chattering and gesticulating. They streamed around her, sweeping her along in their momentum. They were all dressed alike, in plain dark pants and white shirts, open collars, the sleeves rolled up. And each man wore an unusual cap made of some stiff black fabric, embroidered in a complex design of bright colors, and adorned on the right side with a kind of cockade made of small red-and-white feathers. In the midst of the confusion, Annie caught sight of the crudely hand-lettered banners and signs they carried. "Independence Now For Buljornia!" and "Free Buljornia Now!"

Buljornia? The name was new to her. What—or who—was Buljornia?

Even as she struggled to place the name, she was being carried down the broad avenue by the obstreperous crowd. Like a leaf twisting in the flow of a mountain stream, she was caught in the current that swirled her about in tiny eddies of excited, noisy demonstrators. Every now and then they would give her a momentary spin before dragging her farther along their course.

"You big gorillas! Watch out!"

That did her no good. The growing mob pushed and pulled her, and she was struggling—while dutifully remembering that she was supposed to hang on to her handbag and avoid making eye contact—to stay upright on her own feet. In a growing confusion, she was swept across Forty-fifth Street, past the United Nations building and its long array of national flags flying in the breeze. She caught a glimpse at the corner of a small booth marked "Police," and just beyond, the United States Mission to the United Nations. A miniature park, bright with fenced-off patches of greenery and flowers nestled up against a tall, ivy-covered wall and at its center, a tall monument rose up. It was in this tiny bit of green that the crowd was gathering, clumping together into a tight mass. The men filled the little park and climbed around the monument, exhorting the world to free Buljornia, and holding their banners high for the benefit of the television trucks that were positioned nearby to cover the event for the local evening news.

Emotion was boiling up in the dense little crowd and panic was beginning to shiver up Annie's spine; she could feel the chill down her arms. Her pulse was racing, she was confused, and she was hanging on to that handbag as though it were her only link back to a familiar world.

I'm all turned around!

Her disorientation was intensified by the growing hysteria of the demonstrators and the increasing menace in their tone.

I've got to get out of here.

Men were spilling out around the edges of the park, and Annie was an island in the center of a bubbling mass of waving arms and clenched fists.

I have to get out of here! Now!

She looked frantically up the broad avenue, desperate for a safe way out. The city traffic continued to fly by as though nothing unusual were happening, and there were no openings between the stream of cars and taxis to let her slip through. Burly men pressed up against her, their chests and shoulders shoved at her, their fists thrust beyond her at the cameras, as they kept shouting their steady chant.

"Freedom for Buljornia!"

The crowd surged out into the street, carrying her along in its shoving, yelling mass. A fat face, glistening with sweat and excitement, breathed unfamiliar spices at her.

"Free Buljornia now!"

Their tone was growing more fierce. This was definitely not the adventure she wanted.

Suddenly, behind her, a single voice resounded over the heads of the mob, a calm voice, masculine, firm, and full of authority.

"All right, everyone. Let's just back it up there." Steady and clear above the racket. "Everyone back from the curb. We don't want anyone getting hurt."

Annie turned and looked up into the bluest eyes she'd ever seen. A bit of sandy-colored hair curled out from under a light blue helmet—the helmet of a New York City mounted policeman. He was astride a beautiful, powerful, big quarter horse. As he wheeled the animal into position, Annie, pressed up close to the horse's side, caught a glimpse of blue riding pants with a yellow stripe, the Glock holstered at the rider's belt, and knee-high, close-fitting riding boots. Without spurs. He directed the troop of mounted police into crowd-control positions along the curb, and Annie, who knew a thing or two about quarter horses, had a nano-moment to admire the New York police horse at work: steady, unflappable, efficient—and very good looking. But it was only a moment caught in the midst of her panic. The crowd surged forward, pressing her helplessly still tighter against the big bay's chest and she felt her feet sliding out from under her. She grabbed, instinctively, for the horse's bridle near her head. The horse braced, giving her something to hold on to and for a moment, pressed against his shoulder, she was glad of the familiar smell of horseflesh and leather as she began to fall.

"Easy there, ma'am." The deep, steady voice stroked down toward her and she felt a strong arm reach around her waist, holding her firmly upright. "Let's get you out of here."

The rider, leaning way forward in the saddle, held Annie solidly in his encircling arm and lifted her right up off her feet, out of the clutch of protesters, holding her tight up against the animal's body, turning her breathless. He turned his horse away from the crowd, clearing a path for her toward the barricades the patrolmen were setting up in the street. When, at last, her feet touched the ground, her breath came back, and she was about to wave a thank-you up at him.

"Omigod! I've lost my bag!"

Annie clutched at her bare shoulder, looking back helplessly at the melee of flailing arms and shouting, angry faces where the demonstrators were being squeezed back into the little park by the police horses. "Somewhere in there—" She pointed frantically at the ground beneath a hundred milling feet.

"Can't help you now, ma'am." He turned his mount back toward the crowd. "You'd best get away from here." He called over his shoulder as he went back to work. "If we find it, you can pick it up at headquarters, Troop B."

For a few entranced moments, Annie stood alone in the space he'd cleared and watched man and horse work together, a perfectly coordinated team. And she whispered to herself, her words lost in the demonstrators' noise.

I can't believe it.

Bemused, she turned and headed back to the hotel.

He actually swept me off my feet!

And behind her, as his horse blocked the crowd's surge forward, Sergeant Bart Hardin turned in his saddle for one brief moment to watch the slim figure in the little flowery sundress as she disappeared up the street.

Wow! She's the prettiest girl I've ever seen!

Chapter Three

Whew!

Sunday Afternoon

She wasn't used to elevators and she teetered a bit as it began to rise.

Forty-four floors! The tallest building back home is only twelve stories. And that's the tallest building in all Wyoming! This whole day has been a jolt. Never saw anything like this city. How do people live like this? How are they not all crashing into each other? Big and noisy, and everything so fast! And what am I going to do about my bag? Here in New York, without my wallet, my ID. What a mess! Maybe Mitzi can help. Glitzi Mitzi! I've never seen energy like that. And that insane street scene—what was that all about? And now Liz is going to scold me. "I told you so!" I'll never hear the end.

The elevator arrived. She stepped off into a long hallway, thick-carpeted and silent.

I was really scared. If it hadn't been for that cute cop—it was like magic, how he just came out of nowhere. And on a horse, of all things! Never expected to see that, in New York City. And what a horse! He really knew his business—the way he worked that crowd— I've seen cutting horses couldn't handle a herd any better than that horse right there on a crowded city street. A good looking horse, he was. Really good looking.

The cop was kinda cute, too!

So her head was a jumble of visions, but no way was she prepared for the one that waited for her when she opened the door to her suite.

There was Liz, standing stock-still in the middle of the living room, caught in midstride. Her hands were frozen in the act of removing curlers from her hair, and her eyes were riveted to the flickering television, to a report of breaking news. Her mouth was open in astonishment and she didn't even turn as Annie came through the door.

"Come quick!" she squealed. "Come quick! Omigod! It's you! Annie, that's *you*!"

Sure enough, there on the TV, big as television life, her very own self was looking back at her, being scooped efficiently out of danger by a handsome mounted policeman. The reporter's voice was explaining the action:

"—and New York's finest were on hand to quell the demonstration. Here we see a passerby as she is plucked from the crowd by police Sergeant Bart Hardin. New Yorkers will recognize Sergeant Hardin and his horse, the legendary and highly popular Lindy. It was just last February that Sergeant Hardin was honored by Mayor Walter Gideon for his bravery in the daring rescue of four children when their apartment on West 38th Street was engulfed in the flames and choking smoke of a three-alarm fire."

Here, the TV image switched to file footage of the sergeant smiling as the grateful children placed a garland of flowers around the horse's neck and presented him with an extra bag of oats.

"Lindy is well known around Times Square. Theater people there say they consider him one of their own and claim to be his greatest fans. This horsey veteran of New York's Great White Way has been a crowd pleaser for years, and his repertoire of tricks together with his raffish charm have made him a favorite of New Yorkers and visitors to the Big Apple ever since the days when Sergeant Hardin's father, Lieutenant Des Hardin, rode him."

The newscaster moved on to the next story.

And now it was Annie's turn to stand openmouthed. She and Liz stood there like bookends, stiff and soundless, staring at the television as it reported Dow Jones averages and last night's baseball scores.

That was me!

She could hardly breathe.

Not more than an hour in New York City and I'm on the local TV!

Liz's voice ended the stunned silence between them.

"What's the matter with you?" She was registering outrage as only a big sister can. "I tell you to stay out of trouble and look what you do. You go out to 'take a little walk' and right away you get mixed up in some crackpot demonstration." The sound of her own voice set Liz back into motion and she remembered to attend to the curlers in her hair.

"Honestly, Annie, am I going to have to put a harness on you?"

She continued muttering to herself as she disappeared into the bathroom. "And needing to get rescued by the police, for goodness' sake—"

But Annie wasn't paying attention. The TV image was locked in her brain, added magically onto the screen of her fantasies, as though some cosmic finger had hit the pause button and the scene flickered there irresistibly, with a force of its own. She couldn't turn away from it. It was the TV image of her own self—her very own, recognizable self—being lifted to safety by the strong arm of a mounted police officer.

"It was an adventure, Liz," she whispered into the empty room. "And when he pulled me up out of that crowd, he just took my breath away!" The story was taking shape in her imagination: "Annie Cornell, just a simple college librarian from Laramie, Wyoming, was scooped up by the dashing young officer, who reached down from his powerful mount, and she felt the strength of his arm around her. His seat in the saddle was sure and as he held her out of harm's way, she could smell the familiar scent of good leather and horseflesh—"

Liz's voice from behind the bathroom door brought her back to earth.

"We have to get ready for that reception. Mitzi said five o'clock. Better get dressed."

Annie smiled a private sort of smile—just to herself.

An adventure! Yes. Definitely. First day in New York City. A brush with danger. A cute cop. A handsome horse. Oh, I love this city!

Chapter Four

Meanwhile

Sunday Afternoon

Sergeant Bart Hardin tossed his helmet into the in basket, spun the swivel chair around into position, and dropped his long frame down into it. A white straw shoulder bag had just been turned in and he held it in his hands as though it might contain something really precious. He smiled, took one deep breath, and he set the bag squarely in the center of the blotter that covered the desktop. Then he leaned forward and rested his hands on the desk, on either side of the bag, and drummed his fingers thoughtfully. For a long time, he just stared at the bag as though it held the answer to the most important question in the universe.

"Hey, Bart." From across the room, his partner's voice chided him playfully. "You expect a genie to jump out of that bag?"

"You never know, Max. You just never know." Bart kept looking at the bag, his brows drawn together in concentration. "I got a look at the woman who lost this bag." *I got a look into those eyes when she was hanging on to Lindy's bridle. And jeez, the feel of her against my arm, when I grabbed her.* "She just might be a genie," he said thoughtfully. "Just might be a little something—" he paused, "—something special."

Max came over to Bart's desk and parked himself on its corner edge.

"I got a look at her, too. Cute little number in a pretty dress. Flowers all over." He smiled at his buddy. "Go on. Take a look in her bag.

See who she is. Maybe she's married or something. And if she isn't, well, you never know about magic genies—"

"Yeah, I know. They grant your wishes."

"I'm just saying—"

Bart's short laugh acknowledged Max's friendly needling. At the same time, he fingered the clasp at the top of the bag, and wondered why he was hesitating. A cop often has to cross the barriers of a stranger's privacy. Why should it be different just because this girl had eyes like sunlight filtered through sea foam and hair so rich he wanted to bury his hands in it?

"All right," he added, squaring his shoulders and drawing the bag close to him. "Let's see what we can find out about her." He opened the clasp and looked into the depths of the bag. Max leaned across the desk, also curious.

"Well, she's a tidy type," Max said. "Her bag's not a mess. Some of them I've seen—" Max's eyes looked inquiringly as Bart removed a tooled-leather wallet. "And that looks handmade."

"Looks like it." Bart paused for a moment and then flipped the wallet open. From a window panel on one side, a Wyoming driver's license displayed a pale replica of the face that was still reverberating in his head.

Wyoming!

Now that's a coincidence.

"Little girl from the wide open spaces, all alone here in the big, bad city. And she walks right into that crowd scene. Must have scared the hell out of her."

"Well, she sure got a taste of the big city today," Max said. "What else does it say?"

Bart kept his eyes away from the name on the license. As though knowing her name would remove the last veil of her privacy. Instead, he read aloud: "Height, five feet five inches; weight, one hundred and twelve pounds. Blond hair and hazel eyes."

I guess that's the best they could do on a driver's license. You wouldn't expect it to say "like music and sunlight in your arms, with hair the color of buttercups and eyes bright as sea water."

"Yeah, blond hair, hazel eyes. The picture's no good, but that's the one. The girl in the flowery dress."

He read out the birthdate and did a quick calculation. "Just turned twenty-six."

"What's her name?"

Bart hesitated, then read it off.

"Cornell, Annika Elizabeth."

Annika.

He took a breath while he let the name flow through his head, filling his senses, creating a memory.

Her folks probably call her Annie.

"Triple C Ranch. Route 287, Laramie, Wyoming. She must be visiting. Or maybe she's here on business."

He flipped through the plastic inserts in the wallet, stopping for a long time at a snapshot of two little boys, ages about six and eight.

Uh oh! I hope they're not hers.

Bart felt the beginnings of a painful disappointment tighten his chest.

"Anything else?" Max asked.

"I'm looking. Some kids in a picture." He poked through the items in the bag. "Just the usual stuff. A lipstick. Car keys." He held up a plastic card and a folded piece of paper. "A hotel room entry card. And a letter." He unfolded the letter from *Lady Fair* and scanned it quickly. "How about that? She won some kind of contest—"

"Better give her a call," Max said. "Let her know we have her bag."

"Yeah—"

"Give you a chance, maybe, to find out about those kids."

"Yeah—"

Headquarters, Troop B, was on New York's West Side, close to the Hudson River. Only a few blocks away, in a tiny, three-room apartment on the sixth floor of a very old and very seedy walk-up building, a meeting was about to take place. At the same time that Bart was looking into Annie's handbag, two men were puffing painfully as they climbed the last rickety flight of stairs, holding their hands flat against the peeling walls to steady themselves as they ascended. The first man, carrying his more than two hundred fifty pounds with difficulty on his short frame, came to a gasping stop at the top step. He was bent forward, bracing his splayed-out, pudgy fingers on his knees, fighting to catch his breath. Perspiration streamed down his plump face, drenching his thick mustache and running down to the soggy collar of his shabby shirt.

The second man, his head hanging low as he dragged himself up, reached the top without seeing that his companion had stopped, and he blindly butted the rear of the man ahead of him. The impact tumbled him back a step or two and he grabbed frantically for the wobbly railing. The first man was almost thrown to his knees and his brightly embroidered black cap was pitched forward over his forehead.

"Idiot!" The first man whirled angrily, grasping his skinny friend by the front of his shirt. "You can't see your nose in front of you?"

"But Leon." The man behind clutched at the other's wrist, trying to loosen his grip. "It wasn't my nose I ran into. Let me go." He was panting. "I can't breathe. These stairs. I thought everywhere in America is elevators." He continued to try to pry himself loose. "Let go of my shirt, Leon. It's the only one I have left."

"Already you have forgotten. We use only code names. I am not Leon. I am Larry." With a last twist of exasperation, he released the other man. "And you are Harry. Remember that. Harry."

"I remember." He was still puffing. "I remember. Code names." With a couple of shakes of his head and a wiggle of his skinny shoulders, Hugo replaced his shirt in its proper position. He ran his hand tidily down the front of his bony chest a couple of times, and then smoothed his thick mustache with his fingertips. I am Harry and you are Larry. And Boksmer is Barry and—"

"Enough! You want to tell the whole world?" Larry pointed at the closed doors down the length of the hall. "The walls have ears! Just be quiet a few minutes for a change." He took off the black cap and brushed gently with the tips of his fingers at the bright cockade of feathers before he resettled the cap neatly on his thinning hair. He tiptoed to the nearest door and knocked three times, waited a moment, then knocked twice more. He put his ear to the door.

"Who is?" came from behind the door.

"We have come to fix the grandmother's broken cuckoo clock."

Muffled voices could be heard inside and then the sound of multiple locks and chains and bolts being undone. The door cracked open a thin slit and a beady eye and part of a mustache were visible. Leon and Hugo were being inspected. Then the owner of the beady eye stepped back and pulled the door open to admit them into the small room.

Dusty lace curtains filtered the late afternoon sun as it dappled the potted plants and the ragged plush seats of several old straight-backed chairs. Except for a large dining table and a worn sideboard on which a crocheted runner and some chipped, once-pretty china were now gathering dust, the room was almost bare of any furnishings. A couple of roughly lettered posters had been tacked on the old-fashioned paper that covered the walls. From across the room, a harsh voice sliced angrily at them.

"You are late!"

At the far end of the table, a very tall, very thin man looked up from the piles of papers scattered everywhere in front of him. His embroidered cap sat on an absolutely bald head and he was entirely without eyebrows. Had it not been for the thick, luxuriant mustache filling the space between his sharp nose and his thin, tightly pursed lips, he'd have looked like an egg wearing round, steel-rimmed glasses. An empty teacup was on the table in front of him, and he tapped his pencil impatiently on the cloth, waiting for an explanation.

"We got lost. We went to 408 East instead of 408 West." Leon removed his cap respectfully while he mopped his face with a handkerchief.

"And the traffic." Hugo was almost invisible behind Leon and he had to crane his neck around, peering out from behind his fat friend while he added his excuses. "So many automobiles. We couldn't cross the streets. Is not like at home."

"Of course is not like at home!" the seated man snapped at him. "At home are goats and geese walking in the streets! Of course New York is not like at home!" In irritation, he tossed the pencil onto the pile of papers and it rolled away from him. He remembered that he *had* only one pencil and he grabbed it before it could fall to the floor.

He pursed his lips even more tightly. "That is why we are here. In New York the people never heard of Buljornia. In all America no one ever heard of Buljornia! Even here, where is home of United Nations, Buljornia is unknown!" His eyes began to glitter intently and his voice grew more impassioned. "We must change that! We must find a way to *force* people to know who we are and what it is we demand!" He motioned at everyone to sit down at the table. He motioned at his wife, a small woman with huge round eyes, who was peeking around from the edge of the kitchen door, to bring him more tea.

"And today, in this demonstration, our leader is arrested!" His clenched fist pounded the papers on the table. His eyes glistened fervently as he grew more and more impassioned. "We must find a way to free him! We *will* find a way! We will *force* them to free him! We will bring them to their knees!"

He paused and searched the faces of the men around the table.

"There is but one task before us. We must think of a plan that will compel the people of New York—and the nations of the world—to take us seriously! We will make them listen to us. We will make them yield to our demands!"

His wife brought him the tea, and he rapped his pencil on the table.

"So! I hereby declare that the first meeting of the Ad Hoc Committee to Bring New York to Its Knees is now in session!"

Chapter Five

The Green Parrot

Sunday Evening

Their town car was caught in traffic along 57th Street, so the reception had already started by the time they arrived. By some magic trick of design, the Green Parrot managed to be both cave-dark and brightly lit at the same time, and the effect was deliciously festive. Past the hostess's desk, Mitzi steered them into a softly buzzing mass of sleek guests, all bejeweled and beautifully coiffed and elegantly clad, women in little black dresses and men in dark suits. Lively chatter and the clink of ice in glasses mixed engagingly with the soft background music. Tuxedoed waitstaff moved unobtrusively about, bearing silver trays of the tiniest canapés and glasses of wine. Here and there, an overheard bit of French added an international edge to the party atmosphere.

"Oh, Annie." Liz glanced down nervously at her navy dress and pink jacket.

"All the women are wearing black."

"I noticed."

"Do you think we look out of place?"

"Maybe. A little." Annie felt an uncomfortable cloud of self-consciousness darken her mood. Maybe her pale peach dress, with its fitted bodice and flared skirt and the little cropped jacket, which had looked so festive in the shop on Grand Street, wasn't quite what the upper crust was wearing in New York. But she quickly shooed the cloud away. She was determined to enjoy this evening and she wasn't going to let a bunch of big-city sophisticates spoil it. She dropped her voice to a conspiratorial mutter, only loud enough to reach Liz's ear. "I came to New York to have a good time. I'm just not going to put myself down." She picked a wee bite of carpaccio from a passing plate. "And I think we both look just fine. What's more, I don't think anyone here cares at all."

"Absolutely right." Liz joined in with a bit of whispered defiance. "It seems to me no one in New York pays much attention to anyone else."

"Right. You could probably rob a bank and nobody would notice."

"But they're going to notice you, Annie. There's the meeting at *Lady Fair* tomorrow and the ribbon cutting Tuesday, and then the spree. You're going to get plenty of attention. You'll get so swell-headed, I'm going to have to rope you in once we get back to the ranch."

"Don't worry, big sis. After this week, no one will know who I am anymore. There are eight million people in this city. Do you think anyone cares about one little librarian from Laramie?"

Back at the stables, Bart was settling Lindy down for the night. Checked his water and the feed in his bin. Checked his hooves. Ran his hands up and down the horse's legs, feeling for any tenderness, muscle knots, scrapes. And as always during this daily ritual, Lindy was his closest confidant. Silent and attentive, the horse was the best listener.

"Hey, dude. You saw that girl today? At the demonstration at the UN?" He ran the comb through Lindy's mane and smoothed the light hair away from the horse's eyes. "Cute little thing, wasn't she? What did you think? She could have been really hurt, getting caught up in that mob. Good thing we were there. A girl like that, innocent, new to the city, doesn't know her way around.

"Funny about that—her coming from Wyoming. That's where you were born. That's where your whole line was bred, on Grandpa Malone's ranch. We used to spend all our summers out there, when I was a kid. And I remember, we used to drive through Laramie to get to Grandpa's ranch. There's nothing there but a couple of streets and a lot of wind. I bet this girl's never seen anything like a big city before. She must be blown over—maybe scared, too. Yeah, probably scared. I saw how she looked when I pulled her out of that crowd of bozos. All that noise and yelling and a million guys pushing up against her. Little girl from the big sky country, doesn't know her way around, she could get lost—or get herself into trouble. She should have someone to protect her. Someone who's trained to handle trouble. Someone who knows New York."

He gave Lindy a big, proud smile.

"Someone like me?"

The reception was winding down and the slightly tipsy guests were disappearing into the night. Mitzi suggested dinner at a nearby bistro, but the exhausting day had worn them out.

"Thanks," Annie said as they paused on the sidewalk outside the Green Parrot, "but we need a rest. Tomorrow's going to be very full. And I have to be up early for the meeting at *Lady Fair*."

"Okay. No problem. I'll see you in the morning. Maybe I'll have some news about your bag by then. You get a good rest in the meantime. And, oh, for the meeting and the photo shoot tomorrow, wear those cute western clothes—the jeans, the boots, that fabulous jacket." Mitzi walked with them to the waiting car. "You'll be such a hit in that outfit." She stuck a couple of air kisses on their cheeks, called a happy "Ciao" in their direction and was off.

"I just want to drop on my bed," Liz said, from the depths of the car's leather seat, "have room service bring me a hamburger and some fries, turn on the TV and just chill for the rest of the evening."

"Mmmm, I don't know if I can even make it that far. I'm so tired I may fall asleep before we get there."

And sure enough, Annie was practically staggering with fatigue by the time they got through the lobby, up the elevator, and through the door. She kicked off her shoes, peeled off her little jacket, and fell *plop* on her bed. She didn't notice the blinking light on her phone, but when Liz came in to ask about her room service order, she saw that a message was waiting.

"Should I answer it?" she asked.

"Oh, sure. But who'd be calling me?"

Liz picked up the phone. She punched a button, listened for a moment, then broke into a big smile.

"Oh, thanks so much." She was writing something on the notepad. "This is her sister. I'll tell her right away."

"Mmmm?"

Annie was too tired to speak

"That was someone at the police precinct. They found your bag. You can pick it up at Troop B Headquarters. I wrote down the address."

"Oh, thank God! That's a huge load off my mind." Her eyes remained closed. Her head remained on the pillow. "I'll have to let Mitzi know." And she was out.

A little later, when the food arrived and Liz poked her awake, they both stayed up long enough to eat, but were too tired for TV. They brushed their teeth, they said good night, they each closed their windows against the unfamiliar nighttime racket from the streets below, and then they both slept soundly until morning.

So they never got to see the rerun of the earlier news story about the demonstration, and the bit about the rescue of the "bystander," as she was rescued by Sergeant Bart Hardin.

But others' eyes were fixed intently on that report.

In the shabby walk-up apartment on the far West Side, three men stood glumly in front of a black-and-white television screen, each one pulling morosely on his mustache.

"Is crazy," Leon said. "Is saying more about some foolish horse than about our demonstration. I don't understand."

"They don't even say about Buljornia or how our leader is in jail. Only is 'a demonstration,' they say." Leon sagged his fat body into the nearest chair. "All this long way to America we come, and they don't even notice us." He and Hugo turned to Boksmer, who had taken his seat at the head of the table and was passing his hand contemplatively over his shining bald head as though it were a crystal ball, full of portentous messages.

"What we do, Boksmer?"

Hugo slapped his hand against Leon's shoulder.

"*Barry!*" he reminded him angrily. "And you call *me* idiot!"

The tall man looked wearily at his two compatriots.

"What we do? I tell you what we do. We think of something to make them pay attention to us, these people—" he waved his hand at the TV screen, "—these imbeciles here in New York, and all those idiot diplomats—" here he waved toward the window, "—those irresponsible fools at the United Nations. We must think of something they will *have* to notice. Now, quiet, all of you." He included his little wife, who instantly stopped clearing the teacups. With a spoon and saucer in her hand, she sat down timidly in a stiff wooden chair in the kitchen, making herself as small as possible. "Be quiet, and think!" her husband ordered.

For many long minutes, the room was silent. A fly explored the cord that hung from the ceiling light. The curtain at the window moved lightly in the soft spring breeze. Dust settled on the furniture. Hugo made his face look as intelligent as he could. He pursed his lips and furrowed his brow. Leon tried to think, but he forgot what he was supposed to be thinking about. With the soup and dumplings simmering in the kitchen, he could think only of dinner.

Boksmer stared at the TV screen, now blank.

"This horse," he said. "The way these people love this horse, this gives me idea. Be quiet, all of you." No one had said anything. "Be quiet. I am thinking of something—"

And Bart Hardin, getting Lindy settled in his stall, poured an extra measure of the troop's specially mixed feed into the horse's bin.

"Like buttercups," he murmured, stroking the velvet-soft hair along Lindy's cheek. "Hair the color of buttercups, growing wild on the mountain. And light as a feather when I held her. Like a bunch of wildflowers off the mountainside. Like a soft, western breeze blowing across the valley—"

And in the shabby tenement walk-up, plans were being made. By people who had watched the evening news on the TV and had noticed a man and a horse . . .

Chapter Six

A Whole New Person?

Early Monday Morning

They stepped off the elevator into a cream and chrome silence perched high above the heart of the city. *Lady Fair*'s vast, silent, windowless, and stunningly chic reception area was guarded by the room's only occupant, a dark-haired young woman who looked up at them from behind a glass-topped desk. She wore an air of total competence, composure, and congenial calm.

Mitzi barely paused as she led Annie past the desk with a cheery wave and a brief nod to the sleek young woman sitting there. "Morning, Gina. Are they ready for us?"

"Go on in. They'll be along soon." Gina gave Annie a fast up-and-down glance that processed every detail of her appearance, from Frye boots to rodeo buckle and Wrangler jeans, to the blond hair pulled back in a loose ponytail. She noted the pink paisley shirt with the mother-of-pearl snaps, the fringed, deer-hide jacket, and the absence of any jewelry. As they disappeared down the hall, she called her assessment after them.

"Love your outfit."

Annie wondered if this was a universal greeting among these fashion people. But there wasn't time to give the thought much attention. As the door from the serene reception area closed behind them, the scene changed suddenly into a glassy beehive of bustle and nerves. Bright light flooded the room through enormous windows that looked out in all directions; under a crystal blue sky, gargoyle-topped skyscrapers commanded from the north and south, and to the west there was a postcard-worthy view of a broad, vividly bright river. White sailboats, like a child's toys, decorated the river, and opposite, along the Jersey shore, the skyline of Hoboken hovered like a gray shadow. A helicopter patrolled the riverfront and far above, tiny dots led the contrails of planes across the sky, marking voyages to the four corners of the compass. Fifty floors below, at the sidewalk level, a blurry mass of snarled traffic and quick-moving office workers, eager shoppers and dawdling, gawking tourists snaked along the city's streets. But up here in *Lady Fair*'s aerie, where walls of glass sealed off any sound from the world outside, nobody was looking at the view. Here, the air buzzed with activity and concentration, deadlines and competition and a passion for the magazine that were far more compelling. At the most, Annie received a quick look, maybe a half smile, as she walked past serious, intense young women in chic outfits—little skirts, dark tights, ballet flats—girls taping photos to display boards, girls carrying trays of coffee, or trays of earrings, girls carrying plastic-wrapped garments on hangers. Workspaces were lined with seductive racks and shelves filled with fashion items—samples everywhere, on desks, on file cabinets, on windowsills, spilling out of drawers, and jammed up against computers, samples of shoes and bags and lipsticks and hats, sunglasses, belts, gloves. She walked past hundreds of photos taped to the walls, past people on phones, people poring over articles to be edited and proofed, people not even glancing up at them as they passed, too focused on their work to recognize an interruption. Everywhere there was a vibrant sense of energy, of devotion, and of the most careful attention to the minutest detail.

Annie was fascinated. This fashion industry was not only profoundly self-focused but, because its secrets needed to be guarded, also too well protected to be penetrated. And yet here she was, not only being allowed into the beating heart of the fashion industry, but also being the beneficiary of its attention. What angel had landed on her shoulder and dropped her into the midst of this busy scene, this place of brilliant light and high-level talent and energy, rich with surprise and opportunity and an unforeseeable outcome? And wasn't that the very definition of adventure? At the very least, whatever might come, wouldn't she have something to file away safely in memory, to be treasured for the rest of her life—

Her fantasies were spinning out all sorts of variations on the theme of future adventures as they arrived at their destination. Mitzi led her into a large conference room that had an interior wall to their right and to the left an enormous wall of tinted glass, curved to suggest the prow of an ocean liner cruising high above the city. A long table filled the center of the room. Several steel-and-leather chairs were placed along the interior wall and at the table there were twelve more, but only one of these was occupied. A young man with spiky blond hair and a dark gray business suit stood up to greet them. A folder of papers lay open on the table in front of him.

"They'll all be here in a minute." His smile was big, broad, and eager. "I'm Matt. From legal. And you must be our winner, Annie Cornell. We're glad to meet you, Annie, and to congratulate you." He came around the table to shake hands. "Your contest entry just grabbed us right off the bat. An easy winner. Can I get you anything? Coffee? Danish? Fruit?" He pointed to a sideboard that was loaded with goodies. "Muffins, bagels, cheese? There's decaf and regular." He pointed to a couple of coffee urns. "And tea, if you like."

"Not for me, thanks." Annie was too excited to eat. She took the seat that Matt held for her.

Mitzi broke in. "I've got to go. They need me everywhere. I'll catch up with you guys later. You'll be in good hands from here on." And like a leaf in a high wind, she was gone, leaving the door open behind her for two women who were just arriving—two women who were almost clonelike in their similarity, both tall, model-thin and impeccably groomed, except that one was brilliantly blond and the other startlingly black-haired. They were engrossed in some papers they were reviewing, but when they glanced up and saw Annie, they looked over at Matt, who made the introduction.

"Hey there, Dinah. Like you to meet our winner. Annie Cornell—"

The blond one stacked the papers they'd been examining and slipped them into the denim tote bag that hung from her shoulder. The black-haired one interrupted him with a wave of her hand and a big, welcoming smile. "I'm Dinah Featherington," she said. "I'm one of the features editors here. And I'll be doing a piece on you for the next edition, so we'll spend some time together later today. So glad to have you here, Annie." On her way to the treats table, she looked back at Annie. "I just love your outfit. Great look!" She put a bagel on a plate, poured some coffee, and took a seat near the far end of the table next to her blond companion who had already scooped some cut-up melon onto a plate and taken a seat.

"I'm Eugenia Shaw," the blond one said. "I'm Dinah's assistant. We'll be working together on this."

The room was filling up, introductions were being made, names were being tossed at Annie, and she gave up any hope of remembering who was who. Editors of all kinds. Assistant editors. Associate editors. She caught a couple of titles as new arrivals poured out cups of coffee, selected bagels or muffins or bits of fruit or cheese, took seats around the table —"beauty and health director"—"associate fashion editor"— "sales and marketing director." A photographer. Makeup people. The Paris editor (arrived last night with the Galliard's contingent—Annie remembered meeting her at the reception, Sylvie something). She couldn't possibly keep it all in her head. All the seats but one were filled. The chair at the far end of the table was apparently being saved.

And just then, a tall, trim woman blew into the room. She had a mass of dark hair, wore a stunning fuchsia Chanel suit, and moved with the air of a sailing ship slipping elegantly through a high wind. She went directly to the empty chair, stood there a moment to survey the suddenly silent scene, and then focused directly on Annie. Her smile could not have been warmer.

"And you are Annie Cornell," she announced. "All the way from Wyoming. And the winner of our contest. On behalf of everyone here at *Lady Fair* and at Galliard's, I want to congratulate you and to tell you it's wonderful to welcome you to New York."

Annie opened her mouth to say a thank you, but she never had the chance.

"I'm Marge Webster, editor-in-chief here, and we are just so delighted with what we have in store for you, with the program and activities we've planned. It's going to be a terrific week, and the people here are going to tell you all about it. I've got to go now, busy, busy, busy, but I'm leaving you in very good hands."

She'd never sat down and now she was blowing right out again. As she passed Annie, she leaned over and said, "I love your outfit, dear."

The door closed behind her; there was a brief silence following her departure and then, as though at a silent signal, they all seemed to come to life, to inhale again. Papers were rustled, coffee cups were raised to lips, and suddenly everyone was talking at once—until a woman who'd been sitting off to one side left her seat and took the empty chair at the head of the table. She set her Starbucks latte on the table in front of her. All heads turned to her and again everyone stopped talking.

"Annie, I'm Greta Pena and I want to add my welcome to Marge's, and tell you how excited all of us here at *Lady Fair* are about your participation in this marvelous event. We just know that your part in our sponsorship of Galliard's opening here in New York is going to be a huge success, but that also means we all will have a very busy week ahead of us." Greta's big smile beamed on Annie. "So we need to get started right away. We have a full schedule for you, but we also want to be sure you have free time, too, to spend all on your own to enjoy this wonderful city."

A young man sitting just behind her handed her a folder of papers.

"Here's a copy of the itinerary we've planned for you." She handed one copy to Annie and sent the others around the table. "It lays out the program for the whole week. But first off, today's program is at the top of the list. Today you'll meet some of the people who'll be working with you and see some of our home here at *Lady Fair*. You've already met Mitzi—her number's on the program—and she and Jerry here"—she indicated the young man behind her—"will be your guides and trouble-shooters. If you need anything, contact one of them." Jerry nodded, waved a hand in a kind of salute, and gave Annie a big smile. "Then the fun begins. At ten thirty, there'll be a full workup by our makeup people. They have wizards there in that department; you can't imagine what wonders they create. Although," she paused, tilted her head a bit, and did a quick appraisal of Annie's face, "with skin like yours and your coloring, you'll hardly need their magic. But never mind—it'll be so much fun anyway!

"After that, lunch in our cafeteria, and then at one thirty, Damien and Louis from the Vanetta Salon are coming in to do a color and styling. Our color people will assist them and they are absolutely first rate. Honestly, Annie, you're going to take a whole new you back to Laramie."

Oh, Lord, Annie thought, *will this be a spectacular treat? Or am I in for a ghastly disaster?*

But she reined in her anxiety, told herself to enjoy whatever was coming over the horizon, and reminded herself to say thank you to the whole team. She did a quick organization of her thoughts and then let a little speech spill out.

"I just want to let everyone know how excited I am to be here and to get to be a part of this amazing adventure. Back in Laramie, I knew I was the luckiest girl in town, getting to win this contest. Now I know I really am the luckiest girl in all of New York, too. In fact, I feel like the luckiest girl in all America. So I thank you all, I thank *Lady Fair*, I thank Galliard's, I thank the contest people, and I just hope I can make everyone here—and everyone back home, my folks, my friends, everyone—proud of me."

There were smiles all around the table. Annie didn't know it, but she'd just passed a test. Her ability to think on her feet and talk in complete sentences was going to be valuable. After all, no promotion event wants to be stuck with a dummy. And Annie Cornell was, clearly, no dummy.

"So that's it, my duckies. Time to move on." And at this signal from Greta, the room went into motion: chairs were pushed back, coffee cups were drained of their last dregs, watches and smart phones were consulted, and everyone was gone as though in a puff of smoke. Annie noticed that none of the food on the plates had been touched. Not a single bite had been eaten by anyone. Only one person remained: a tall, dark-eyed woman who held out a hand to Annie. "I'm Annelie Magano," she said. "I'm *Lady Fair's* beauty editor and I'll be in charge of your makeover starting right now—that's on the next floor down, so we'll just take the stairs—and I'll be working with Sandi-K. and Richard, who really are a couple of wonder workers. Later on, the Vanetta team will be here to do beautiful things with your hair." She paused on her way to the door in order to give Annie's hair an appraising look. "I've been watching how the light works through your natural highlights. I don't think our colorist is going to want to do much with it. Your hair is already one of your great features. Such a rich variety of tones. I just love it!"

Annie was feeling some trepidation.

"Will I still look like me when you're done?"

"Don't worry." Annelie was familiar with the fear of drastic change. "Your friends will still recognize you when you leave here. Our experts know what they're doing."

And those were probably the last coherent words Annie heard for the next couple of hours, as she sank into a maelstrom of activity and attention. As though she was a precious egg being packed for special handling, she was led down a flight of glass stairs and escorted into a deep leather chair that reclined, tipped forward and back, cradled her head, raised her legs, massaged her spine, and rode up and down like a slo-mo carousel horse. There were mirrors all around, hand-held, wall mounted, backlit, magnifying. There were powerful lights picking out every square millimeter of her skin and its every variation of hue, texture, and tone. Eyes peered at her through magnifying glasses, hands worked creams and lotions into her, seriously analytical evaluations were being discussed by apparently expert consultants and miracle workers. Muds and herbs and foams and gels were packed and smoothed and scrubbed into her pores. And when they'd finished with her face, they started on the rest of her. A manicurist sat to the side, a pedicurist at her toes, a masseuse pummeled her, first painfully then lovingly. There were ice packs and hot lamps.

And then, when they were done, it was time for the makeup.

Beyond the blindingly bright lights that were trained on her, she could occasionally catch a glimpse of human faces studying her, and snatches of voices in consultation, conferring, disagreeing, agreeing, making choices about her.

"I want to go with cat eyes—no, no, totally wrong—just a thin stroke of dark liner here along the upper lid—what do you think?—I'd like a light dusting of lavender above that, too—or lilac?—a line of gold along the lower lid—"

She felt like a specimen fixed onto the glass under a microscope's lens. An odd sensation, at once both gratifying and terrifying. Never had so many eyes been so intimately, and yet so dispassionately focused on her.

"– and look at those eyebrows, they're perfect—don't need a thing, just a bit of gel—such a fresh look, don't want to mess with that—go easy on the blush—she has great skin—not what I expected—isn't she from a ranch in Wyoming?—shouldn't she be all leathery?"

Annie didn't know whether to laugh or to be indignant. She knew what every western woman knows: if you live in a super-dry climate, where the humidity is single-digit, the winds are powerful and the sun is even more so, you learn to slather on the moisturizer. That's a no-brainer.

But at last her handlers were done, and with a flourish and many big smiles, they released her from their clutches. They returned the chair to its upright position and gave her a chance to look at the re-vised Annie Cornell.

She was stunned. Without changing anything about her, they'd turned a normally pretty girl into a photo-ready, fresh-looking, lovely beauty!

What a confusion of exhilaration, embarrassment, pride, and discovery swirled through her. With a warning to herself not to get too full of herself, she decided everything—so far—was all right with the world, and she was in good hands. She gave herself a men-tal thumbs up.

"I love it," she said. "You guys really are miracle workers." She lifted her chin, turned her head this way and that, admired the en-hanced Annie that preened for her in the mirror. "But I'll never be able to do this on my own. I couldn't possibly have kept track of everything you were doing—all the creams and lotions and things you were using—"

"Oh, don't worry about that." Sandi-K. handed her a colorful can-vas *Lady Fair* tote bag and a thick sheaf of papers. "We keep notes as we work. These are the handwritten pages, but I've made copies and I'll be transcribing them. You'll get a fully typed printout. With trac-ings of your face so you'll know what goes where. And *Lady Fair* and Galliard's will send you home with a full supply of each beauty prod-uct we used today, and guidelines and suggestions. You'll be able to reproduce our work any time, on your own."

"I told you these guys were good, didn't I?" Annelie was ready to escort her to lunch for an hour's break before the next batch of spe-cialists could have a go at her. "The food in our *Lady Fair* cafeteria isn't exactly scrumptious, but nobody eats anyway. Also, it's handy so there's no need to go anywhere else. Dinah will be joining us so she can chat with you and get background for the piece she'll be writ-ing, and you and I can talk about the program for the rest of the week. After that, the hairstylists and colorists will be waiting in our studio upstairs. They should be done by about three or three thirty. That will leave you free for the evening."

Thank God for lunch! What a morning this has been! And then my hair. What can they possibly do to my hair? But whatever—as long as they finish with me by three thirty.

She hadn't forgotten the other matter, also on her agenda for the day. *There'll be plenty of time for me to get to Troop B Headquarters.*

And thank God for the New York City mounted police.

The whole outrageous mob scene from yesterday flashed through her memory.

I could have been trampled into mush. He really was cute—and the TV said he's sort of famous—the horse, too—what was the horse's name?

Like the *Lady Fair* reception space, the cafeteria was all interior. It reminded her of the Green Parrot from last night—full of sparkly lights and yet somehow a dark space.

How do they do that? And why *do they do that?*

She loaded up her plate with a pasta-and-tuna salad, a big bunch of carrot sticks, and a couple of tiny corn muffins. She made one stop at the coffee urn to add a tall French roast with sugar and cream to her tray, and followed Annelie to a table up against the wall.

The muffins were okay, the pasta salad was routine cafeteria quality, but the carrot sticks were fresh. She ate most of them and wrapped the rest in a napkin to be saved for later.

Maybe it's a way to keep people's minds on their work, and not on their stomachs. Not that anyone around here seems to feed their stomachs. I don't see so much as an ounce of body fat.

She looked around. Sure enough, the super skinny, super chic types who worked at *Lady Fair* seemed to have no interest whatsoever in what was on their plates. She'd noticed, at the meeting that morning, they'd put food on their plates, but no one had eaten anything. With one exception. Now Annie remembered: she'd been mystified by the bagel-eating technique of the food editor—a gorgeous Asian woman with a perfect cut of the shiniest, straightest black hair. But she was so thin, Annie had wondered where in her body there was room to store her vital organs. With meticulous care, the woman had pinched off infinitesimal bits of the bagel, and nibbled on each bit as slowly and thoughtfully as a medieval scholar trying to calculate the weight and age of the earth. By the time the meeting had ended, she'd made her way through less than one eighth of the bagel!

I've got to try that sometime. It must be a dieting technique.

Across the table from her, Annelie was consuming a plate of steamed kale on which she'd sprinkled some lemon juice. And a glass of iced tea. Silent moments passed while Annelie focused all her attention on chewing down her allotted portion of greens, seeming to view them more as a penance than a pleasure. When she'd eaten up the last bits, she was ready to talk.

"You have the itinerary for the week," she said. She laid her copy on the table between them. "We've tried to leave you time to be on your own, without being tied a hundred percent to *Lady Fair* and Galliard's. New York is a great walking-around city, and even if there isn't time to see all the sights, or go to a Yankees game or whatever, if you do nothing else but walk and walk and walk, you can have a marvelous time here. You'll find the city is a show a minute just walking around, and whatever you do, it will be an adventure. But we do also have a schedule of planned activities, and we can go over those now."

With one perfectly manicured fingernail, she indicated, point by point, the schedule of events that would fill up most of Annie's week in New York.

"Tomorrow, at nine thirty, there'll be the ribbon-cutting at the store, with TV coverage. The mayor will be there and Galliard's president. Also Greta, our events director—you met her this morning— and some others. You'll be asked to say a few words, so have a little speech ready. I do mean *little*." She looked up from her schedule to check Annie's reaction. "You don't have a problem with that, do you?" It had just occurred to her: Annie Cornell is a librarian from a small western city. Maybe public speaking is too unfamiliar, too intimidating, all those cameras, the attention—

"I'll be okay." Annie tactfully suppressed her smile. Hadn't she led thousands—whole stadiums—full of fans, cheerleading for Wyoming U's teams? If she could do that, dressed only in her skimpy little brown and gold outfit, she was certainly not now going to be shy about appearing or speaking in front of small gatherings. And anyway, at that moment, her attention had been deflected to the bit of kale that was stuck between Annelie's front teeth, and she was figuring out the best way to let her know. Her first thought was to get her little makeup hand mirror out of her bag and offer that as tactfully as possible. But of course, her bag was not with her. It was waiting for her at Troop B Headquarters, and as soon as *Lady Fair*'s elves were finished with her hair, she'd have to grab a cab and get over there.

"I'll be okay," she repeated. "Actually, you have something—" She gestured toward her own mouth.

"Omigod!" Annelie whipped out her own makeup kit, checked her teeth and used that well-manicured nail to capture the embarrassing green bit. "Thank you, thank you. I could have gone around with that all day and no one would have said a thing."

Annie just smiled, openly this time. "What's next on the agenda?"

Back to the agenda page. "After the ribbon-cutting, you'll have a two-hour tour of Galliard's, with cameras following. You'll go floor to floor and choose fifty thousand dollars' worth of clothes, accessories, perfumes, whatever you like. You won't be rushed, but you'll have to be efficient." She checked Annie's face to watch her reaction and saw Annie close her eyes and take a deep breath.

Annie had seen enough high fashion this morning to know that her usual L.L.Bean and Eddie Bauer wardrobe might need a rethink. Would a tour through Galliard's high-end displays turn her self-image upside down?

This still isn't real. But I've got to get my head around it by to-morrow morning.

All around her, *Lady Fair* people were picking at their leafy rabbit-food lunches, sipping at their stevia-sweetened drinks, keeping themselves rail-thin and couture-chic. Would that be a good thing? Was she ready? Would she be sorry she'd won this damned contest—or would it turn out to be the big adventure she'd been eager for?

"And on Wednesday," Annelie was saying, "you'll be here at *Lady Fair* for fittings of all the clothes you've chosen, so our wardrobe staff can have them ready for your TV runway appearance on Friday."

Annie took a deep breath.

"Don't worry," Annelie went on. "Our people will be right at your side. They'll do your makeup and your hair, and they'll see to it that it's a wonderful day for you, for us, for Galliard's, and for the audience. It'll be fun, you'll see." She took a quick look at her Black-Berry, where a message was waiting. "That's Dinah. She's on her way now to interview you. She'll need about a half hour, and after that, Damien and Louis will be ready for you."

Dinah arrived, bringing her notebook, a Starbucks latte, and a staff photographer. She parked the coffee on the table, she set the photographer in motion around Annie getting shots from all angles, and in twenty minutes, she learned enough about Annie's life to write many thousands of words about this lucky winner. She also learned that, though Annie could be very forthcoming about growing up on a ranch, making better than average grades in high school, and loving her work in the university's veterinary division as its head librarian, she could be circumspect when she chose. She could twist gracefully away from allowing more than the simple information that both her parents had died before her seventh birthday, that her sister, Liz, who had been only a teenager herself at the time, and their aunt Velma had taken over her care, and that no, there was no man in her life. Dinah was not entirely satisfied—she rarely was—but she knew she'd gotten all there was to get; she left the cafeteria with her latte untouched and a notebook full of usable information, but she left the photographer, assigned to get a carload of shots to be available for the final version of the story.

"Oh, honey. This is going to be so much fun." Louis was already preparing batches of color, like a wizard stirring up a magic potion. "You've got such great color to start with—look at this, Damien." Louis ran his fingers through Annie's hair, lifting it as though it were a fragile veil. "So bright and natural. And not a sign of fading yet, like a ten-year-old's. But still, I think we'll add a tiny bit of highlights, just to make it more magical, and maybe some lowlights, too, just for a touch of drama." He spun Annie's chair so he could face her. "What do you think, honey?"

Annie just nodded helplessly. She'd already been divested of her shirt, robed in a neck-to-toe black robe, and handed over to Louis like a plate of pastries. Whatever was going to happen here, she knew it would all be new to her and she'd best just let the experts have their way with her. In minutes, Louis was all happy chatter as he expertly separated thin sections of hair, painted each with its carefully selected compound, and wrapped it in a square of foil. Annie laughed at the effect when he was done; the reflection in the mirror showed a cartoon character, silvery and metallic, ready to be beamed up into some galaxy far, far away. Assistants, like elves, scurried around her, eager to keep her comfortable, offering her coffee, magazines, anything to amuse her while she waited through the setting period. Twenty minutes later, she was transferred to an improbably big leather chair that apparently had a mind of its own; throughout the removal of the foil squares and the rinsing out of the chemicals, the chair massaged and pummeled her back and neck. And then she was combed out and handed over to Damien.

Damien was all gentle charm as he ran his magic fingers through Annie's hair, fluffing it and familiarizing himself with its texture.

"This is going to be such a pleasure. For such fine hair, it has more body that I'd expect. And it even has some wave. Unusual in such fine blond hair." He had his iPad ready for her to skim through. "Now, what are we going to do with you? Let's see what you'd like and what would work best with your hair." He tapped through a voluminous array of photos, commenting as he went. "Side parts are in. Everyone's wearing them this season. The center part, the vampire look, that's so out. And it would be so wrong for you with your bright sunny color. Maybe swirly down the side—how would you like a light braid, just near the ends? Very casual?"

"Oh, I'd rather not."

"A chic chignon—?" But before she could respond, he nixed that. "Nope. Sophistication is great," he said, "but you've got years to go before you get to that. Let's go fresh and lovely."

"Yes, I like that."

She liked Damien's style. Easy and comfortable, as though he always knew just what he was about. And he was sensitive not only to a woman's hair; he was sensitive to the woman herself.

He stood behind her, studied her reflection in the mirror, stepped around from right to left and back again, examining her profile, the shape of her head, her reflection in the mirror, her "good" side, her "other" side, found she was pretty symmetrical, confirmed his initial impressions and choices, and then proceeded to do his special magic with comb and scissors. And all the while, the photographer was darting around her, here and there, busy with before-and-after shots, a few of which would be culled and used in the magazine's Galliard Sweep-Spree story.

When Damien was done, there wasn't a whole lot of hair on the floor, and yet what remained on Annie's head was unquestionably the best job of hair styling in all New York, loose and soft and young and innocently seductive. Damien held the hand mirror for her to inspect the rear view, but she didn't need to—she was already in awe: how had her familiar self just disappeared, before her very eyes, into the stylish Annie she saw in the mirror; how had her formerly adequate ponytail-do been undone and transformed into something glamorously simple yet glamorously up-to-the-minute?

"Damien," she said. "They're right. You do have magic fingers."

Damien just smiled. He'd heard that many times. Now he just

whisked away the towel from her shoulders, gave a last pat to the top of her head, and said, "I'll look forward to seeing you in *Lady Fair.*"

Annelie rode with her down to the lobby and took her leave. "You look so fabulously great," she said. "Every guy is going to fall totally and completely in love just looking at you."

These folks all talk in superlatives. Do they ever just say something is nice? Does everything have to be "great" and "fabulous" and "so totally awesome?" She raised an arm as an empty cab cruised by.

And I'm not sure I'd like it if "every guy" fell in love with me just like that.

"Troop B Headquarters," she said to the cab driver. "I hope you know where that is."

I've had guys in love with me. It doesn't always work out so well.

Chapter Seven

Headquarters, Please

Monday Afternoon

Ikechukwu Ndibe hadn't been long on the job, so he needed a rapid-fire conference with his Igbo dispatcher to find out where he'd find Troop B's headquarters.

Which gave Annie a minute to sit back, catch her breath, and think things over. She settled into her seat and enjoyed the first restful moments of this extraordinary day. The mirror told her she was looking her very prettiest. And for once in her life she had no complaints about her hair—thanks to the wonders worked by New York's humidity, Louis's chemical wizardry, and Damien's magic scissors. She flipped her hand through her new hairdo and felt generally very pleased with herself.

And even losing my bag turned out okay. And what's more—

Annie was determined to not let anything spoil the good time she was having.

You don't expect to come to New York and wind up at a real New York police station. Maybe it'll be like something out of Law and Order. *With Mafia types and crooks of all kinds being dragged into the precinct in handcuffs.*

And here I am listening to a conversation in some African language and I haven't a clue—can't get even a single word. Five years of school French and two of German, and they're no use to me now.

The driver clicked off his phone.

"Okay, miss. We go to Pier Seventy-Six—on Twelfth Avenue." With a single motion he started the meter and drove into the heavy flow of traffic. Annie read the driver's name off the license mounted on his seat back.

IKECHUKWU
NDIBE

Again, not a clue. Does the license list family name first—like "Doe, John"—or is Ikechukwu his given name? She felt shy about asking, and his accent was so heavy, she wasn't sure they wouldn't misunderstand each other. She abandoned the idea of making conversation. But it was he who spoke first.

"I know you, miss." With his head at a quarter turn toward her, she could see his big, genial smile. "On the TV," he said. "You lucky lady. You saved by policeman. So you bring good luck to my taxi. Now I am lucky, too."

I can't believe the way this trip is working out. In town for one day, and I'm a TV personality.

She returned the driver's smile and he turned his attention back to the road.

And there's another thing. What about that crazy scene yesterday? Who comes to New York and gets practically trampled by a wild mob? With posters and yelling—what was that all about? What's Buljornia? Or who? Is it a person? A place? I could have been killed. If not for that cop—

The television scene flashed through her memory. And with it, the sudden sense of his arm around her—the pressure against her ribs—her feet off the ground—the familiar horse-and-leather scent—animal and man working together, a single force—a gallant knight—riding to her rescue—

How many girls come to New York and get rescued by a cute cop?

Too bad she had no souvenir photo. Only the fleeting glance, the blue eyes and strong voice and the quick memory of a uniformed horseman riding herd on an ornery crowd. That would be all the souvenir she'd have to file away in her memory. Well, even that would be more than most girls got to take home with them.

But, gee, he absolutely took my breath away—

Ten minutes across town and now they were at the river's edge, in a neighborhood that seemed not to belong to the densely packed, vertical New York she'd seen until now. Here it was an empty scene of river-borne breezes and salt-scented air. Here, with only sparse traffic on the broad avenue that ran parallel to the river, with not a single pedestrian in sight, they rode through a silent waterfront neighborhood that was almost uninhabited. Here, instead of skyscrapers, the skyline was flat and close to street level. Long, low structures, like soulless warehouses, marched down the avenue's length, one after the other, as far as she could see. Annie felt she was riding through a different New York.

The driver pulled over to the curb.

"This is Pier Seventy-six," he said. He reached over and turned off the meter.

Set well back from the street, behind a great length of chain-link fencing, a few cars and vans were parked and beyond those, a bleak, gray, windowless structure stretched down the length of a couple of long city blocks. Along the top of the building's façade, there were great white letters:

UNITED STATES LINES

There wasn't a single person in sight and she wondered why the driver had brought her here. As she peered out at this unpromising sight, Mr. Ndibe apparently recognized her apprehension.

"Would you like me to wait while you go in, miss?"

"I don't know. I'm not sure this is the right place. I thought—"

But just then, as she peered through the cab's window, past the fence and the parked vehicles, she spotted the somewhat obscure sign, rather modest for such a vast structure and barely visible behind tree branches and chain-link fencing:

NYPD
MOUNTED UNIT
HEADQUARTERS TROOP B

"Oh, no. That's okay. I see it now. This is the right place. No need to wait. Thank you."

She paid him and got out, and he drove off, leaving her alone within an apparently uninhabited landscape.

Great place for a crime. If it weren't a police station, I'd be a little scared.

She was, in fact, a little scared.

There was an opening in the fence wide enough to allow a van to drive through and just beyond that, she saw a small hut.

Hardly any security here. Anyone could just walk right into this place. Maybe they rely on the isolation of this place to create their security.

She started across the parking space toward the glass door under the NYPD sign.

I just walked right in here—

But before she could take another step, a uniformed officer stepped out of the hut.

"Yes, miss. Can I help you?"

He was a big man in an NYPD uniform. He had a broad face and a wide, jolly smile and he seemed glad to see a person, any person, and especially a pretty young woman. His lonely job in this quiet, uneventful place could get really boring.

"You come to get your car, you'll need to go back there."

He pointed to the other end of the structure, a good fifth of a mile back in the direction she'd just come from. His smile was sympathetic and he shook his head, as though he felt sorry that she could have gotten herself into a really expensive error. "That's the impound back there."

She was momentarily puzzled, and then she sorted it all out.

"Oh, no," she said. "I'm not here for a car. I'm looking for Troop B headquarters."

His smile became even broader.

"Oh, sure, miss. Right over there. The general public doesn't come down to this end very much. Just go right in."

She went through the glass doors and into a space as bright and almost as spacious as the average high school gym. And almost totally empty. To the right, along the wall, was a reception desk, and behind it sat a young officer, casually T-shirt-topped, sitting way back in his precariously tipped-back chair. The name plate on the desk said "Caleb Kim."

"Can I help you, miss?"

She walked across the wood floor, aware of the sound of her boots echoing back at her.

"Hi," she said. "I lost a bag at a street demonstration yesterday. I had a message that it's been turned in here."

"You'll have to see the sergeant," Officer Kim said, "but he's with someone now." He gestured toward a door just behind him. "You can wait here." He pointed to a couple of folding chairs against the wall. "Sorry about the accommodations. We're moving to new quarters soon, so we're a little underfurnished right now."

"That's okay. I'm glad for a chance to just rest for a few minutes and take it all in. This city can be overwhelming."

Officer Kim brought his chair upright and he straightened himself up, too. Annie knew, from the way he was looking her over, she must be looking pretty good.

"So you're visiting here? Where from?"

"Wyoming. Laramie, actually."

"No kidding! Hey, I've seen that bucking bronco on your license plates. Does everyone out there ride horses?"

"Well, not exactly *everyone*—"

"Then maybe, while you're waiting, you'd like to see the stables."

"Well, yes. I'd love to. That would be great."

Just then, across the room, a set of broad doors opened and a couple of officers came out. Annie caught a glimpse of stables behind them.

"Hey, you guys," Officer Kim called across to them. "We've got a visitor here, from out west. She's waiting to see the sergeant. Maybe, while she's waiting, one of you guys could show the lady around, show her the stables." He turned to Annie. "I'd be glad to do it myself, but they need me here at the desk."

"I have some time," one of the officers called to her. "I'd be glad to give you the tour."

"Thanks so much. I really appreciate it." As she crossed the room, she was congratulating herself on the continuing flow of good luck.

I just know this is not on the usual tourist agenda. This is so great.

"No problem, ma'am. We like to have visitors here. Public relations is part of our job."

His companion said, "Sorry I can't join you, miss, but I have to get to a meeting," and with a quick, appraising look at Annie, up and down, he added, "I'm really sorry about that. Maybe another time." Under his breath, to his friend, he added, "Nice move, Chester. She's a cutie." And he was gone.

Officer Chester held the door for her and she stepped through into a veritable equine palace.

Wow!

The Cornell ranch back home had a barn for its horses. The barn had stalls. It had baled hay. It had feed bins and a feed trough. It had a tack room. It had corral space out back.

But it had nothing like this.

These stables were definitely the ultimate in luxury, the Ritz Hotel of horsedom.

"Wow!"

It was a whispered—but heartfelt—exclamation.

To her left was a training ring as big as the corral back home. To the right were rows of spacious box stalls that must have been designed for elegance as well as service, and obviously maintained fastidiously. Gleaming steel posts were topped by well-burnished brass finials. Mounted across the top of each stall was a brass plaque with the occupant's name in raised letters. Each stall was occupied, and each occupant kept a lively eye on Annie's movements as she walked past.

"We bring tours through these stables all the time," Officer Chester explained. "As you see," he said as he guided her past the aisles of stalls, "these horses are in first-rate condition. They've been very carefully selected and trained for the work they do, and they're cared for as if they were royalty. Each horse has its own feeding trough, and the department employs a team of civilian hostlers to care for the animals. Their shoes are specially created for high traction on city streets. Even their feed is specially designed and mixed for them."

Annie could tell he'd made this speech many times before.

He led her to the first stall in the nearest aisle. The horse lifted his head in an obvious greeting.

"This here is my horse," he said. "This is Ballyhoo." The horse lifted his head and nuzzled Officer Chester's shoulder.

"Sorry, buddy," the officer said. "I don't have anything for you today." Then to Annie, he explained, "I usually have a treat for him, but I didn't know I'd be coming back in today." He chuckled. "He won't starve. These guys get plenty to eat."

Just then the door to the stables opened and Officer Kim looked in.

"Hey, Chester," he called. "Some visitors just walked in and I'm going off duty now. We'll need you to show them around."

"I'll be right there," Chester said. Then, to Annie, "Sorry about that, ma'am. I'm going to have to leave you now. But feel free to walk around, say hello to the horses. Stay as long as you like."

"Oh, sure. I'll be fine," Annie said.

And he was gone.

Alone in the stables, she was free to take a leisurely stroll up and down the rows of stalls, to greet the horses as they put their heads out of the stalls to examine her, to pat a muzzle here or there, stroke a mane, enjoy the familiar pleasure of running the back of her hand along that lovely, soft place along a horse's cheek, to say a word or two of greeting to these beautiful animals. She recognized at once that these were horses of remarkably gentle and unflappable dispositions—as of course they would have to be—but they were also the four-legged royals of the NYPD. They seemed to know they were a special breed, a cadre of highly trained "officers," ready to do their invaluable job with the valor, dignity, and intelligence that come with good genes, good training, and a willing spirit. Though they were pretty much uniform in color, some were quarter horses, some were mixed breed, she saw a couple of Arabs, and even one thoroughbred. But each was beautiful, each was clearly an intelligent animal, and each one seemed comfortable with strangers, some going so far as to nuzzle at her, as though expecting to receive a treat.

She paused at one stall, responding to what seemed to be the demand of a big bay who shook his dark mane at her and lifted his head as though he wanted to be friends.

She couldn't help smiling at the mischievous quality of his invitation.

"Well, you're a smart one, aren't you?" He was pushing against her shoulder, as though he expected something from her. "Sorry, I have nothing to give you," she said, showing him her empty hand. He tapped his hoof a couple of times on the floor of his stall, as though he had a Morse code message for her; she touched her forehead to his, as though maybe they could communicate that way. She stroked her hand along the side of his neck. "Oh, you're a beautiful thing," she whispered. The horse twitched an ear in response. She pressed her face against his, and even more softly, she said, "You sure make friends easily."

"That's Lindy." The voice was just over her shoulder. "He recognizes you."

Her hand on the horse's shoulder stiffened. She recognized the voice instantly. Just coming up behind her like that, without any warning—it wasn't the first time he'd taken her breath away.

She didn't turn around. She needed a moment to take in—to enjoy—the swirl of pleasure and surprise, the interesting combination of feelings his presence, so close to her, had produced. Through her hand, pressed even more firmly against Lindy's dark coat, she felt the strong pulse of the horse's blood and it matched the sudden throb of her own response. She closed her eyes; she took one deep breath. She needed another moment to feel steady again.

Then, slowly, looking casually over her shoulder, not making any real move toward him, she said, "Oh, hi. It's you." Her hand continued to stroke Lindy.

"Yes, ma'am," he said. "It's me." He was enjoying her surprise. He stepped around to her side and the horse stretched out his neck in greeting. "I see you two are getting reacquainted." He held a hand to Lindy's face, and she saw he had a bit of carrot for the horse.

There again was the merry expression of his face, the twinkle in his eyes, and she thought of leprechauns. Horse and rider seemed to be a good match.

"Oh, yes, we're practically old friends now. He's a beautiful horse."

"Oh, you betcha," he said. "Lindy here is a very special animal." He fed the horse another bit of carrot. "You must be Annie Cornell. I'm Sergeant Hardin. Bart Hardin. Glad to see you got here safely. I wouldn't want you to have any more adventures. You gotta be careful in this big, bad city. You can't count on having a police officer on hand every minute to pull you out of danger."

"Well, Sergeant Hardin, I—"

"And we have your bag."

"Yes, I got the message that it had been found."

"One of our officers picked it up right after that demonstration. That crowd had its own problems to think about and weren't noticing ladies' handbags. I've got it right back there in my office." He held the door for her as they left the stables to cross the big reception area. "You'll have to identify the contents and everything—we'll need some paperwork taken care of." His voice had become official as he led her out of the stables, passing Officer Chester, who was bringing the visitors into the stables.

The group wasn't very large—not more than seven or eight people. A little girl—she couldn't have been more than seven—had on a child-size helmet, and at Ballyhoo's stall, Officer Chester said, "Hey, you want a ride?" Her face lit up, her mama signaled okay, and she was hoisted up bareback onto Ballyhoo. The officer led the horse and his little rider for a short walk up and back in the aisle of stalls.

The little girl's older brother looked on enviously and her mom and grandma took photos with their cell phones while Chester talked about the program, the selection and training of the horses, the amenities of the facility.

Three tourists from upstate asked questions, and an earnest woman who was writing a children's story about a police horse was taking notes, doing her research, being careful to miss nothing.

And at the edge of the group, the last member of the little party also took pictures, using an old film camera that hung from a strap around his neck. He was a tall man with a thick mustache. He wore round eyeglasses, he had no eyebrows at all, and his head was as bald as an egg. And he, too, took notes, writing unobtrusively—on the lined, pale green pages of a small spiral notebook. Each page had a light red line running down the center of each page.

Chapter Eight

Pride and Prejudice

Monday Late Afternoon

Compared with the deliberate elegance of the stables, the sergeant's office looked like a grudging afterthought. In one corner a couple of battered metal file cabinets leaned against the wall. Wire bins of scattered papers perched atop one of them. A precinct map, half torn and retaped, was tacked to the wall along with a calendar from a local body repair shop. Two desks, also battered and scratched, were against opposite walls, facing away from each other. Like everything else in this office, the two desks had lived through generations of mounted police and more than one move around town, changing locations as city administrations changed and the city's real estate values went through its ups and downs. Clearly, though no expense had been spared in providing for the animal troops, the human ones—well, they managed with the space and the furniture they were given.

At the desk on the left, an officer was at work on a stack of reports. He looked up as they came in and swiveled his chair around to smile at Annie. She glanced at the name on the brass plate on his desk.

SERGEANT MAX WOZINSKY

"Don't mind me," he said. "I'm just the gofer around here. You go ahead with whatever the sergeant here is doing to earn his pay." He gestured toward Bart.

Bart pulled up a chair next to the other desk, a chair that was worn and torn, its leather seat repaired with duct tape.

"Just sit here," he said. He held the chair for her and she sat. His own chair was of the swivel variety and he spun it once before he dropped his big frame into it. "And don't pay any attention to that guy over there," Bart said airily. "We just keep him around to run errands for us."

"Yeah, he's the cute one. I'm the guy that does all the real work around here."

Max Wozinsky looked to be about forty years old. Clearly, despite the difference in their ages, the two men were good friends.

"I have your bag right here," Bart said. He pulled at the bottom drawer. It didn't open. He pulled again, with an irritation showing around his mouth. The drawer was old, sticky, and recalcitrant. It wouldn't open. He struggled with it and Annie saw that he was embarrassed. It's hard for a man to look cool, authoritative, and masterly when his own desk drawer is fighting him. What should have been a smooth move had turned awkward. She smiled to herself and kindly looked away. She studied the items on his desk. Beginning with the nameplate.

SERGEANT BARTLETT HARDIN

He continued to struggle with the drawer, and she continued to study the items on the desk: a clutch of papers in a metal letter tray waiting for his attention; an old Starbucks cup holding a bunch of pencils, mostly sharpened; a framed black-and-white snapshot of someone's home—a pretty, clapboard two-story house, sun-dappled, with trees and shrubbery and a planting of flowers along the entrance pathway—and a big desk blotter that covered most of the surface of the desk with a couple of business cards stuck under its edges. She also noticed there were no pictures of kids or, possibly, a wife. Or girlfriend. She smiled again to herself.

At last, the drawer gave in and slid meekly open. Bart glared at it and reached in for the bag.

"Here it is," he said. "The department provides all sorts of great equipment," he added, with some irritation, "but just not to us here in this room. Sorry about that. I guess the city has bigger problems than the desks at Troop B headquarters. They've moved us around so much, we're lucky to still have a mailing address." He put the bag on the top of the blotter.

Annie's gesture indicated "no problem."

"No need to ID the contents. I saw your photo on the driver's license. But I will ask you to examine the contents—see that nothing's missing. You can do that while I get the report ready for you to sign." He started a two-finger job of completing the report. "I had to examine the contents of your bag," he said, "so I could locate you. To let you know it had been found." He didn't tell her that the more usual procedure would have been to just hold any lost property until someone came around to claim it. He didn't tell her he'd gone out of his way to identify her. And he didn't tell her that back there, during the demonstration, he'd had one quick look at her scared face and, as he'd lifted her out of the melee and felt her warm body against his arm, a current of strength ran up to his shoulder and down his spine. And he didn't tell her that, when he'd had one more quick look, as he'd turned Lindy back to that crazy crowd, as he'd called after her, his mind's eye took an indelible picture of her. He didn't tell her she'd looked so pretty in her flowery dress, but so lost out there in the street—

And while he filled in the required form, and spun his fantasies of rescue and his own nobility, Annie was thinking her own less elevated thoughts. Annie was making a more earthy observation of the man who was sitting there, pecking awkwardly at the keyboard.

She decided "cute" was not quite the right word for Sergeant Hardin. The shoulders were a little too broad, and the arms and chest a little too muscular—evident even in the light blue shirt that was his summer uniform. His manner was altogether too self-confident and commanding to be called cute. And "cute" was definitely not the message of authority and skill that went with the uniform and its reminder of a trained and armed protective force. But still, there was something about the improbably curly flare of reddish hair—sandy, really—and the deep crinkles around the wickedly blue eyes, and the broad mouth and its happy, easy, even mischievous, grin.

That face has done a lot of smiling, she thought. *There is definitely something cute about that expression, as though maybe his grandfather was indeed a leprechaun.*

In the meantime, Bart had finished preparing the form for her to sign. "I'll just read you the list and you check that it's all there," he said.

The list. Oh, yes. The things in my bag!
She was shaken out of her daydream.
He took each item from the bag as he read from the list.

"Contents as follows: One small pack Kleenex tissues." He placed the tissues on the desk blotter, to be followed by each item in turn. "One small makeup case containing one lipstick and one mirror. Three nickels and one quarter. One stick Juicy Fruit chewing gum. One iPhone in pink case. One wallet, leather, tan, containing eighty-three dollars cash, one hotel room entry card, one Wells Fargo Bank credit card, one Wells Fargo debit card. Also one photo ID, Library Staff, University of Wyoming Department of Veterinary Studies."

He looked up at her. "You're a librarian?"

"Yes, in the veterinary department at the university."

"No kidding. I once knew a girl who wanted to be a librarian. Way back in high school."

She didn't say anything. What was there to say?

He went back to the inventory.

"One Wyoming driver's license number 670452-635."

Oh, Lord! Now he knows my age, my height, my weight. And that awful photo!

"And also one color snapshot. Two boys." He held the wallet open to display the boys' picture. Without looking at her, he asked, "Are they yours?" He said it as casually as he could. As though it was the idlest question in the world.

"Oh, no. They're my sister's boys. Brandon and Buckley. Bran's eight and Buck's just turned six." She was mad for those boys and the picture held her affectionate attention for a moment. And that's why she didn't notice the relieved little smile that passed over Sergeant Hardin's face.

He leaned back in the chair, letting the official manner drop away. "Right," he said. "And then there's the last item in the bag—there's a letter. From *Lady Fair* magazine. I see you won a contest. Sounds like a really big one. Congratulations. Is that what brought you to New York?"

"Yes, it is."

"Have you ever been here before, Miss Cornell?"

"No, this is my very first time. I've never been out of Wyoming."

He said nothing for a few moments, as though he had something on his mind.

"My sister's here with me," she added. "It's a first for her, too."

"Mmm hmmm."

He looked over the form, made sure all was in order, and hit "print." Neither of them spoke while they waited for the old machine to crank out the paper.

"So I guess that's it, Miss Cornell. If you'll just sign this form"— he handed the paper over to her—"and that's all we'll need. You're free to leave."

But even as she signed the paper and handed it back to him, she felt that he paused, that there was more he wanted to say. She waited a moment, then slipped the bag over her shoulder and stood up.

"Well, then—"

"Actually, Miss Cornell, it's much too far to walk back to your hotel, and the taxis don't cruise much in this neighborhood."

"Maybe I could take the subway? I've heard so much about the New York subways. Or one of the buses across town."

His laugh was quick and easy.

"No, I wouldn't want you to take the subway, what with your being new here in the city and not yet familiar with its ways. Too easy to get lost. Anyway, it's a long walk to the nearest subway from here. Tell you what, ma'am." He stood up, pushing the chair so that it rolled back on its casters. "I'm off duty in a few minutes. I'll drive you back to your hotel. I don't want you out wandering around this part of the city alone. Don't want you getting yourself into any more trouble." He came around the desk and stood close enough for her to look right into those blue eyes. "That way, I'll know you got back to your hotel safely."

"Oh, I'm sure I'll be fine. I'll just—"

And there was that leprechaun grin again. "Please, ma'am. I'll take you back to your hotel. See you get there safely." He stood up and headed out of the office. "You just wait here. I'll change and be right back." And he was out the door before she could get out a single word of protest, leaving her standing there, openmouthed and contemplating the empty space he'd just left.

Well! He sure is full of himself! Like I need to be ferried around like some fragile little creature.

She turned to Max, who'd been watching them with a little smile on his face.

"Is he always so bossy?"

"I guess he does seem that way."

"He didn't even wait for me to say yes or no."

"He's a pretty take-charge kind of guy."

"And I suppose that's a good thing, in a policeman?"

"Yes, it is, ma'am. And Bart Hardin comes by it naturally."

"Oh? That sounds like there's a story there."

"Yes, there is. But I'll let him tell you himself. I have a feeling he's going to get around to it."

"Oh?"

"Well, you're going to be here for a few days, aren't you?"

"Yes."

"Well, like I said, I think he'll have a chance to tell you about it."

He turned back to his work and Annie didn't want to interrupt him.

Bart was back in about fifteen minutes, in jeans, jacket, and biker boots. He'd also managed to take the fastest shave on record, but Annie couldn't have known that—unless she'd caught a whiff of the aftershave.

He handed her a motorcycle helmet.

"Here. Put this on."

"But— I thought—"

No car?

"You'll be safe with me, Miss Cornell."

"Oh, I didn't mean—"

"You'll be okay," Max said from across the room. "The sergeant's a good driver."

"Yes, I am a good driver," Bart said. "And I don't want you wandering around alone, Miss Cornell. I'll get you back to your hotel safely."

Was he being condescending? Or just gentlemanly? Should she tell him she was capable of getting herself back to her hotel without an escort? Or just say thank you and accept the ride?

"Well. Thank you. I guess."

"Go on," he said. "Put it on." He was pointing to the helmet.

"Oh. Right."

And they worked so hard on my hair. Now it'll be a mess.

He was holding the door for her.

Don't make a fuss, Annie. He's being generous, driving you back to the hotel. Just put on the damn helmet and say thank you.

"Thanks for the ride. It really is very kind of you."

"No problem, Miss Cornell. Public relations is an important part of our work, and I'm happy to give a ride to a visitor from the wild west, someone who might get lost or get herself into trouble here in the big city." He turned to Max and winked. He made no effort to hide the wink. "I wouldn't want that to happen to you again, Miss Cornell."

"Oh, please." She could hear the sarcasm in her tone. "And I wish you would just call me Annie."

He gave her a big smile, as though he'd just received a wonderful gift.

"You got it, Annie."

He followed her out into the big reception area. But just before he left the office, as he passed through the door, he turned and flashed a huge grin at Max who, with an approving smile in return, lifted two fingers to his eyebrow and snapped them away in a quick salute.

Chapter Nine

Getting Closer

She'd have figured him for a big Harley, or maybe even a fancy Ducati, something show-offy and macho—something predictably self-important. So she was surprised to see the bright blue Yamaha FZ1 that was waiting for them among all the parked vehicles—a good, serviceable machine with not a shred of show-off about it. And probably bought used, too, by the look of it.

Who'd have thought?

She hung her bag across her body, made sure the helmet was se-cure—

"Hop on," he said.

—she climbed onto the bike behind him—

"Hang on," he said.

—and she wrapped her arms around his body.

"Okay," she said. "Let's go!"

Back home in Laramie, lots of folks had motorcycles. Men and women. Old and young. Annie had been riding around, hanging on, ever since she could remember. She'd owned a bike herself for a few years, until she got her Jeep. Many times she'd climbed on behind a boy, and always she'd put her arms around him to hold on while they rode from here to wherever. But never, *never* had she had this experi-ence. Never before had the contact, body to body, connected like a flow of current running between them, like a gently electrified synergy, this warm suffusion—a physical reality that spread through her chest, and down her arms and along her spine.

She was so startled, she needed to take one long, slow breath to let the extraordinary sensation settle throughout her body.

This was so unexpected. His body felt so *comfortable* against hers. As though they matched perfectly, as though the rhythm of the blood flowing through their two bodies, her front against his back, was in perfect sync. She could have closed her eyes and dreamed herself all the way across the city, back to her hotel, clinging to this suddenly magical man, but she felt too alive to close her eyes and she wanted to miss no moment of this remarkable experience. So with eyes wide open she hung on as he wheeled out onto Twelfth Avenue and headed for 42nd Street.

It's funny how that is—a man who'd only minutes ago seemed so officious, with his irritating air of macho posturing and unquestioning command, now felt appealingly manly and all warm and desirable in her arms. With the speed, and her needing to hang on securely, there was an unmistakable thrill, an intimacy, a definite connection, body to body, that was much more sensual than she'd expected. Maybe more sensual than he had any right to make her feel.

Is this why guys buy motorcycles?

All the way along 42nd Street, whipping through traffic and zipping past buses and vans and taxis, surrounded by the city's racket, the sounds of horns and sirens and diesel engines clacking away around them, she heard nothing, as though it had all receded into a fuzzy, warm blanket of friendly activity. He was taking them through it all and she was happy to just be there, contentedly hanging on, enjoying the really nice feel of him in her arms.

It would have been fine with her if the ride lasted longer, but there she was, too soon, in front of her hotel, and she had to get off. So she did. And he did, too.

She was unwilling to look at him directly, unwilling to reveal what she'd experienced. But she needed to force herself to face him as she unstrapped the helmet and handed it to him.

"Thank you, Sergeant."

He was looking at her funny. Intently. Searching into her eyes, as though he'd find there an answer to a question he wasn't ready to ask.

"Call me Bart," he said, taking the helmet, but still giving her that deep look. "Call me Bart. Forget the sergeant stuff."

"Okay. Bart."

Then, as though he was waking up, he said, "Listen. You haven't had dinner. I'm going to take you to a place just up the street here—makes great soup. And sandwiches. And Irish shepherd's pie. Best in the city."

Suddenly, there he was again—Bossy Cop, Know-It-All, Take-Charge-Macho-Man, ready to run her life. Not even consulting her first. Went and spoiled all that nice warm and fuzzy feeling.

Still. She'd had nothing since those tiny corn muffins and the pasta salad, she argued to herself. And the carrot sticks. Hours ago. And an unplanned dinner would be a nice addition to the twists this day was taking, wouldn't it?

"I'll have to run upstairs and tell my sister."

"You do that. I'll wait for you here. Tell her we won't be late," he called after her as she disappeared into the lobby.

"Run upstairs" meant, of course, another heart-thumping elevator ride up forty-four floors. But she was getting used to it, and she took the moment to check the mirror and see the damage the helmet and the ride had done to her hair.

Oh, Lord! After all Damien's good work. He'd shoot me if he saw this.

She raked her hands through her hair—and was then surprised to see the magic of a first-rate cut: the wild tangle settled right into place; nothing more than a light touch with a brush would be needed.

"Go ahead, honey," Liz said. "I've been out sightseeing all day and I've had enough excitement. I'll have room service bring me a hamburger and I'll just veg out here. A quiet evening alone—oh, God!—when was the last time I had a quiet evening alone? Someone to bring my dinner, and the TV all to myself." She folded herself up on the sofa and looked as comfy as a cat. "Go. Go. Have a good time. Take your cell phone. Don't get into any more trouble."

"No trouble," Annie called over her shoulder. "How can I get into any trouble? I have police protection."

Chapter Ten

A. J. Keenan's

The tables at A. J. Keenan's were thick wood slabs, rough-hewn, and varnished to a high gloss, and the seats, too, in the booths, were solid and comfy. The lighting was gentle—a large antique chandelier above all and a small candle at each table—and the bar was far enough from the diners that the soccer on the TV was not intrusive. The decor was Irish and friendly—masses of old photos on the walls, and posters including notices of age-old political rallies and theatrical performances of plays by Synge and O'Casey; small cabinets and shelves on all the walls all full of knick-knacks and figurines, wood carvings and homey teacups and teapots, an arched brick fireplace at one wall and an antique pendulum clock mounted on another. And against the wall of their booth, a few fresh flowers in a glass.

The waitress, too, was Irish and friendly. She put a basket of soda bread between them and handed them each a menu. Before she could even look at it, Bart took it from Annie's hand.

"We'll have the shepherd's pie," he told the waitress. "And a Guinness."

What!?

Annie's mouth fell open, but no word came out.

"And a green salad on the side." He handed the menus to the waitress. "And how are you doing, Katie? And the kids?"

"We're good. And how's yourself? And your mom?"

"All good."

"And that noble horse of yours?" She smiled at Annie, including her in the talk. "When am I going to see him around here? You're always keeping him across town at Times Square."

"I go where they send me. But we were just here yesterday—that demonstration over by the UN."

"Oh, the kids saw that on the TV. Was that you?"

"Were we on the news? I didn't see. But then, maybe they saw Annie here. She got herself caught up in it. Needed a bit of rescuing from those bozos."

"Ooh." She turned a kind eye on Annie. "Not hurt, I hope?"

"I don't—"

But again, before she could answer, Bart was speaking for her.

"Oh, she's all right. Just shaken up a bit."

Annie's indignation was beginning to show.

But this time it was Katie's turn to break in. She turned sharply on Bart.

"The girl does have a mouth, Bart. She doesn't need you to speak for her." She turned again to Annie. "You can speak, can't you, dear?"

"Of course I can speak. I do just fine on my own."

"Sorry about that," Bart said briefly, not at all sorry. "Katie, this is Annie, visiting from Wyoming and new to the city."

"And obviously in need of some big lummox to do her talking for her." Katie smiled affectionately at him and then, to Annie, said, "Don't mind this big ox. He gets so used to being in charge, he forgets his manners." She tapped Bart's arm with the menus. "Shame on you, Bart Hardin. If I tell your mother on you, you know what she'll say."

"Katie's a neighbor from way back," Bart explained. "Three houses down from us in Windsor Terrace in Brooklyn. She's known me since I was a little tad and she gets to scold me when I'm out of line. I wasn't out of line, was I?" He expected no answer and turned to Katie. "I'm just seeing to it that she gets a better impression of our city than she had yesterday."

And who appointed you? Annie thought, but she kept her mouth shut. He was among friends and she wouldn't embarrass him by arguing with him here.

"Well, Annie. Bart's a good one to show you around, so long as he behaves." And to Bart, she added, "You see you behave, you hear me. No getting all bossy, like you do. Let the girl enjoy herself, you hear," and she gave him another parting tap on the shoulder with the menus.

"Glad to meet you, Annie. You two have a good evening, now." And she was off.

"I really could have ordered for myself, you know," Annie said quietly, glad that it was now just the two of them. "We do have restaurants in Laramie and I've been reading from menus ever since I became a big girl."

"Ah, but you wouldn't have known about the shepherd's pie. The best in town, here at Keenan's. I couldn't let you go back to Laramie without ever trying the shepherd's pie at Keenan's."

Bossy is right, she thought. *Look at him. Sitting there, like all's right with his world. Just so full of himself.*

It was true; Bart was sitting back in the booth, expansive, self-satisfied, the king of the hill.

And looking at me like I'm a chocolate chip cookie and he's the five-year-old who's going to eat me up. The nerve of him. I ought to—

But before she could decide what she ought to do, Bart interrupted her thought.

"So tell me, Annie Cornell. Shouldn't you be wearing glasses and have your hair in a bun?"

Omigod! I can't believe he said that!

"Just kidding," he added, laughing. "But you are an innocent librarian from Laramie, aren't you? And I worry about you wandering around this city without a proper escort. Look at what happened to you yesterday. You don't know your way around here. You could have been really hurt. And not only from crazy street protesters; there are plenty of bad guys around just waiting to take advantage. You need a man like me to keep an eye on you, see that you're safe—"

"Now wait a minute, Mr. Big-City Policeman! I'm sure I could get around perfectly safely without needing a special police patrol to take care of me. And what's more, whatever you think of librarians, I promise you, you got it wrong. You think we're prissy old maids with horn-rimmed glasses, saying 'Shhh!' all the time. That's so old!" She could feel her hackles rising. "That's so *wrong!* It's such a stupid stereotype!"

"But I was just—" he tried to break in.

"And furthermore—"

"Whoa, there! Hold your horses! I didn't mean to get you all ruffled." He'd come forward in his seat, leaning toward her. "I don't see what I said that was so awful. I wasn't trying to put down librarians.

I've got nothing against librarians. I think librarians are just swell. A bad joke, I guess. But really, I was serious about—I mean, I just meant that you don't know your way around here, being new to the city and all, and I didn't want you to get yourself into another bad situation. And I'd kind of like to be the one who—the one to—I mean—"

Now he was getting tangled up in his apology.

She was still rankled about the librarian thing but was calming down.

Well, so what. Not my business to educate the world.

She told herself to ease up—to remember that he actually had come to her rescue (was it only yesterday?) and after all, he *was* being generous with his time and attention. Obviously, he liked her, and there was no need for her to be ungracious. And he looked so earnest, with the light from the little candle on the table adding a cherub-like glow to his face, and the light sandiness of his hair darkened a couple of tones in the pub's soft lighting, he seemed to have an air of almost little-boy innocence. Not quite little boy, of course, but if she looked closely, she could see the younger version of him. Maybe the one Katie could see. Not the uniformed mounted rescuer he'd been yesterday, and not the one across the table from her with the holstered sidearm she'd spotted under his jacket, but the boy who would one day grow into that man.

Enough of snap judgments, she decided. And, with a sly little smile deep down inside herself, she remembered the warm buzz she'd felt on the ride across town. The feelings she'd had then certainly earned him a few more points.

Maybe she ought to get to know him better.

She broke off a bit of the soda bread, put a bit of butter on it and nibbled at it thoughtfully.

"Okay," she said, taking off on a new tack. "I guess we could start over." She leaned back in the booth, letting herself relax.

And as though on cue, Katie arrived just at that moment with their beers.

"Glad to see you two getting along so well," she said, putting their glasses on the table. "Enjoy your Guinness," she said cheerily. "I'll be back with your dinner in a few." And she was gone.

"So," Annie restarted the conversation, "tell me more about that wonderful horse of yours. Why is he so wonderful? And how did he get his name? Was he named for the Lindy Hop?"

Bart leaned back, too, glad to see that the storm clouds had passed and that the subject had been changed to one he really loved to talk about.

"No, it was nothing like that. Though I guess he could have been, come to think of it. The choice of his name does kind of go back to the swing era."

He raised his glass toward Annie in a gesture that acknowledged her—and his subject—and he began.

Chapter Eleven

Lindy's Story

Monday Evening

"Lindy is well known around town, especially in the theater district, around Times Square. He's a big favorite with the actors—they like to stop by before a performance and chat with him a little. They say he brings them good luck. They give him treats and they teach him tricks, and have their pictures taken with him. And the tourists, too. They all stop and ask about him. My mom keeps a scrapbook of his photos and his newspaper clippings."

"He's a beautiful animal," Annie said. "And I could see he's well-schooled."

"I'm guessing you know something about horses—I saw the ranch address on your license. So you know a good quarter horse when you see one, don't you?"

"Yes, I do. And I saw your work with the crowd yesterday. Just like our horses—trained for cutting and herding, which is really no different from crowd control. Just that here in New York, it's people instead of steers."

"Well, yes. Similar. Except Lindy has to deal with maybe a little more danger. Armed attackers. Terrorists. Crazy people." He laughed. "And the press. And TV personalities. He gets interviewed a lot. And photographed. So he has to know how to be polite and how to show off for the public."

"On the TV, they said something about an award you both got. I didn't get to hear the whole story, but I had the impression it was for something heroic."

Bart looked both embarrassed and a little proud. "Oh, that." He made a face, as if to say it was all in a day's work. "It was really Lindy, more than me. Back in February, I guess it was. There'd been a fire, in one of those old brownstones just off Broadway. Some of those houses and hotels have been there a long time and are pretty run down. I was patrolling along Ninth Avenue and Lindy smelled smoke down the street. He knows to signal me when there's danger—he kind of pulls his head up and bares his teeth—and he led me to this place where a fire had started in the basement. I got there fast as I could but it was already moving to the floors above. I called for police backup and the fire trucks. But in the meantime, I heard kids crying inside. The front door was locked and the smoke coming out from under was black and thick, and the kids were screaming so I had to work fast. Most of us cops wear a quick-deploy survival bracelet, so I had about twenty feet of paracord. Just pulled it loose real fast, knotted it round the doorknob and then to the saddle and Lindy pulled that door right off the frame. I got right inside and found those kids, four little ones, all hanging on to each other, screaming and so scared. Got 'em out right away, piled 'em up on Lindy and by the time the fire trucks arrived, Lindy and I had those kids out of there and up the street. Turned out their mom had gone to the corner to buy some groceries and she'd locked them in so they'd be safe. Almost lost them all. There were some folks upstairs, too, but the firemen got them out in time. I figured Lindy was the hero that day, and the media was all over the story."

"That's very impressive," Annie said. "So along with all his charm, he's also got a good story to tell his kids." She laughed and corrected herself. "I mean, for you to tell your kids."

Bart paused. Then, quietly, he said. "Lindy's a good police horse. That story is just the most recent. There have been others. He knows how to do his job."

Annie sensed that something had stopped the flow. So she tried a different tack.

"So how did Lindy come by that name?"

Bart's attention returned to her.

"Lindy?"

Again he paused, as though deciding where to start.

"Well, to begin with, this Lindy used to be my dad's horse. And there were other Lindys before this one. "

He saw she was surprised.

"Oh, you didn't know, of course. See, my dad was a mounted policeman before me. The first Lindy was a gift to him and the others just followed naturally after. It's a long story."

They both got ready for the long story. She put her elbows on the table and rested her chin in her hand. He stretched his arms expansively along the back of the booth, as though he was about to take in years of history. His eyes took on a storyteller's distant gaze.

"Back when my dad was a kid, there was a restaurant on Broadway, in Times Square, that was owned by a guy named Gus Lindberg. Now, everyone called him Lindy, so when he opened the restaurant, he decided to call it by his nickname. Now, I'm not saying Lindy Lindberg was a shady character, because I don't know that for sure. But I do know he opened the original place during the speakeasy days, back in the twenties, during Prohibition, so he must have had the right connections. And I know the place was popular with the old-time Broadway crowd, including gamblers and mob types. Also, theater people, the old vaudeville acts, comics. Newspaper people, too, the theater critics and sports writers. And later on, when television came in, the TV producers, too. They came to hang out with each other, to trade jokes and stories and catch up on the latest gossip.

"And they also came to Lindy's for the cheesecake Lindy's wife made. Lily Lindberg's cheesecake was something special and pretty soon Broadway folks were all fans of the cheesecake at Lindy's. In fact, I think it was Lindy's cheesecake that started America eating cheesecake."

Annie looked quizzically at him.

"Really?"

"Really! You could Google it."

"Okay. If you say so." She made a mental note to do a little research on the subject.

Bart continued, past the interruption.

"Now, when Prohibition ended, Lindy continued to run it as a regular restaurant. And it continued to be a hangout for the Broadway regulars—shady and otherwise. And, like I said, that included sports writers. And it just so happens that one of the very best sports writers of that time was my mom's dad, my granddad Malone. Jimmy Malone wrote for one of the old New York newspapers, long gone now, like most of the old great ones. Maybe you've heard of some of them—like the *Journal-American,* the *World Telegram,* the *New York Herald-Tribune.* Well, sometimes Granddad Malone's columns were about Lindy's and the guys—and the dolls—that hung out there. And because they were a very mixed and interesting bunch of people, and because the stories my granddad wrote were so great, the columns got a lot of attention for the restaurant and Lindy was convinced my granddad's stories were what made it the famous place it became. And, being an honorable man, Lindy figured he owed Granddad a special thank you. So right around that time was when my dad was born, in 1950, and old Lindy was so grateful, he wanted to give the baby— my dad—a special present, something that would live on, long into the future. And what he did was he wrote in his will that when the baby grew up, on his twenty-fifth birthday, he would receive a sum of money, held in trust for him, which was to be used to help him in whatever career he would have chosen for his life's work. It was a hefty sum, and of course it had accrued interest over the years. By the time my dad was twenty-five, he was already in training to be a mounted cop, and he knew how he wanted to use that money. What he wanted was to have his own horse.

"Now it just so happens that when my mom's family, the Malones, came to this country way back in the early 1800s, they'd settled out west, in Wyoming, up north of where you're from, up by Casper."

That took Annie by surprise. "So of course," she said, "you noticed right away that I'm from Laramie—not far from your people. Small world." She made another mental note to check out the Malone ranch— see just how close these "neighbors" were. "Is the ranch still operating?"

"Sure is. When I was a kid, we used to go out there every year. I spent most of my summers on the Malone ranch. And my dad did, too. So he knew, if he was going to get his own horse, he couldn't do better than to head out to Wyoming and get one out of that herd. So he went and chose what turned out to be the first of the Lindy horses, a beautiful, smart bay yearling, and of course he named him Lindy, after his benefactor. He brought that Lindy back to New York, and donated him to the force to be trained for police work. When that one—the first Lindy —was too old for police work, Dad returned him to stand at stud on the ranch. And he sired the Lindy I'm riding now."

"That's a real coincidence. So you've got Wyoming roots, too," Annie said.

"That's why I noticed right away from your driver's license that you were a Wyoming girl. And that your home address was a local ranch near Laramie. So I figure you know horses."

Annie smiled. "We're a cattle ranch, but of course we have some horses. Good quarter horses. Like Lindy. Maybe, if it's okay, I could— oh wait—"

She was interrupted by the arrival of Katie and their food.

"You could what?"

"Never mind. It can wait."

Katie set down their plates. "Enjoy," she said, and she was off.

The aroma of savory lamb stew under the browned topping of mashed potatoes replaced all thought of horses and ranches and police work. She'd save her question till later.

"This looks great," Annie said, "and it smells great."

"I promise you," Bart said, "this is the best you'll get anywhere in New York." He held up his glass of beer. "And here's a toast to your visit, and to your winning that contest. And maybe to more visits some time."

They clinked glasses. She smiled, he smiled, they tucked into their shepherd pies, and a few minutes passed before Annie said anything.

"Do you suppose I could get the recipe?"

"I doubt it. No way Keenan will share. But I could ask my mom. I think hers is even better, though I wouldn't say it out loud around here." Then he remembered. "There was something else you wanted to ask, wasn't there?"

"Yes, there was something else I wanted to ask." Annie hesitated, because she knew she might be overstepping. But this whole trip had been so full of extra treats, she decided that maybe her good luck hadn't yet run out. "I'm going to be all tied up tomorrow, and probably the rest of the week, too. I don't expect we'll meet again while I'm here, and I was wondering if it's possible that maybe tonight we could go back to the stables and you could introduce me properly to Lindy. I'd love to take a couple of pictures with him—as a memento of this trip?"

"Hey, that's a great idea." He restrained a satisfied little fist pump. "But I meant what I said about seeing to it that you get a proper tour of this city. And I didn't mean just tonight. You shouldn't be wandering alone without a proper escort and I'd like to be your escort for the rest of your time here."

Am I pleased? Amused? Irritated? What am I to make of this guy?

She looked into her shepherd's pie. What was left of it. She scooped up a forkful of lamb.

But he is really cute. And I think he means well, even if he is all full of himself. And I do want to see that stable.

She hit the mental rewind button and went back to where she'd left off.

"Does that mean you have access at headquarters any time?"

"Why, sure. I can go in there whenever I'd like. Tonight would be great. It's quiet. Only the night shift is on. Let's do it. I'd like you and Lindy to get better acquainted."

"Then let's skip dessert," she said. "It's been a couple of really packed days and I have to be up early tomorrow for more of the same." She finished the last bit of her Guinness, Bart did the same, got his credit card charged, and with a warm good night to Katie, they were heading back across town on the blue motorcycle.

Chapter Twelve

Making Friends

Yes, the stables were quiet. Quiet for the moment, at least. Some of the stalls were empty, their usual occupants out on the night shift and not due back until after midnight; those present had been fed, groomed and bedded down for the night, at rest after a days' good work. But alertness was both bred and trained into these animals, and they all came to attention when Bart switched on a single small light and led Annie to Lindy's stall. In the soft illumination, all heads turned toward them, all ears pricked up, all eyes scanned the unexpected visitors.

Annie felt the thrill of being a special guest, with doors being opened just for her. With just a casual nod by Bart to the officer on duty as they passed through the reception area, just a quick, "Hey, there, Morgan," and a brief explanation, "Taking a friend in to meet Lindy," and an answering wave of the hand from behind the desk. "No problem, Bart." And they passed through the big double doors into the stable. Good luck seemed to be following her everywhere on this trip.

"He's such a big ham," Bart said, as Lindy reached into Bart's shirt pocket, snuffling there to find a treat. "Sorry, fella. Nothing tonight. Just brought a lady to visit you, so remember your manners." Lindy bowed his head, as though in response, and Annie realized this was one of the tricks he'd been taught.

"Is it a voice signal, or do you use physical cues?"

"Both," Bart said. "He's a super smart horse and loves to learn new stuff. He catches on faster than any horse I've ever worked with. Back on the ranch, before I got him, my cousin, Janice, she was training him in dressage. He was just a yearling and he was already winning blue ribbons in some of the local horse shows."

As they talked, Bart had slipped a halter on Lindy, led him out of his stall, and brought him around so Annie could get a good look at him.

"He has such an intelligent face," she said.

Lindy lifted his head and gave his mane a little toss.

Annie laughed. "You're a fine-looking animal," she said to Lindy. "And I see you know when you're being praised."

They were getting to know each other, she and Lindy, becoming friends.

She didn't see how Bart was looking at her—and only at her—with an expression so gentle, so tender, she'd have wondered where the bossy, take-charge, macho-man had disappeared to.

Her face was softly shadowed by the single light and to Bart, she was so lovely, so sweet and vulnerable and innocent—a strand of her hair shadowed the curve of her jaw and neck, the shadow of her eyelashes fell on the smooth curve of her cheek, and there were delicious shadows in the slight parting of her lips as she talked to the horse—he wanted to reach out his hand to touch that hair, that face, that soft mouth—

But instead, he said, "If you'd like to walk him around—"

And he offered her the halter.

Annie understood the etiquette of his offer. Without Bart's permission, she would not have touched the horse, not even to stroke his mane or the soft side of his cheek. But now, as she took the halter from Bart, she put her free hand against the horse's neck, then ran it down his shoulder, feeling the animal's strength, his controlled power, and his quick responsiveness. She understood, too, and was pleased, that with the offer came Bart's vote of confidence.

"He'll let me?"

"As long as he knows it's okay with me." He was being careful. "Just take him along the stalls here."

So Annie led Lindy the length of the stalls and back again and Bart saw how she observed Lindy's moves, how she talked to him, how comfortably she handled him. And saw, too, that Lindy was comfortable with her; he knew that Lindy would never let anyone lead him like that unless he knew he was in experienced hands.

"Take him over to the training ring," Bart said. "I'll let him show off for you, show you some of his tricks."

Bart was doing her a very special favor, having his horse perform for a private audience—for just her alone.

As they stepped into the ring, she said, "Oh, I'd completely forgot." She took the packet of wrapped-up carrot sticks from her jacket pocket. "I've had these all afternoon—forgot all about them. They were left over from lunch." They were a bit dried out and soft, but still edible. "Is he allowed a treat?"

"Sure." To Lindy, Bart said, "Say hello to the nice lady, Lindy. She has some carrots for you. If you mind your manners, she may give you one."

Lindy made a small toss of his head and then bowed it toward Annie and placed his right hoof forward on the floor of the ring.

"And hello to you, too," she said, and let Lindy have one of the carrot sticks.

"He has a whole bag of tricks. His favorite is a sort of dancing thing he does. The show people, from the Broadway musicals, get him to do it to the songs from their shows. Only, he'll only do it for the one who taught him the song. So if you have a favorite, you just sing it for him and he'll do his dance. But it'll be just your song; he won't do it for anyone else. Go ahead and sing something."

"Oh, you don't want to hear me sing. I'm absolutely tone deaf." Annie knew even a horse would stop up his ears if she started singing. It was an old joke in the family. "But I can whistle," she said. "I don't know why—but I could always whistle."

"Go ahead, then. Pick a tune. It'll be just yours."

She thought a minute—and then said, "Okay, here's one that's special for a Wyoming horse."

She puckered up and whistled the last few bars of Wyoming U's traditional fight song. Lindy wasn't accustomed to his music being whistled, but he heard something song-like and made a tentative swinging motion of his front quarters.

"What you're whistling," Bart said. "That sounds familiar."

"Oh, sure. Everyone knows that old western song. That's 'Ragtime Cowboy Joe.' The words got changed a bit for our team. But our football players are the Wyoming Cowboys, and our team mascot, Pistol Pete, is a 'highfalutin, rootin'- tootin', son-of-a-gun from ole Wyoming . . .' just changed the song a little bit. And now maybe Broadway Lindy can join in the song, too."

While holding the halter firmly in her left hand, she leaned down and, with her right hand, she stroked down Lindy's shoulder, down his off front leg down past his knee to the cannon bone, and stopped a couple of inches above his hoof.

She heard a tiny gasp of alarm from Bart and smiled to herself. She knew she was scaring him.

So what! Let him be scared, the big macho-man.

"Now, pay attention, Lindy," she said softly.

And while she whistled the first bars of the song's chorus, she grasped the cannon bone firmly, putting just a gentle pressure with her thumb below his knee and—just enough pressure to hold his attention—lifted his leg and made him make a pawing motion, making him tap the floor firmly a couple of times in time to the music. Then she stopped, stood up, looked him in the eye, and said, "Do you get it, Lindy? Are you that smart?"

Lindy turned an attentive eye to her, and Bart could have sworn they were talking to each other.

"Okay," she said. "Let's try it again." And she repeated the whole combination, whistling and stroking and lifting Lindy's leg, making his hoof tap the floor three times in time to the music.

"Are you kidding?" Bart said.

She stood up straight and brushed her hands off on her jeans. "Well, you told me he does tricks. I bet he can pick this one up easily enough. Let's see if the third time is the charm."

Once more she went through the routine and this time, she could feel the horse was helping her, understanding what was wanted.

By George, I think he's got it!

She stood back, giving Lindy a chance to let it all sink in. Then, without touching him, she whistled the song again, clearly and firmly, and sure enough, Lindy lifted his leg and made one pawing motion, three times against the ground.

"Oh, you really are a wonderful horse," she said, and got another carrot stick out of her pocket. He nibbled it out of her hand; she saw that he understood perfectly. He looked at her with an expression that clearly said, "That was fun. Let's do it again."

And again she whistled, and this time he responded right along with the ragtime rhythm of the song and pawed the ground firmly, making a good solid *clop-clop* on the floor. Four more tries, four more carrot sticks, and Annie and Lindy were working together like an old vaudeville team.

"That's amazing," Bart said. "I swear. It's like you two were talking English to each other."

"Well, some horses are very musical. You see it all the time. I figured Lindy was a likely candidate for a musical trick, from what you said."

"Yeah, well, you're lucky he didn't stomp you, bending down like that in front of him, picking up his leg in your bare hand when he hardly knows you."

"He wouldn't stomp me. He knows we're friends." She nuzzled her face against Lindy's cheek. "Don't you, Lindy?" And Lindy nuzzled her right back. She handed the halter back to Bart and the three of them walked back to Lindy's stall. "I was pretty sure he'd be quiet, as long as you were standing by. He'd seen you hand me the halter, so he knew I had your approval. And something else—my jeans and jacket have spent plenty of time around horses and cattle. I probably smelled right to him."

"Yeah," Bart said very quietly. "I guess you do smell just right."

Annie didn't turn, but she felt Bart lean in close, taking in the scent of her hair.

Thank you, Cartier, she thought.

Now Bart did reach his hand to her hair, a shy touch, just a cautious lift of a strand away from her cheek as she turned toward him.

"You have such pretty hair," he said.

Omigod, he's going to kiss me!

And he would have kissed her, right then, but suddenly a bright light went on, startling them both.

"Hey, you guys. You finished up in here?" It was Officer Morgan, looking in at the stable door. "Just want to let you know, I'm going off duty now. My replacement's here."

Bart looked quickly away from Annie.

"Yeah, we're on our way out now."

From the closing of the stable doors as they left the precinct until they pulled up in front of the entrance, neither one was willing to speak.

In front of the hotel, Annie got off the motorcycle, handed the helmet back to Bart, and paused as she smoothed her hair into place.

Bart looked into her eyes and saw the question there.

"You're going to be seeing me again," he said quietly.

And he made a quick U-turn and zoomed away into the crosstown traffic.

Chapter Thirteen

Ribbon-Cutting

Tuesday Morning

Sunny skies, gentle breezes, birds singing—the day was shaping up to be a winner all around. Bart's face revealed nothing, but he was pretty sure the gods were smiling on him. Captain Simon's morning assignments had just detailed his unit to the event over on Fifth Avenue, the grand opening of Galliard's, that new store from Paris. Annie would be surprised—he'd get a chance to show off a little, and maybe have the opportunity to set up a date. As the men headed for the stables, Bart hung back, preoccupied with his good fortune.

"Hey Bart." His buddy, Max, had been trying to get Bart's attention. "You off in dreamland?"

"Sorry about that, Max. Just thinking. Nothing special. Just thinking it looks like it's going to be a nice day. That's all."

"Yeah, well you have a funny look—like you just won the lottery."

"Nope. Nothing like that. Just feeling like all's right with the world. Ever have days like that, Max?"

"Not often enough," Max said. "Anyway. We need to get going. Time to get over to Fifth Avenue."

They were heading for the stalls to saddle up for the day, just as Captain Simon stepped out of his office.

"Hey, Bart, can I see you a minute." It was not a question. He pointed his chin toward his office. "In here," he said.

In his office, behind the glass-paneled door, the captain walked around his desk and sat down. His moves were quick, a busy man with a busy day ahead of him. In his hand he held a ragged piece of paper which he scanned quickly to refresh his memory, and then handed to Bart.

"Do you know what this cockamamie thing means? Someone shoved it under the door last night."

Bart frowned at the paper.

He read the message a couple of times.

Police man HARDIN

pay Attention!

we are WATCHING YOU

and your Horse!!

Bart put his trained eye on the paper; he fingered it expertly. Pale green paper, lined, cheap quality, torn from an ordinary spiral steno notepad, with a faint red line printed down the center. The handwriting was recognizably foreign, all in thick pencil. Irregular torn edges curled like snaggle teeth along the top of the paper. He held it up to the light looking for a watermark. He didn't expect to find one and of course there wasn't any. Could have come from any one of tens of thousands of cheap notebooks, easily available in any one of thousands of stores, anywhere in the country.

"The handwriting looks foreign."

"What does it mean?" Simon repeated.

"Beats me. Sounds like some loony-toon."

"Yeah. Well, maybe. Probably just some goofball who saw you on the TV the other day—that kind of publicity always brings out the kooks. But just so you know to keep your eyes open. And we'll go ahead and process it anyway. Leave it with me." He took the paper back from Bart. "Go on, now. Get out of here. I'm busy."

Bart headed for the door.

"Hey, Bart," the captain called after him. Bart paused as he was about the close the door behind him. "You watch yourself, you hear?"

"You bet, Captain. I'll keep an eye out."

Some loony-toon, he thought. They all come out in the spring.

Max was already up on Hip Hop and he waited while Bart brought Lindy out of his stall. By eight thirty on this perfect morning, the unit was headed up Twelfth Avenue, on their way to their morning assignment on the East side.

And while Bart was feeling pretty satisfied with the way the day was shaping up, Annie was approaching her big event with nerves she wasn't accustomed to. There'd be cameras and TV coverage and she'd have to be the center of more attention than she'd ever faced before.

What to wear? What to wear?

"Oh, Liz. Help me. What should I wear? I don't know what to wear."

"Honey, I've never seen you so dithery. This isn't like you."

"I know. I didn't expect to feel this way—sort of intimidated. Now I feel like I don't look sophisticated enough for New York."

"Oh, that's silly. That blazer is very attractive and you brought a skirt, didn't you? And what about—" The phone interrupted her and she paused to answer it. "Here, honey," Liz said, handing her the phone. "It's Mitzi, calling for you."

"Oh, Mitzi. Just in time! I don't know what to wear. Do I go casual—I have a simple sundress with me—or pants and a blazer, a little more dressy—"

Mitzi didn't skip a beat. "Oh, jeans, Annie. Absolutely. And boots. That whole super outfit you had on yesterday. With that great leather jacket and the belt with the silver buckle. God! I would kill for that jacket. The cameras will love that western look. So authentic. Girl from Laramie dazzles the big bad city. Trust me. New Yorkers will eat it up. I'll have the car at your hotel in half an hour. Ciao." And there was silence.

Annie stared at the phone.

"Liz, these people are so weird. What is it about the jeans and leather jacket? What they call the 'western look'? They all wear black, like it's a uniform, and they want me to dress up like a cartoon character? Honestly! I'll feel like a cardboard cutout."

But Mitzi's advice helped calm her down. Jeans and the leather jacket were everyday wear for Annie, so for sure she'd feel more comfortable.

And Liz reminded her that this day was the climax of the whole trip—the interviews, the TV coverage—and the sweep! And the clothes! She had to be at maximum energy.

By the time Mitzi arrived, they were dressed and ready to leave for the Galliard's opening, the speeches, the cameras—and the shopping spree!

Nine thirty a.m., and they were perched on folding chairs out in front of Galliard's, just behind a podium that was banked with media mics. Annie squeezed Liz's hand.

"Just don't let me make a fool of myself."

Annie was giddy with the realization that she was the center of all this fuss and she was doing her best to keep a lid on the excitement that kept bubbling up from her toes, totally unaware that the nervous energy that was bursting out of her made her an even more radiant and attractive target for the cameras. Liz, at her side, was practically crouched in her seat. She held on to Annie's hand as if to keep herself from sailing uncontrollably up into the blue sky. Poor Liz, she was totally overwhelmed by the noisy commotion that surrounded them: busy traffic continued to shoot down Fifth Avenue, completely inattentive to the big event in front of Galliard's; towering buildings, with their thousands of sun-flashing windows, marched up and down the avenue, shouldering up against each other like a horde of enormous egos, each trying to be the main one; and a vista of glittering storefronts, all brass and glass and high society, showed off their wares—diamonds at Harry Winston, crystal at Baccarat, emeralds and sapphires at Cartier, leather at Mark Cross.

The morning was perfect for a ribbon-cutting. A light breeze was fluttering the flags outside Galliard's; the sky was bright blue and totally cloudless. Mitzi, in a simple suit and her usual stiletto heels, her hair in a slick French braid, and wearing a chunky gold bracelet that must have weighed three pounds, was there to guide Annie through the day. Greta Pena, *Lady Fair's* events director, was there. Mayor Gideon and assorted dignitaries had turned out to make speeches and get their pictures taken. Galliard's president, Jean-Claude Aumont, had flown in from Paris to preside over the event. A crowd of passersby gathered on the sidewalk and camera crews from all the local TV stations were pressing around, getting in everyone's way.

And there were mounted police on hand to keep the event under control.

She took a quick look and sure enough, there he was. Involuntarily, she brushed a stray buttercup-colored wisp out of her eyes, smoothing it into place.

And Bart, who'd seen the gesture, caught her eye, tipped a quick little salute to her from the saddle, and put Lindy through his snappiest paces, making him look good for this special audience of one. Lindy, who always knew when he was being displayed, tossed his mane as though it were a flag in the breeze and flaunted his special, rakish charm.

She felt a rush of reassurance. Not only were Bart and Lindy familiar faces, they also represented law and order. Their presence seemed to make the surrounding racket and commotion calm down a couple of notches, and she felt a little more secure that maybe she wouldn't trip all over herself, after all. And as her usual self-confidence began to return, a song started to play in her head. That same song she'd whistled to Lindy last night. Her alma mater's fight song. The melody of "Cowboy Joe" came to her now like an answer to her prayers.

This is game day, Annie. This is what you came here for.

She imagined she heard the roar of a crowd; the team was running out onto the field, and Pistol Pete, their mascot, was whipping up the spectators. She actually glanced down, expecting to see the yellow and brown of her cheerleading uniform.

Don't let these big-city people think you're some scaredy-cat yokel who's afraid of a bunch of skinny girls in little black dresses and a shop full of high-priced merchandise. Okay, so it's not quite the Knothole back home. So what. You come from pioneer ancestors and big sky country. You've been up on bucking broncs and you've faced down angry bulls. You've hauled hundred-pound sacks of feed. You've mucked out stables and shoveled tons of snow. You've lived through weather that would flatten most cities. You can handle this, Annie. This is your special day. A once-in-a-lifetime experience. This is a day to enjoy—not to run away from.

The butterflies in her stomach settled down a little. She could stop being nervous and just go ahead and focus on all the fun this once-in-a-lifetime day was supposed to bring.

Just be sure to pay attention. You'll want to remember this always. To tell your children.

She nodded a little smile at Bart. And for his part, with Annie smiling at him, he couldn't help showing off a little, so he had Lindy do a couple of the sidestepping moves that always made them both look snazzy.

And while they were being snazzy, they didn't notice the three men who were standing off a little way from the crowd. Three men who were clumped together; three men who whispered to each other behind their hands, and who would, every now and then, point surreptitiously at Lindy, keeping their heads low and their hands as unobtrusive as they could manage. Three men—one skinny, one short and fat, the third tall and totally bald. All with thick mustaches. And the tallest and baldest one of the three was intently taking notes on a scruffy steno pad.

Mayor Gideon was at the mic and was grandly proclaiming his own cleverness at bringing yet another major enterprise to the city. He acknowledged Monsieur Aumont, with thanks for bringing a major French label to New York, reminding everyone that when it comes to panache, New York and Paris are sister cities. He invited Monsieur Aumont to make a few additional remarks of welcome. And then, with a great flourish, he took up the ceremonial scissors, about three feet long, and invited Annie to say a few words and join in on cutting the broad blue ribbon that stretched across the front of Galliard's gleaming door.

She took one deep breath. Then, one more.

Here I go!

With a little toss of her hair—and a little nudge from Liz—Annie stepped up to the podium. Greta Pena now materialized and whispered into Annie's ear.

"Go ahead, dear. You look wonderful. Just say a quick thank you to the crowd. And *smile!*"

Annie waved, a little timidly at first, with butterflies doing a couple of gentle flips inside her. Then, picking up steam, she was able to give it her full cheerleader all. The crowd waved back eagerly, enjoying the pretty scene. She took a deep breath.

"Thank you, Mr. Mayor." She nodded once at him and he glowed. "Thank you, Monsieur Aumont, and thank you for bringing Galliard's to New York. And thank you to all the wonderful people at *Lady Fair*." She turned and smiled at Mitzi and at Greta. "You've done so much to make us feel welcome. And by the way, I want to introduce my big sis. Liz, stand up, honey." And Liz did a half-rise from her chair, managed a weak, self-conscious smile, made a half-wave of her hand, and gave Annie a look that said, *I'll get you for this!* Liz sat down quickly, while Annie went on. "And thank you, *thank you,* New York!" She tossed a quick smile at Bart. "This really must be the most exciting day of my life. And when I get back to Laramie, I'm going to tell everyone, *New York really is Fun City!*" The spectators clapped enthusiastically.

And Bart smiled, as though he was the one who'd won the prize.

And Mitzi and Greta also beamed as though they had single-handedly given birth to a brilliant prodigy, especially because *Lady Fair* had gotten a proper plug.

"Now," Greta whispered, "keep smiling and put your hand on the scissors while the mayor does the cutting. Look at the camera."

Annie did as she was told, the mayor made the ceremonial cut, the crowd cheered happily. Liz applauded madly. All the dignitaries crowded around, pushing their faces into camera range. And then it was Greta's turn. She planted herself in front of the bank of microphones and invited the gathered crowd to attend to her.

She introduced herself, and then said, "Now listen up, folks. Galliard's is inviting you all to watch us on national television while our lucky Sweeps-Spree winner from Laramie, Wyoming, Annie Cornell, sweeps fifty thousand dollars' worth of fabulous, fresh-from-France, fantastic furs—faux or real, as she prefers—shoes, evening dresses, whatever she chooses, all the latest Paris fashions, right here in Manhattan's newest, brightest, glitziest, seven-most-wonderful fashion floors, the fashion floors of Galliard's."

Applause, applause.

"And we're not putting any pressure on her," here she turned and smiled at Annie, then back again, wickedly to the cameras, "are we, folks?"

Laughter from the crowd.

"We're going to give Annie a full two hours to make her selections. And we'll be checking every step of the way while she gets to live out the dream, a free prowl through all the fashion goodies a girl could want. So stay with us, America, as our cameras check in on Annie's progress. We'll be there every half-hour, just after the regular news breaks with our very own tally-man keeping score. And be sure to be tuned in to the runway show on Friday morning, when Annie will show her selections to everyone out there, all across the country. That's fifty thousand dollars, folks. So be sure to be with us."

And she was done.

The ribbon-cutting came to its end, the milling crowd broke up in all directions to continue on to their interrupted errands, camera crews organized their gear, and dignitaries pulled out their cell phones to check their messages, make their calls, and return to their heavily scheduled days.

Bart moved Lindy through the confusion to lean close to her. He had to lift his voice as she was being delivered to Galliard's front door.

"Dinner tonight. I'll call you."

She could do no more than stare, openmouthed, as he rode away. *Talk about take-charge! Never have I ever—*

But her astonishment got no further, for Mitzi was chattering in her ear and practically prancing as she led Annie toward Galliard's threshold, and she had to concentrate on the big event of this big day. For wasn't it supposed to be, indeed, the biggest day of her life?

And off to the edge of the crowd, the tall, bald man with the mustache watched them closely. He had already noted the interest Lindy's rider was showing in the winner of the contest. And he saw the smile that passed between them.

"Very interesting," he murmured.

He licked the tip of his pencil, stroked his mustache once, and made another note on his pad.

Chapter Fourteen

The Spree . . . Wheee!

Tuesday Mid-morning

S he stepped into a place of golden light and subtle scents—scents of bergamot and sandalwood, of ambergris and lavender and musk— perfume fragrances that carried with them subtle hints of leathers and fine furs and tobacco. It was the scent of money. It stopped her in her tracks.

I've died and gone to heaven.

Like Dorothy, stepping into the Land of Oz, Annie knew she wasn't in Laramie anymore. This was a long way from her usual western-wear store back home on Grand Avenue. This was a fantasy turned real.

As far as she could see, from inside the great glass doors where she was standing to the elevators along the back wall, there were rows upon rows of glass-topped vitrines displaying—most tastefully—jewelry and cosmetics and perfumes. Names she knew only from magazines. Lanvin and Patou and Lalique. Handbags and small accessories, gloves and scarves and belts by Chanel and Prada and Burberry, all enriched by that same seductive scent, all suffused with that same ethereal light.

She approached a perfume counter. A slim, black-clad, perfectly coiffed woman smiled upon her, appearing to have been placed on earth specifically to serve. Annie picked a crystal flacon from a mir-rored tray.

"Would you like to try it?" The saleswoman's voice was gracious, with a musical French lilt. "It is a lovely scent."

Annie held out her hand, palm up, and the saleswoman placed a drop from the glass stopper on Annie's wrist.

Annie sniffed at it. "Oh, that really is nice," she said. "How much is it?"

"Three hundred twenty-five dollars. For the half ounce. Of course, there is a larger size, if you prefer."

Annie gulped. It took a heartbeat or two to let that sink in. How easy it would be to rack up $50,000 worth of selections. But what a gloriously indulgent way to begin her spree. "Oh, yes. I'll take it." But, careful as always, she added, "The smaller size, of course."

And Galliard's tally-man made a note.

What next?

"Bags," Liz had said. *Yes, bags!*

At the Chanel counter, she looked at bags. She picked up bags. She quickly scanned the interiors of a couple of bags. Back in Laramie, she and Liz had read about handbags that cost thousands, but couldn't imagine such things really existed. Now, with a real specimen in her hand, she realized this was of a different species. The softness of the leather, the quality of the stitching, the beauty of the hardware, it began to make some sense. Not a lot of sense—but some.

She fell in love with a Burberry alligator bag, but at $24,000 it would have taken too much of her spree budget, so she went with two less expensive Burberry totes—one in black and one in the signature Burberry tartan—and she and Liz could fight later on over who got which.

And now, with her heart beginning to race, she realized that if she spent a lot of time on each item, she'd be turning this adventure into a leisurely shopping day, instead of a giddy "spree," which is what this was supposed to be. The fun of it all would be to run and—sort of—grab. And later on, when it was all done, discover what she had.

And in that spirit, she sprinted for the escalator, pausing only to grab a rope of crystals from a display of costume jewelry, a cashmere Hermès scarf from a stack in a Lucite tray, and a pair of burgundy suede gloves, lined in silk, from Italy. The TV people had to run; the staff people jogged along, with Mitzi bringing up the rear, herding them hectically along. There weren't any escalators in Laramie, so

Annie needed a moment to adjust her pace, but a girl who's ridden broncs can figure out a staircase that does the climbing for you, and in a minute, she was racing up the moving stairs, eager for the rest of this great adventure.

From there on it was a whirlwind of Louboutin and Jimmy Choo, of parkas lined with real fur, and skinny, gorgeous jeans, a Vera Wang dress in a soft fog-gray wool fabric so thin and fine it could have been silk, a long tweed coat from Finland, a short camel hair coat by Max Mara, a biker jacket lined with shearling by Alexander McQueen, and an absolutely-must-have black-and-white Chanel blazer. A spectacular sable coat brought her up short with its price tag of $80,000, so she gave it just a couple of obligatory reverent strokes and then moved on. In the kids' section, she got a set of real drums for Liz's Brandon and a brightly-colored go-kart for Buckley. Liz might not thank her, but the boys would love her forever, if they didn't already. For Craig, she took a minute to choose between a brightly-colored Scandinavian-style heavy-knit sweater with images of reindeer and fir trees, and a plain but classic cable-stitched crew neck. She had a momentary vision of Liz's husband's dismay at the former and his genuine pleasure at the latter—and she chose the gray cable stitch.

She was feeling breathless, as though the whole world had gone into slow motion and she'd lost track of time, lost the feeling of her feet under her, lost her usual sense of centeredness. She'd almost forgotten that there were people right there, following her, paying attention to her. People for whom she was the center of attention. This was really a weird experience.

She turned to Mitzi, whose professional focus was looking a little frayed. A few strands of hair had slipped out of the French braid.

"How am I doing?"

"You still have a couple of thousand to go."

"Okay. I want the baby department."

"Baby?"

"A couple of the women I work with have new babies. I'd like to bring back something for them. And then I want to look at lingerie."

"Lingerie is on this floor. Babies the next one down."

"Okay. Let's hit the nightgowns first."

Lingerie at Galliard's was not like anything she'd known about, and it wasn't just the prices. She'd never seen a garter belt before. She hadn't known there were things like low-beam adhesives and cleavage cupcakes, and she needed a little instruction from Mitzi as to their function. She'd never seen such exquisite lace as she saw on one pair of skimpy panties. And she hadn't known a pair of panties could cost $380. Neither, apparently, had the TV producer. She heard him whisper to his cameraman, "Hell, for three eighty, I could buy the whole girl!" Which was a bit of New York cynicism that would probably fly in Wyoming, too.

But the nightgowns were beautiful, and she added an outrageously tiny teddy and a slinky, sexy, cleavage-to-the-navel bit of pale froth, both from La Perla, and a brilliantly red silk nightshirt from Donna Karan. In a moment of good sense, she added a totally sensible pair of flannel pajamas from Bedhead.

"Now to the babies," she said.

Down one flight to the babies department, and there she selected a couple of silver baby mugs and a silver piggy bank.

"And you've done it!" Mitzi said. "Only seven minutes left! And you've just hit fifty thousand dollars!"

"Wait, Mitzi. I just want to take a couple of minutes here. Don't say anything yet."

Mitzi's expression was quizzical, but she was willing to indulge her, at least for the last minutes.

Annie's eye had been caught by the displays of tiny dresses for tiny little girls, and she needed to pause, if only for a few moments, to touch the sweet little frocks. Is there a woman on earth who doesn't get drawn into the fun and fantasy of dressing a baby girl? Annie couldn't just walk past all those precious little outfits. Even Mitzi recognized the dream that lay in that pause and she let Annie have her moment. "I know it's silly—but I just love this little velvet party dress," Annie said. "I'll just pay for this one myself and put it away. Maybe someday—who knows—maybe—"

Mitzi smiled and whispered a couple of words to the salesperson.

And the TV's on-air correspondent, who just couldn't wait any longer, was almost breathless with excitement. "She's done it, folks. Annie Cornell has had the spree of a lifetime. She's going to leave Galliard's with fifty thousand dollars' worth of the most expensive, most glamorous, and most exciting items that any young woman could want. Tune in to the runway show on Friday when we're going to show you everything she collected on this fabulous adventure, this spree of a lifetime."

The spree of a lifetime? She was going to have to let it sink in. With all the hugs and kisses from Liz, and the cheering and fussing-over by Galliard's people and assorted spectators, and Chanel-scented air kisses from Mitzi, it was clear this was supposed to be the most important day of her life. But she was numb with spent adrenaline and the never-before experience of being the center of so much public attention. And deep down inside her intelligent head, she knew that there must be more to life—to her life—than a day in the sun of television fuss and the accumulation of a truckload of fancy clothes.

And in the car, on the way back to the hotel, Liz said, "Honey, when you get back to Laramie, you're going to have a really super story to tell everyone about this day. Not many people come to New York and have a story like this to tell everyone back home."

"I know. Nothing for the rest of this week could top this day."

Chapter Fifteen

In the Park

Tuesday Late Afternoon

B ack in their hotel room, the telephone light was flashing. Its mechanical computer voice announced, "You have three new messages."

The first, it turned out, was from Craig and the boys, wanting to know how they were doing.

"I'll call on my cell," Liz said. "And give them a full report." She retreated into the bedroom.

The second call was a rapid-fire message from Mitzi. Annie was getting used to listening fast when Mitzi talked.

"Annie, sweetie. We've had a look at the TV coverage. Everyone just loves how you come across on camera. You were born to be on TV. Now here's the thing. We've decided to follow up today's coverage with an expanded piece for the magazine and we need shots of you in the outfits you picked out today. But that's just part of it. We'd already been booked next week on *Good Morning America*, doing a regular summer fashion segment, and now we'd like to include a bit about you and your spree things on that show. *Lady Fair* will pick up the costs for you and your sister to stay the extra days. Also, the clothes you picked at Galliard's may need some altering, so we've scheduled you early tomorrow at *Lady Fair* for fittings. Our tailors and dressmakers can have everything ready in time for the show. Pick you up at eight thirty tomorrow. Any questions, call me back. Ciao!"

When do these people breathe?

Annie looked toward the bedroom. She could hear Liz's voice in the next room, muted behind the closed door, rising occasionally to an excited level. She and Liz would have to plan around this new development, but she wouldn't interrupt Liz's phone time with Craig and the boys.

And, also, there was the third message. She clicked it on.

"Change of plans." It was Bart's voice. "I have to stay on tonight. One of the guys got sick and I'll be doing his shift in the park. So instead, meet me in front of the Tavern on the Green at six thirty. I'll buy you a hot dog. With sauerkraut, even. Best hot dogs in the world. And a Coke. Or whatever. Get a pencil." He waited a few beats, Annie grabbed a hotel pencil off the desk. "Sixty-sixth Street entrance into the park from Central Park West. Can't miss it."

End of message.

She stood there, dead phone in her hand, transfixed. She spoke aloud to the empty room.

"Does anyone ever say 'no' to that man?" She waffled for a minute. "He just assumes I'll be there."

And I was so worn out. This day has been so exciting—just took everything out of me. I thought I'd stay in—get some rest. But still—

She could hear Liz talking to the boys. She opened the door, stuck her head in, and signaled she needed a brief consultation.

Liz told Brandon to wait a sec—"Just hold on"— and covered the phone with her hand. "What's up?"

"I have a date," Annie said. "Do you mind? Just a quick dinner— with that cute cop—and I'll be home early."

"Oh, no. Go, go. No problem. I really like these quiet evenings here after all the hurry-up stuff all day. I'll watch TV here. Go. Have a good time."

"Thanks, Liz. You're a peach. I'm going to take a quick power nap. Wake me at five thirty."

And she closed the door.

In her own bedroom, she sat on the bed and took a couple of moments to savor the fact that this had, indeed, been quite a day. Then she pulled off her boots and dropped them on the floor. She closed her eyes and fell back on the bed. She did not have another conscious thought until Liz came in to wake her up at five thirty on the dot.

* * *

Ten minutes in the shower. Then another five to decide on the proper outfit for a hot dog in the park, definitely *with* sauerkraut—dinner *al fresco*—and decided on the little sundress and sandals. A few quick strokes of a brush through her hair, a dab of lip gloss, and a wave to Liz.

"I've got my phone. Don't worry. I'll be fine." And she was out the door.

At the concierge's desk in the lobby, she paused to get directions.

"Tavern on the Green?" He selected a map from his assortment. "Right here," he said, his pen circling the location. "You won't have any trouble finding it."

"Is it far from here? I have to be there at six thirty."

"Just across town. You'd probably prefer to take a taxi. But you have plenty of time. I'd suggest you ride from here just as far as the entrance to the park here"—with his pencil he indicated an entrance along the southern edge of the park—"and then go by foot the rest of the way." He marked the route for her. "The weather's so mild this evening and it's a lovely walk. Visitors to the city always enjoy it. So much to see."

"And is it safe?" She'd heard stories.

"Yes, Miss Cornell. Perfectly safe. Not, perhaps, at three o'clock in the morning, but at this hour, you are entirely safe. Nothing dangerous could possibly occur. Trust me." He handed the map to her.

She got out of the cab and turned right, into Central Park. With map in hand, she made her way, choosing among a dizzying assortment of paths, keeping herself on a northward heading. The hotel's concierge was right: it was indeed a lovely walk, past bridges and stone arches, a pond and playgrounds, a zoo and a skating rink, countless statues of famous people, and numerous enticements that deserved far more time to explore than a single evening would allow. Unlike Wyoming's sere, spare growth—its beige palette of sage and scrub oak and aspen—here all was rampant lushness, well watered, rain-abundant greenery, great swaths of verdant lawn and a numberless variety of trees, none of which she could identify.

And in this green haven, she made a discovery. The stereotypical fast-moving, fast-talking, hard-working go-getter New Yorkers who seem to suck up energy out of the very sidewalks they strode along all day were magically transformed when they entered the park. Men slipped off their jackets, stuck their ties into their pockets, opened their shirt collars, and slowed their pace to a leisurely amble. Mothers chatted with each other as they pushed baby strollers along the paths. Nannies walked little ones home for dinner, friends sat on the grass, shared a picnic supper, a bit of wine, reviewed the events of the day, and old folks whiled away a peaceful hour or two in the late-afternoon sun. On the roads, streams of joggers jogged, cyclers cycled, and online skaters skated in an unending flow of motion along the many paths and roads, a ribbon of motion through the lassitude of the day's end. Miraculously, despite the thousands of people enjoying this lovely early evening in the park, there was no crowding. There was room for all within the beauty of an extraordinary urban treasure.

The charm of this urban oasis was seductive. Surely, only good things could happen in this idyllically peaceful place. With cell phone in hand, she took photos as she walked, making a record to be treasured back home.

She was just crossing the bridle path at the place where, her map told her, the Tavern on the Green should appear ahead of her, and, indeed, there it was, an inviting sprawl of elegant brick and glass, trees draped and summery, with black-coated waiters moving smoothly among the outdoor tables. Her watch showed six thirty exactly. She looked to her right, and right on schedule, there was Bart. Not mounted, holding Lindy's reins, while an enthusiastic cluster of kids surrounded him, asking questions, asking if they could pet the horse, asking if Lindy does tricks, getting teased lightly by Bart, who seemed to be drawing the kids magically from the nearby playground and from the pre-dinner strollers along the paths. Mommies and daddies and nannies stood around, watching, enjoying the show, enjoying this friendly break in the day's activities.

And Annie watched, too, enjoying the unexpected side to this man. Obviously, he was naturally comfortable in this press of children and she found herself wondering about his family. Is he an only child? Or one of many siblings? Is he the oldest? Or is his bossiness the pampered self-confidence of the baby of the bunch. What sort of parents does he have? What sort of parent would he be?

Just then he looked up, saw her, and waved. He detached himself from the little crowd of admiring kids and led Lindy across the path to join her.

She snapped a quick shot of them as they approached—the two of them, man and horse, so striking, he in his uniform, boots polished, his trim blues emphasizing his good body, and his horse, so powerful and regal, so perfectly groomed, with the late afternoon sun falling across them, lighting them up dramatically—it would be a great Instagram for the folks back home: "My dinner companions for tonight." And slipped the phone into her bag.

"Hi," he said. "I'm glad you got my message."

She realized people were noticing them. Not staring—New Yorkers would never do that—but heads turned a bit as folks strolled by and expressions warmed. She also realized that Bart was used to the kindly regard and paid it no attention.

"I'd planned something a little different tonight," he was saying, with a gesture toward the Tavern, "but a hot dog in the park on a great night like this—that's pretty good, too. I wouldn't let you go home to Laramie without having had at least one hot dog from a street vendor."

"I couldn't resist your gracious invitation."

Her light sarcasm went right past him.

"I'm patrolling now, so I'll have to mount, but no problem if you walk along with me and I can show you the sights. We'll take a dinner break in a little while. "

"That's fine with me. I've had such an incredible day—and I'm so bushed, I'd planned to just fall into bed. But your offer of a hot dog sounded better than room service, so—here I am. As long as we don't make it a long trek. I'm going to need to get back to the hotel soon. I left my sister alone—again—and I need a good night's sleep. *Lady Fair* has more plans for me early tomorrow."

"No problem. A little walk, a little dinner, an hour to see the park, no excitement, I promise you. And I'll put you in a cab back to your hotel in an hour."

And so they strolled. And so they melted into the peaceful flow that surrounded them, accompanied by the *clip-clop* of Lindy's hooves, the muffled background sounds of playing children, birdsong from the treetops, the light swish of leaves lifted by an occasional breeze. Bart was a good guide and explained points of interest, while never forgetting that he was on patrol, keeping his eyes scanning as they walked. Then, abruptly, he stopped.

"I wanted you to see this," he said. "Take a look."

She looked around her. All she saw was great, tall, rock outcroppings, thick trees, and a rather empty path.

"See what? I don't see anything."

Bart just smiled.

"Keep looking."

She looked.

Still nothing.

Bart still smiling.

Then she saw it.

"Oh, my God!"

A cougar, crouching on the rock above her, ready to pounce.

Her heart had jumped and she needed a few beats and at least two deep breaths to realize the cougar was bronze but so naturally executed, so skillfully placed, it could not have been more realistic.

"He's called 'Still Hunt,' and if you're not prepared for him, he's a shocker."

"A shock is right. When I see a cougar, I prefer to have my twelve-gauge with me."

"I figured a western girl like you would appreciate him." Bart was smiling mischievously.

"And you promised me no excitement tonight."

"I did," he said as he dismounted. "And I apologize. Let me make it up to you by stopping now for dinner. There's a hot dog cart down there," pointing to a vendor's umbrella ahead of them, "out in front of the boathouse. May I escort you to a quiet dinner on a park bench?"

"You sure can," Annie said. "I'm starved. And I'm dying for a hot dog."

And together, with Bart leading Lindy, they walked toward the hot dog stand, where the vendor greeted Bart like an old friend.

"This is Sergei," Bart said. "Sergei here makes the best hot dogs in the whole city."

Sergei laughed. "Yeah, sure. Like the water I boil them in is different from all the other carts."

"I'll take two of them now, with the usual, mustard and sauerkraut. And whatever it is, water or whatever," Bart said, "yours are still the best." He turned to Annie. "How many?"

"One will be enough. But I'd like one of those soft pretzels, too. And a bottle of water."

"And maybe take some chips, too?" Sergei said. "For you, miss.

With my compliments. To go with your drink." He said it as though he was addressing a duchess. "And who is this pretty lady, Sergeant Bart?"

"This is Miss Cornell. Visiting from Wyoming. That's out west."

"I know where is Wyoming. I know where is every state in America. I studied the map before I come to America."

"Where did you come from?"

"Poltrovnea—little village you never heard from—in the mountains. Very high. Very far away. Famous for our riders—great warriors long ago. Best horsemen in the world."

"Annie knows horses, too," Bart said. "She should show you the trick she taught Lindy."

"The trick?" These days had been so full, she needed a moment to remember. "Oh, yes." She positioned herself in front of Lindy. "Okay, Lindy. Let's see how smart you really are."

Lindy was all attention.

She puckered up and whistled the fight song.

And Lindy tapped the ground three times with his right front hoof. And, for good measure, he tossed his mane as though asking for applause.

"See?" Bart said, as proud as a prodigy's daddy. "See. Is that a smart horse? He learned it after only one try. And now that fight song is going to be how he knows you, Annie. I bet he never forgets it."

"Ah, yes," said Sergei. "Lindy is very special horse, very strong, very handsome. And you are very special lady, I see. You should know, Miss Cornell, this is first time this young man brings a lady to dinner here at my hot dog stand. So I am very happy to meet you."

Bart was one of those men who blush when they are embarrassed. And Sergei had just embarrassed him. So he was in a hurry to change the subject.

"This guy has been selling hot dogs here since I was a kid."

"Yes," Sergei said. To Annie, he added, "His papa used to bring him here for lunch every Saturday, when he was young like little toad."

"That's enough, my friend." Bart's color deepened further. "If she's going to hear my life story, she's going to hear it from me."

"Of course. Of course. I talk too much. Go now. Enjoy your dinner."

"Thanks. We'll do that. We'll find a place in the Ramble. Maybe up by the lake."

"Just be careful."

"Of course."

"Good-bye."

"Good-bye." Annie nodded. "And thanks for the chips."

"Any time. Come again."

Hot dogs, pretzel, chips, and drinks in hand, with Bart leading Lindy, they left Sergei and walked on past the boathouse.

"What's 'the Ramble'?"

"It's where I'm taking you for dinner." Bart pointed into the thick tangle of growth that stretched out ahead of them. "Thirty-six acres right here along the lake—all wild and very beautiful. It was designed that way right from the beginning, to be like a wilderness, all dense and tangled. You can walk through here for hours, paths in all directions, and feel as though you're almost in a jungle. No monuments here, no attractions, just some benches and raw nature. Not many people come through here, maybe because of its reputation. Except the bird-watchers, of course. Birdwatchers love it. Trouble is, it also attracts unsavory types, bad guys who—well, who want to do bad things. It's safe enough during the day, but I wouldn't let you come into the Ramble after dark."

Annie smiled.

There he goes again, she thought. *He wouldn't let me! Who does he think he is—my daddy? Still, she felt the protectiveness and it pleased her. It's true—this guy really would protect me—if I needed protection.*

"But it's safe enough now," Bart said, leading her into the woods. "It's still light, and you're with me and Lindy, so you'll be okay. We won't let anything happen to you."

In moments, they were in a kind of alternate universe. Who knew, in addition to all the attractions the city offered, it was also possible here to disappear into a sunlight-dappled woodland, a tangle of trees and harsh rock outcroppings and a network of dirt pathways? With Bart guiding her, choosing their course, they walked silently through this magical forest, with only an occasional bike rider or jogger passing them, and accompanied only by the whisper of the breeze through the trees, the distant birdsong from the green canopy above, the sound of their own footsteps, and the muffled beat of Lindy's hooves.

After about ten minutes, the path led them along a lake's edge, and a broad vista of sunlit water appeared before them. An enormous willow tree curtained one side of the view, a couple of rowboats moved lazily along the surface, and beyond, the towers of distant sky-scrapers peeped hazily through the trees. To complete the scene, a rustic bench, fashioned of tree limbs and deep enough for them to make a table for their meal, had been set to face out toward the lake.

"This is where I wanted to bring you," Bart said. "It's always quiet here, and I wanted to be sure you got to see it."

Annie smiled to herself. The setting was lovely and it didn't take a genius to know why he brought her here. But they wouldn't be totally alone—there were the occasional bike riders, the joggers, the arm-in-arm couples—and she was curious to see what would develop.

She settled back comfortably and let the beauty of the place record itself in her memory, something to add to the memories going back to Laramie with her.

Bart unwrapped her hot dog and handed it to her.

She took a bite—and a pungent blast of mustard and kraut and garlic and salt hit her palate and filled her sinuses. Probably un-healthy. Instantly she forgot the idyllic scene around her.

"Oh, wow! That *is* good!"

Bart grinned. "Yeah. Isn't that something? I told you—the best in New York."

She grabbed a napkin and dabbed at her mouth. "I'm impressed. You really know this city. You could write a guidebook. "

"That's because my dad and I spent a lot of time together. He took me all over, used to show it all to me."

There it was again—another mention of his dad, along with that faraway look and a sudden quiet. If she really wanted to get to know Bart better—she knew she might be probing a difficult place—but she asked anyway.

"Tell me about your dad," she said.

He didn't answer right away. She watched him think it over. What was he struggling with? She saw the jaw muscles work, she wished she hadn't asked, but it was too late to take it back.

"My dad was killed in the line."

She saw it was an angry memory—not yet healed. She was about to say she was sorry she asked, but Bart stopped her.

"No, that's okay," he said. "It was five years ago." Then he paused. He studied her face, looked deeply into her eyes, as though trying to answer some unasked question. Then he smiled, changing the sub-ject. "I'll tell you about it someday. Not now. Right now, we're going to enjoy our dinner. Enjoy this great view." He gestured out toward the lake. "And tomorrow, I'm going to take you somewhere more formal. Some place you'll have to get dressed up for, maybe in one of those fancy outfits you picked out today. And if those handlers of yours let you out of their sight for the afternoon, I'm going to take you on a tour, show you some of this city—the *real* city." He took a man-sized bite out of his hot dog. "And I'm going to get to know you better. Starting right now. So you tell me, Annie Cornell, tell me about yourself."

Now what was it about this man? She felt perfectly comfortable and didn't hesitate at all.

"I think you already know everything about me. You've been all through my handbag. You saw everything in my wallet. You saw me being a jerk the other day, getting caught in a mob scene. Losing my bag. Scared out of my wits."

"Yeah. I saw that."

How odd. He hadn't made a move, but she felt as though he'd leaned closer to her. Funny about that.

"And I grew up on the family's cattle ranch just north of Laramie. Been around cattle and horses all my life. Went to Wyoming U, got a master's in library science, and I've been a librarian in the veterinary school at the university for the last three years."

"Is there a boyfriend?"

"Not anymore."

He didn't even try to conceal a smile.

"And no, it's not a tragic story. His name was David. We'd gone to high school together, everyone figured we were destined for each other. Only, the truth was, we really weren't. And after a few years of being an item, we both realized it, and that was the end of that. No tears, no fuss. He's married now, has a little girl, they moved to Grand Rapids and we send each other Christmas cards. I have a bunch of friends, done some dating, of course, but no serious man in my life. I'm afraid, even at a big university, I haven't been much attracted to anyone."

Funny. There was that feeling again. That he'd moved closer, when he really hadn't.

"And what about you? Anyone special in your life?" She felt herself getting light-headed.

"No. No one at all."

This time, he really did lean toward her, just a little, and he was not smiling. He was concentrating on her face, examining her eyes, her hair, her mouth.

A confusion of feelings was slithering all through her. She took another bite of her hot dog.

He was closer.

"You know I want to kiss you, don't you?" he said.

"I'm all garlicky."

"So am I."

"You look so serious," she said.

"You have the prettiest hair." His eyes were locked on hers. His finger lifted a strand away from her forehead. "It's the color of butterscotch."

"That sounds sticky."

"I know. But still . . ."

. . . and closer . . .

And then he did kiss her.

And she closed her eyes. And it was the motorcycle ride all over again.

When she opened her eyes, he had his arms around her and he was staring at her, as though he was stunned.

"I never felt anything like that," he said. "Like yesterday—"

"I know," she whispered. "On your bike."

He looked as though he couldn't breathe. And this time, he closed his eyes first. And he kissed her again, holding her close as though he wanted to drink her all into himself, and she felt his heart beating against her chest.

And then, something happened. She felt a change in him and she pulled away a little. His eyes were opened and he was looking puzzled. He was looking past her and he'd moved back a little. A tiny lift of his head, like an animal testing the wind.

"What is it?" she said.

He didn't answer. His attention was focused out beyond her. Into the trees.

Lindy was fidgeting. Pawing lightly, ears erect, nervous.

"I don't know," he said. "I don't see anything."

He stood up. "It's time to leave." He crumpled up their dinner detritus and tossed it into a trash bin. "Let's get you out of here."

"Trouble?"

He didn't answer. He had Lindy's reins in his hand. He flipped them up over Lindy's head, had his foot in the stirrup and was up in the saddle, all in one gesture. "I want you up here behind me. Hop on. We're going to ride out together."

He reached a hand toward her. She asked no questions. He cleared his foot out of the stirrup, she took his hand, put her foot into the empty stirrup, and he had her up behind him onto the saddle pad, all in one smooth motion. A few minutes and they'd passed silently through the Ramble, with Bart scanning the forest right and left as they rode.

Once out onto the busy roadway, Annie slipped down quickly.

Bart said, "I'm going to leave you now. Walk straight out to Fifth Avenue," he indicated the direction, "and get into a cab. I'll be in touch tomorrow." He was all business now and she knew he must have seen something in the woods. And would be going back to investigate.

There was no flourish. He merely turned Lindy back toward the Ramble and disappeared into the trees.

They're right about this city. It certainly is a show a minute.

And I've had enough entertainment for one day.

Ten minutes and she was back at the hotel. Liz was curled up in the corner of the sofa, glued to a reality show on the TV.

"Have fun?"

If she told Liz about her evening, she'd have to answer a million questions—maybe get a scolding for who knows what?

"Yes. It was a nice evening. But this day has been too much for me. I've got to get some rest. And *Lady Fair* needs me early tomorrow. Want to come?"

"No. You don't need me along, and I decided to be brave." She barely took her eyes off the TV. "I might sign up for one of those bus tours around the city, so I'll just go off on my own, if you don't mind."

"No, but are you sure? You've been kind of neglected. I want this trip to be fun for you, too."

"Are you kidding? First of all, this trip is your treat and I'm just along for the ride. Second, I've already got enough memories to fill a big suitcase. And third, I'm beginning to feel a little less skittish about getting around here. The city's not really so scary, the way I thought it was. I'll be fine. You go. Have a good time. And I'll get lots of pictures to take home."

Liz's attention was already back on the TV.

"That's good," Annie said. She was in the bedroom by now. She called back to the living room, "You do that. Take your phone and I'll keep in touch." She yawned, she tossed her bag onto her bed, she sat down in the deep armchair in the corner and kicked off her sandals. "I'm so tired, I may fall asleep right here."

What a day this has been.

The ribbon-cutting, with all those cameras, her little speech, the spree though the store. And then Bart and Lindy and their stroll through the Ramble. His arms around her, the extraordinary physical connection between them. And oh, that kiss. She'd have let it go on forever. The memory took her breath away.

What made him stop? Just at that moment.

She went into the bathroom and brushed her teeth. She washed her face. She left a wake-up call for seven thirty. The night was warm. She tossed her PJ's onto the chair and chose to sleep naked.

In twenty minutes, Annie was in bed, totally worn out by her most extraordinary day.

Bart, however, was not in bed. By the time Annie reached her hotel, Bart had turned Lindy back into the Ramble and loped quickly to the spot he and Annie had just left. He dismounted and led Lindy into the woods that rimmed the cleared space where they'd been sitting. He tethered Lindy to a tree off to one side so hoofprints wouldn't compromise any useful evidence. But evidence of what? His instincts told him it wasn't just a random peeping Tom who'd been watching them, some weirdo park denizen or curious bird watcher. Maybe teenagers, out for an evening of adventure. No, his gut feeling, reinforced by years of experience and good training, told him to check this out carefully. He examined tree branches, up close and up high, and scanned the ground closely. And found what he was looking for.

Back at troop headquarters, he made his report and forwarded to forensics a plastic evidence bag that held a small cluster of red-and-white feathers, stitched together. A couple of trailing black threads suggested it had come loose from whatever it had been sewn onto. A black cap, perhaps? With an embroidered design of bright colors? He hadn't forgotten that weird note and he'd not written it off as a prank or empty threat. The cluster of feathers convinced him this Buljornia bunch was following him. He decided they needed to be taken seriously, and he included that analysis in his report.

What he didn't include in his report was how mad he was. Mad that those creepy stalkers had shown up when they did. What was happening to him with Annie was a first-time-in-his-life experience. There'd been some magical connection. He'd sensed it from the first moment he'd seen her during that street demonstration, felt it when he'd grabbed her up from out of the crowd. Felt it as he watched her disappear up First Avenue, so unprotected and at risk. And felt it, for sure, on the motorcycle, with her body against his, a kind of sweet, gentle electricity. No, it was more mystical even than that. More like an angelic message, telling him, telling them both, *"This is special. Pay attention."* And in the park, in the moments of their first kiss, he knew the magic messengers were right. Now, here at his desk at troop headquarters, he could still feel her in his arms. He could still feel her mouth against his, remembered how he'd felt his breath leaving him, felt time stopping. His heart had been racing and he'd needed to catch his breath and so he'd paused, and as he'd opened his eyes, he'd seen through the trees' camouflage what seemed to be watching eyes, a couple of bodies, and he felt their menace. His immediate thought then was not to keep holding Annie in his arms, not to keep kissing her forever; he needed to get her out of there right away, and only then come back as soon as possible to investigate.

But now, with his report and the evidence forwarded on to forensics, he could put that aside and think about tomorrow.

He picked up the phone and dialed Max.

"Listen, buddy. How would you feel about swapping a day tomorrow? Something's come up."

"Yeah, I saw what came up. She's a cutie. But remember—we have tickets for the three of us, you, me and Chloe. For that show at the Booth."

"I remember, Max. But here's what I was thinking. Your shift would end at three thirty. Annie's sister has been pretty much left on her own with all that attention on Annie. I'd gladly give her my ticket if you'd be willing to offer to show her around for the afternoon, after your shift, and then have her join you and Chloe for dinner and the show. I bet she'd appreciate the chance to see a Broadway show and get a little attention for herself."

"That show is the hottest ticket in town. You know how much trouble we had getting good seats."

"I know, Max. I'll see it another time. It would mean a lot to me—"

"This girl must be something really special."

"Yeah. Something really special."

Chapter Sixteen

The Fitting

A nnie was usually an early riser, but when the morning call came she was barely able to open one eye. A reluctant hand came out from under the sheets and fumbled for the phone.

A mechanical voice spoke.

"This is your call for seven thirty a.m."

"Mmmmm."

She fumbled some more, replacing the handset into the cradle.

The phone's ring had interrupted her dream. She could still hear the rustle of breeze-stirred leaves, and she was riding through a dense forest, bareback on a beautiful palomino; the foliage parted and a big bay horse came toward her, and his rider was a man wrapped in a dark blue cape. The forest was dark, but a strong sunlight filtered through in random shafts and she was sure there was a woodsy scent wafting around her. It was a dense dream, with many levels, and she didn't want to wake up.

But the other eye opened, and she was forced to realize it was Wednesday and a car was coming to take her to *Lady Fair* in an hour.

She shook off her dream, slipped out from the sheets, and into the shower.

Room service brought breakfast to them—a good, hearty breakfast. Sausages and eggs and hash browns, toast and jam, and plenty of coffee.

"So," Liz said, "tell me about your date last night."

"Oh, we walked. We talked. Nothing much to tell. He was on duty, so we just—rambled—a bit. He bought me a hot dog." She paid attention to her sausages as though they were especially interesting. She concentrated on her eggs. She broke off a bit of toast and buttered it. With her head still lowered, she looked up at Liz, a little mischievously, with a tiny smile.

Liz examined her sister's face with an experienced eye.

"Hmmm. So?"

"So?" Annie was all innocence.

"Oh, come on, Annie. You're looking all sly. You had a good time with this policeman?"

"Yes, Liz. I had a good time. He's still sort of officious, but there's more to him than that. He has a nice, protective quality. I like that part. And he is kind of cute."

"And he kissed you, didn't he?"

"How could you tell?"

"Annie, how long have I known you? All your life, right? So I can tell. He kissed you and you liked it."

"Okay, Liz." Annie's smile was now totally open. "Yes. It was nice. Only—"

She paused, holding her toast halfway toward the next bite.

"Only?"

"Something happened right then. I think he saw something in the trees. And then he was all anxious to get me gone. Actually rode me right out of there—on his horse! And sent me home before I could even figure out what was happening." She ate the toast. "Funny about that. One minute, it was all sweet and just the two of us. And then, suddenly, he was all business, like he had to get back to work."

She took a last bite of breakfast, a last gulp of coffee, and got up from the table.

"But he said he'd call. And if he does, I'm definitely willing to see him again."

They were waiting for her at *Lady Fair*. A team of elves with magic fingers, working the fabrics with pinches and stretches, a basting stitch here and a couple of pins there, a push and a poke and a "How about this—?" They worked with a focus and intensity that made her think of a roper tying down a calf for branding. No nonsense, no daydreaming. But here, she was the calf. And, instead of down in the dirt, they had her up on a pedestal—an actual *pedestal!*—and they moved around her murmuring to each other, slipping each item on, doing mysterious things with chalk and pins and quick consultations, then off with the garment, then on with the next, repeat, then off—

The leader of the elves was a slight, fortyish woman with dark hair in a messy chignon and great dark-rimmed glasses riding low on her nose. "I'm Dvorah," she said, her voice raspy with years of cigarettes, "and oh, honey, you just don't know how interesting it is to work on a body that's not all bone. At least you have a little bit of natural, womanly body fat on you."

"What?"

"Oh, you're not fat, dear. Not at all. Not the least little bit. But be glad you're not a stick. You've got a nice shape—like a real person. The models here, they can't wear anything right off the rack. We need to take everything in to practically a minus zero size. Tailoring your things will be a snap. We'll just be sure the seams drape at the right spot—at the point of the bone here,"—her finger touched Annie's shoulder—"and the neckline here"—she traced an arc along Annie's clavicle. "And it's nice to fit a real bust for a change. You do have a real bust, dear. Be glad of that. We have girls who would kill for a real bust." She took the dressmaker's tape measure that hung round her neck and wound it around Annie's chest. "Oh, God," she said, "I haven't measured a real bust in ages. Thank you, dear. You've made my day."

She took the Vera Wang from the hanger and slipped it over Annie's head. The exquisite light wool floated down over Annie's body like a gentle waterfall, and the mirror on the opposite wall showed her an Annie she'd never seen before. Sophisticated, elegant, graceful.

Wow! I didn't know a dress could do that!

"This one's perfect," Dvorah said, taking a couple of pins from between her lips and sticking them into the pincushion strapped around her left wrist. "This one was made for you. It doesn't need a thing. And that color is exquisite with your hair and your eyes. Just a tiny hint of seafoam in the weave. You're going to live in this one."

Annie smiled at the thought.

Oh, yeah. Just the thing for mucking the barn!

But with a variety of accessories, it definitely would be a favorite for many occasions. "I do like it," she said. "I can see that I'll be wearing this one a lot."

And as they slipped it off, over her head, and the whisper-soft fabric brushed along her bare skin, so luxuriantly sensuous and comforting, she felt as though she couldn't possibly be anything but perfect in this perfectly beautiful dress.

Next it was the long tweed coat from Finland. She hadn't realized, when she grabbed it from the rack, that she'd picked an excellent complement to the Vera Wang dress. Woven of yarns of gold and green and gray with a thin strand of maroon, it made a subtle frame for Annie's hazel eyes.

"Look," said one of Dvorah's helpers. She held up a large mirror to show Annie. "The color match couldn't be better. Look what it does for your eyes. Brings out all the complexity of the hazel coloring—the green and gold and brown. And with your hair, corn-silk blond, with those nice lowlights, sort of caramel. No, not so dark, more like butterscotch. I love it!"

Caramel? And butterscotch? Where had she heard that? *Oh, yes. Bart had said—*

Her cell phone rang. She signaled one of the elves to retrieve it from her bag and it was handed up to her on her pedestal perch. While adjustments were being made to the set of the sleeves at the shoulders, she answered and heard Bart's voice. Magic, as though her thought of him had summoned him by wi-fi.

"Hey," he said. "Are they finished nipping and tucking yet?"

"I think it'll be about another half hour."

"Great. Because I got the day off. Did a little wangling with Max and we swapped some days. Call me as soon as you're done. I'll pick you up downstairs. I've got everything planned. You're going to see this city like no one gets to. Dress casual. See you soon."

He didn't wait for her to say good-bye. She was holding a silent phone in her hand.

"Well, that sounds like—"

She was going to say "a great idea," but realized she'd be talking into the air. She handed the phone back to the waiting elfette who dropped it into Annie's bag.

Dvorah was making chalk marks at the shoulder seams. "It needs a little more room here," she said. "No problem. Plenty to work with. And I'm going to move this button—" She made another chalk mark. "It drapes perfectly down the back. You're going to wear this for years."

After that it was quick work of the Chanel blazer ("It's perfect—just a tiny tuck here at the side") and the camel hair coat ("I don't like these buttons. A little bigger, I think.") followed by some rummaging in one of the notions drawers built into the wall ("there, that's better, don't you think?" as though Annie would have dared question Dvorah's judgment), and then the parka, a simple design from Austria, with useful inner cuffs and a neat built-in gaiter at the throat. Nice and practical, Annie thought, with a fur-trimmed hood and inner closing under the zipper. And then she glimpsed the price tag and gulped.

"Six thousand and eighty-three dollars!"

She took a better look and realized not only was the parka extremely well made, but the fur trim on the hood was *sable*!

"Well," she said, "I guess at that price, it *should* include these accessories clips and the ski pass pocket."

Sable didn't impress Dvorah at all; the outrageous prices were old hat to her. "But the hood is a bit too big at the back. We'll just nip it in a bit, and it's perfect."

The biker jacket was too broad across the back—that would be a major alteration, but the elves assured her that it—and all the rest— would be ready in time. And with kisses all around, she put high fashion behind her and hurried to the elevator, texting as she went:

I'm done now. Meet me down in the lobby.

Chapter Seventeen

The Tour

A nd there he was. Looking natty in jeans, chambray shirt, and light-weight summer blazer. And carrying two helmets.

"First, I have to tell you—I've made some arrangements. I know your sister has been kind of neglected, what with you being the center of everyone's attention. Which can't be much fun for her. So here's what I'm suggesting." And he told her his plan for keeping Liz busy for the rest of the day and evening. He tried to look innocent, but she saw the mischief in his eyes and she had to laugh.

"You sly dog," she said. "Liz will see right through you. But if I'm willing, she will be, too. I know she'll be glad of some attention just for her. Especially if she gets to see a Broadway show. I know she wanted to. It will be a treat for her." She was already getting her phone out of her bag. "I'll call and let her know." When Liz answered her call, she said, "Listen, honey. The sergeant and his partner have a great surprise for you—" and she explained the plan. "And they'll pick you up at the hotel at four o'clock. His partner is Max Wozinski and Max's wife is Chloe. Chloe Watkins. Nice people. You'll like them. And stay out as late as you like. No need to rush home."

She listened for a moment as Liz took it all in, then said "Bye bye. See you tonight. Love you," and dropped the phone into her bag.

"There. She loves the plan. She says thanks for arranging this. It'll be fun and she's looking forward to meeting Max and his wife."

She didn't add that Liz had also whispered into the phone, "And don't think I don't know what you're up to, honey. Just be careful, you hear me?"

"So we're all set," Bart said as they crossed the lobby. "I'm your tour guide from here on. You have any questions, just ask." They passed through the revolving doors and out onto the sunbaked street. "I left the bike parked uptown because I want your tour to start with the subway, so first we'll ride up and get it." He guided her up the street toward the corner.

"The subway? You're sure it's safe?" There were, after all, all those stories she'd heard.

Bart beamed at her. He put an arm around her shoulder, a reassuring gesture.

"Of course it's safe. And you're with me. I wouldn't let anything bad happen to you."

And then, at the subway entrance, he stopped her.

"But first, before we go down there," he said, "there's something I want to take care of."

And right there, with crowds hurrying around them, Bart broke the first law of street etiquette: he blocked the flow of the surrounding pedestrians, getting in their way, becoming a roadblock in the stream of people in and out of the subway entrance.

"We got interrupted last night," he said quietly, "and we left something unfinished."

And before she could say anything, on a teeming city sidewalk in the middle of Times Square, with hurrying crowds and the city's racket swirling around them, he turned her to face him. He slipped his hand down her back and drew her close to him.

His kiss was casual and familiar, as though they'd been kissing like this for years, like a husband saying, "Hi, honey. I'm home."

And Annie, totally surprised, didn't know or care that passersby were glancing at them, some of them irritated and others smiling, as they hurried on.

He absolutely takes my breath away.

Bart stepped back, holding her at arm's length, and his smile said he knew he'd surprised her and that he'd meant to.

"Now let's take that tour, Annie. You're going to have a good look at my city."

And so they joined the stream of people flowing down into the underground labyrinth that is the Times Square subway station.

And in that great rushing mass of humanity, who would have paid attention to the little cluster of three furtive-looking types who had been keeping pace with them, always at a careful distance behind them, three men, unobtrusive, unremarkable, quite unnoticeable in the diverse and utterly ordinary throng of subway riders? Three men who, being unfamiliar with the subway system, didn't know about Metrocards, got themselves tangled up at the turnstiles, and with much confusion and blaming of each other, watched helplessly as Annie and Bart disappeared down another level where the arriving train opened its doors, took them in, and carried them, all unaware, far away from their baffled stalkers.

Midday on the subway and every seat was taken. Annie wasn't accustomed to the train's motion, rocking erratically, clattering along at what felt like a dangerous speed, and she was unsteady on her feet and clung hard to the metal pole she shared with three other riders. She also wasn't accustomed to the bodies of so many strangers so close around her. So intimately close, and yet each person seemed to be surrounded by a zone of privacy that protected them from intrusion.

How do they do it? How do they keep themselves so separate from each other? Like a school of fish. Without getting in each other's way.

And the racket. You could yell at full decibel level in here and still not be heard.

On the seat in front of her was a woman with a little boy next to her. The child was sleeping, snuggled up to his mommy.

How can he sleep, with all this noise?

Farther down the car, she saw another sleeping child, this one a baby in a stroller. A stroller, somehow making room for itself in the midst of the press of people. No one caring at all.

I guess they grow up with so much noise around them, so much stimulation, it becomes ordinary.

The train lurched and she was jostled up against Bart. He smiled at her as she clutched at his arm. She smiled back, a little embarrassed.

"You'll get used to it," he said.

She looked around her and knew he was right. Though she was very much aware that she was hurtling along at high speed, underground, inside the bedrock of a great city, along with hundreds of others, none of those others seemed the least bit impressed by the enormity of what they were doing. She took a good look at her fellow travelers. Most were occupied in some way, some attached by wires to a device, listening to music, or playing a game on their smart phones, or reading a book or a folded-up newspaper. Two kids, heads bent together over their books, busy with their pencils, were doing their homework. A few riders were just resting, alone with their thoughts, staring empty-eyed into space. Here and there, a man or a woman asleep, catching a few zzz's on the way home or on to their next activity of the day.

And the *diversity*! From all over the world, there seemed to be representatives here in this one subway car, of every color of skin, every style of dress, including hijabs and saris, Sikh turbans and African headwraps, and—from the newspapers she could see—every language. A veritable United Nations, right around her. And no one was paying the least bit of attention to anyone else. Back home, people would be staring. Here, no one was even interested.

No wonder Bart wanted her to see this. These few minutes on the subway were worth hours of lectures.

And it was only minutes, fifteen, perhaps, and they were in Harlem.

"This is our stop," Bart said. Along with the multitude, they left the subway and came out onto a wide, sun-filled boulevard, where his bike was parked at the corner, waiting for them.

And they were off, slipping through the buses, the taxis and trucks, the autos, making a big turn onto 125th Street, riding past the Apollo Theatre—yes, *that* Apollo Theatre!—on to a zigzag tour through Harlem, with a stop for lunch on Lenox Avenue, enjoying the early afternoon sunlight outside at a landmark restaurant where she burned her tongue on hot "wild" chicken wings and soothed it with cornbread and a bowl of the best New England–style chowder she'd ever eaten. From there it was back on the bike and uptown to the Dyckman House ("This is a farmhouse, the oldest one still in Manhattan—a museum now," Bart explained), then downtown to the 79th Street marina, where people really live on their houseboats. Then over to the East River, a slow pass around Gracie Mansion ("Our mayor lives here") and finally down the FDR Drive toward the Financial District.

By then, she must have racked up a hundred pics on her cell phone.

"I want you to see this," Bart said, parking the bike and taking off his helmet. "There's a spot here where you can almost feel the beginnings of this city, where the streets must have been just dirt paths. And look at what's grown up on those dirt paths." They stood at an intersection where narrow streets twisted away from them, seemingly at random, unlike the regular grid of the streets farther uptown. On these very narrow, very irregular streets, enormous skyscraper office buildings rose into the perfectly clear blue sky, packed so tightly together, so towering, they seemed ready to fall around them.

His arm was around her and his face was turned up toward the soaring buildings, and she felt his pleasure in showing this all to her, like a kid sharing his treasured secrets with a very special new friend.

"I understand what you mean," she said, seeing the winding, narrow streets connecting and curving away from her. "Here's the financial center of the world grown up on top of these very streets that were once farm roads and dirt paths. It's like a time-lapse film happening right in front of your eyes."

"Right!" he said. "That's it, exactly. See how they didn't even straighten out the streets, or make them wider. Just let this financial giant of a city grow up right on top of those dirt paths. I always get a kick out of standing here, thinking about those centuries, and imagining cows and Dutch farmers walking around me and I want to go up to them and whisper in their ears, 'Look! Look what's coming! Look what you're starting here.' Behind all those windows, in all those buildings, thousands of people are churning out the deals and the plans and the schemes that make this world go round."

His pride in being a citizen of the very center of the universe and his pleasure in showing it to her were evident. Annie hadn't the heart to remind him there was a wide and very effective world functioning well beyond the city limits.

But some day, if I get to know him better—

"It's only three thirty." Bart was checking his watch. "We're going across the bridge now. You haven't seen New York if you haven't seen Brooklyn. And I want to show you where I grew up."

Chapter Eighteen

Across the Bridge

Wednesday Afternoon

It was a quiet street, with a row of comfortable-looking clapboard houses, each set back from the street, each behind its own low iron railing. At the corner, a small grocery store. Across the street, a school, the kids leaving in little clusters, their after-school chatter a hum of buzzing anticipation at the approach of the summer holiday.

Bart pulled up in front of a house about midway down the street.

"Here we are. This is it. Where I grew up. And that—" he pointed across the street "—is the school I went to. Till middle school, a couple of blocks from here."

"Is this your home now?" She recognized it from the picture on his desk.

"You mean 'do I live with my mother?'" He laughed. "No, Annie. I have a place in town. Near the stables. But I lived in this house all my life till I joined the force."

"It looks like a nice house. And I see someone's got a green thumb."

She pointed at the shrubbery planted inside the iron railing and along the little walk that led up to the front steps of the house. Lilac bushes were flowering along the narrow driveway by the side of the house that led to a garage at the back, and there were roses growing along the front of the porch.

"That's my mom's doing. She's good at keeping things green." He took off his helmet and helped Annie off the bike. "Maybe she's home now. Would you like to meet her?"

"Meet your mother?"

That was a surprise. And yet he had said it so casually, so naturally, she had to read no meaning into the suggestion.

"Well, sure. I'd love to. But she's not expecting us, is she?"

"Oh, that's all right. She won't mind. Come on." He held out a hand. "I'll take the helmet, so you can fix your hair."

She handed it to him, surprised—and pleased—to see that he understood about helmet hair. A quick fluff with her fingertips and she was ready.

"I really like your hair," Bart said. He reached out a hand and stroked a stray strand back from her face.

No one had ever said nice things about her hair before and she mentally thanked Louis for the color, Damien for the cut—and New York for its humidity.

They went up four steps to the front porch on which, at the far end, were a couple of slat-backed wooden rockers and between them a small wicker-topped table. There was a mailbox nailed up next to the front door, and a couple of big tubs at either end of the porch filled with more flowering plants, and the cinnamon-and-yeast smell of something good in the oven coming from the interior of the house. While Bart stopped to get his key ring from his pocket—and to riffle through the mail he took from the mailbox—Annie had a moment to imagine sitting in those rockers, greeting neighbors, keeping an eye on the kids at the school, enjoying an afternoon breather. This homey setting was a long way from the rush of the Manhattan streets and she filed it away in her collection of memories to take back home with her. She was glad Bart had given her a chance to see it.

He opened the door and called, "Hey, Mom. You home? We've got company."

"In the kitchen," came a voice from inside the house.

It was cool inside the house, and the lighting was dim, but the entryway led to a large living room, where big windows at the far end opened to a sun-filled garden at the back of the house. To the right of the living room, through a wide, arched opening, there was a dining room, and beyond that, a swinging door to the kitchen, and there was Bart's mother, coming out to greet them.

She was a tall woman, broad-shouldered and straight-backed, with long, reddish-brown hair beginning to go gray, pulled back casually into a sort of a bun. Annie saw where Bart got his eyes from, for hers were just as bright and blue and twinkling, and there was the same small, mischievous smile animating her face.

"Well, dear," she said, "this is a surprise." She had an apron on over her T-shirt and jeans and she was wiping her hands on the front of the apron. "I'm in the middle of trying out a new recipe."

"This is Annie Cornell, Mom. She's visiting here in New York and I'm just showing her the city. I thought she ought to see Brooklyn, too."

"Nice to meet you, Annie." She held up her hands apologetically. "I'm all wet and floury, so I won't shake your hand. But come on in. We can sit here in the living room and Bart can tell me all about what he's been up to." She turned to Annie and, as though just for her ears, said, "I never know what new adventure he's getting himself into. We're an old police family, and I should be accustomed to it by now."

Mrs. Hardin tucked herself cross-legged into the corner of the big comfy sofa, patted the cushion next to her, and said "Sit here, next to me. And Bart," turning to her son, who took the big blue wing chair opposite them, "don't tell me you've been driving this girl all around the city on that bike of yours. That can't possibly be fun for her, getting all windblown and gritty. Why don't you use your car? It's such a nice car, so much more comfortable, and it's just sitting there in the garage out back. You practically never use it. If I didn't borrow it sometimes, it would just be gathering dust."

"A car is just a hassle in the city, Mom. You know that. Costs a fortune to park and traffic's always jammed up. And you don't need to worry about Annie. Anyone from Laramie is used to a little wind in her face. Anyway, she's got limos carrying her all around town, so she's getting plenty of pampering." To Annie, he said, "Go on. Tell my mom about the contest and how you're on TV and getting all that fancy treatment, the clothes, the makeover, all of that stuff."

Before Annie could say anything, Mrs. Hardin stopped her, looking at her closely.

"But haven't I seen you somewhere?" She leaned back, tilted her head slightly and sort of squinted. "Maybe on TV?"

"There was some coverage of the contest. Maybe you saw that?"

"No. It was something else." She concentrated for a moment. "Oh. I know. Aren't you the girl who got mixed up in that protest down in front of the UN? I saw Bart scooping someone up out of that crowd. That was you, wasn't it?"

Bart answered for her. "Yes, that was Annie. She lost her bag, it got turned into the station and I took pity on this little lost lamb, alone—well, almost alone—in this big, bad city and I'm showing it to her in a safe and sound way. And I don't think she minds riding on a motorcycle. She seems pretty hardy to me. And wait till you hear this, Mom. Annie's home is in Wyoming. Near Laramie. On a ranch. Not so far from Granddad's place. How's that for a coincidence? And she and Lindy are already old friends. He let her ride him a little. And she even taught him a trick."

"Well," said Annie, "I guess that's pretty much my whole life story. He just left out that I'm a librarian at the university and I won a contest and that's why I'm here. With my sister."

"Hmm." Mrs. Hardin looked closely at Annie for a moment. Then she looked at Bart, carefully, as though thinking him over, looking for something new in his face, some change in his bearing.

Then she said, "Bart, dear, I'm going to make us some coffee. And I need you to run down to the corner and get us a cake. Or some doughnuts."

"But you've got a cake going in the oven. Can't we have that?"

She gave him a look. *That* look. Her son was being dense.

"The cake in the oven is for a bake sale at the church." With her lips a little pursed. A little irritated. "I already promised them a babka. Go to the corner and get us a cake."

"Okay, okay." At the door he called to them, "I'll be right back." And the house was quiet.

"Come, Annie. You can help me in the kitchen."

"Cups and things are in that cabinet." She pointed to the paned-glass doors above the countertop. "I'll start the coffee going. There's a tray on the other counter. Use that." The room was warm and filled with the scent of the cake baking in the oven. "It should be ready now," she said, as she took a cake tester from a drawer, opened the oven door and reached in to check the cake.

"Perfect," she announced.

A cake rack was ready and she put on a couple of oven mitts to carry it to the rack.

"I always say, 'When it smells good enough to eat, it's done.'"

Annie had the cups, saucers, and spoons ready on the tray and carried it to the kitchen table. Mrs. Hardin brought out a creamer and sugar bowl. She pulled out a couple of chairs from the table.

"Now," she said, "let's sit here while the coffee brews and you can tell me more about yourself."

"Not really much more to tell. Bart pretty well summed it up. I won a contest. I'm being treated like a princess. This is my first trip to New York, and I'm having a great time here. Bart is showing me the city. And he wanted me to see the neighborhood where he grew up."

Mrs. Hardin smiled kindly at Annie. "And you've been here only a few days?"

"Yes, just since Sunday."

Annie knew she was being sized up.

This is so bizarre—I hardly know Bart and I'm already meeting his mother. She must be wondering what's going on.

"It's such a coincidence—your coming from Wyoming. My family, the Malones, have been in that part of the world for generations."

"Is your property near Laramie?"

"We're farther north, toward the Montana border. We used to spend our summers on the ranch. But not so much nowadays. Everyone's so busy here, and Bart can't take those long vacation months away anymore, now that he's on the force."

"He told me his dad was also a policeman. A lieutenant, I think he said."

"Yes." Mrs. Hardin seemed to straighten up a bit more. "Yes, Bart's dad and his granddad Hardin before him. And a couple of uncles, too." She stood up. "Let's take these things into the living room"—she picked up the tray of cups and saucers—"and I'll show you a picture of Bart's dad."

Annie followed her through the swinging doors.

Mrs. Hardin put the tray down on the coffee table and took a framed photo from its place next to the sofa.

"This is Des Hardin. Lieutenant Desmond Hardin. I suppose Bart told you. He was killed in the line." She betrayed no sign of the pain those words must have cost her.

"Only that—and that his horse, Lindy, had been his dad's horse before him. I sensed that he didn't want to tell me more."

"I understand. And in that case, I'll say nothing more. He'll talk about it when he's ready." She paused for a moment, her eyes on the photo, and then returned it to its place on the end table. She sat on the sofa and, as before, patted the cushion next to her. Annie sat down and Mrs. Hardin gave her a big smile.

"And now tell me more about you."

Annie smiled broadly. She understood what Bart's mother wanted to know.

"I'm twenty-six. Never been married. No boyfriend. There were a couple along the way, but nothing serious. I live on the ranch with my sister and her husband and their two boys. I help run the ranch. I've a master's in library science, and I'm a specialist in the veterinary library at the university. I was a cheerleader in college. I have no chronic ill-nesses and like all Wyomingites, I'm accustomed to straight talk."

Mrs. Hardin was beaming.

"Oh, Annie Cornell, I really like you. And," she added with a little smile, "I think my son likes you, too."

Annie returned the smile.

"But he seems to think I need protection. Does he always treat women as though they're hothouse flowers, like they'll be easily crushed if he doesn't come riding to the rescue?"

"Oh, they're all like that, the Hardin men. They outgrow it as they get older and wiser. Time and experience are the cure."

The front door banged open.

"I'm back," Bart called. "I bought a cheesecake."

"In here, Bart," his mother called back. "In the living room."

He joined them, bearing a red-and-white-striped box.

"Best cheesecake in the world," he said.

"But it's not Lily Lindy's cheesecake, is it?"

"No. That's long gone now."

Two hours later, they were back on the bike, crossing the bridge into Manhattan. He'd given her a quick tour of Brooklyn, from its busy downtown to its oceanfront communities, its scenic harbor views, its cultural and ethnic enclaves. He'd kept up a running account of Brook-lyn's history—and Annie tried to take it all in. But with her arms around him, and her cheek resting against his shoulder, her interest in the educational aspects of the ride was minimal. Back in Manhattan, the streets, the traffic, the crowds, all spun away from her as the bike twisted in and out, past City Hall and north along Centre Street, through Chinatown, then Little Italy, Soho, the Village and more and more, too much for her to take it all in, the swirl of shops and luxury residences, elegant brownstones, decaying warehouses, imposing official buildings, crumbling ancient tenements and multimillion-dollar lofts, all jammed up against each other in a rich but overwhelming tangle of impressions. Bart was shouting back to her, explaining it all as he pointed to *this* and *that* and *the other* interesting site, while she, with eyes half closed and an agreeable half smile, continued to rest her cheek against him and to murmur her acknowledgment of the tour he was providing.

They stopped, at last, in front of her hotel. He took the helmet from her.

"You want to get fixed up before we go to dinner?"

"Dinner?"

"Well, sure. I made plans. I've got us a reservation at Charlie Wu's."

"Chinese food?"

"The best. And not far from here. We can walk. So your hair won't get messed up."

"Do I need to get all gussied up?"

"You look great. But Charlie's place is a little bit fancy, so if you want to change, wash up a little after riding all over the city today—"

"And that's why you wore a jacket?"

He grinned.

"Yes, ma'am. With a tie in my pocket."

"Okay. I'll run up, wash my face, maybe make a quick change."

He put a hand on her arm.

"Maybe I could come up, too." There was that nice, gentle smile again. "You could help me get my tie on straight."

Annie was only a little surprised. They exchanged a long look. She remembered that Liz was out for the evening, with Max and his wife. And she made a decision.

Quietly she said, "Not yet."

And she turned and went into the hotel, while Bart remained outside, watching her go.

Chapter Nineteen

Dinner—and?

Charlie Wu's restaurant was a large, dark cave of crimson and black lacquer slashed with gold. Banquettes were black leather, deep, soft and spacious, and the thick carpeting was, like the walls, a seductively dark crimson. And here, like the Green Parrot, there was again the magic of producing bright light and a dark ambience.

How do they do that? she wondered.

They followed the maître d' to their table in a dark corner, almost hidden behind a large planter full of ceiling-high live bamboo.

"I asked for a little privacy when I made the reservation."

"It's beautiful." Annie looked around her as she slid into the seat curved into the wall. "Like a stage set."

"And it's quiet, too. All carpeted and no music, so we can hear ourselves talk. I didn't want to be in one of those state-of-the-art places, all glass and noise and everyone screaming to be heard. And I wanted you to have the best Chinese meal in New York. I bet outside of San Francisco and—well, China—this is the best Chinese food you can get."

She took the menu the waiter handed her and started to scan it.

"I'd read that the best Chinese food in New York is in Chinatown."

"Mostly, that's true, though you can get great Chinese food all around town. But this is Charlie's second location. He already has a restaurant way downtown, near Grand Street. It just did so well, people got him to open another Charlie Wu's up here, in Midtown. Lots of folks from the UN come in here, just a couple of blocks away. Charlie's made it a fully Asian menu; he serves dishes from Thailand, and Vietnam, even Mongolia. Look around. You can see, not just for Chinese folks. Customers from everywhere. This place brings people together. Like a UN annex."

"I can see why. This menu looks great."

But Bart took the menu from her and handed it to the waiter.

"I already ordered ahead for us," he told the waiter. "And we'd like a bottle of the Riesling," he added, pointing on the wine list to a good spätlese with a name rich in umlauts and too German for him to try to pronounce.

To Annie, he said, "You have to have the scallops. They do them in a sauce," he shook his head, "no words for it—"

"You already—?"

"And some dim sum, too. My favorite—"

"Bart, you didn't need to—"

"But we'll start with the ribs."

"Bart!—"

"—and I'm going to teach you how to eat with chopsticks."

This was too much!

"Oh, for goodness' sakes, Bart! You are really too much! Can you *possibly* understand? I don't need you to order for me. And I already *know* how to eat with chopsticks."

That brought him up short. He looked disappointed and the word "crestfallen" went through Annie's head.

"Well, how would I know that?" he said.

"*Everyone* knows how to eat with chopsticks. Even in Wyoming! After all, Bart, there really *are* Chinese restaurants beyond the Hudson River."

"Well, not good ones. Not like here in the city."

She was getting irritated. This man definitely needed to be reined in.

"Well, I would invite you to come to Laramie and come with me to Tommy Yao's place."

"Chinese?"

"Yes. Chinese. And not only authentic Chinese, but also authentic, old-time Wyoming, as well." She poured a little tea into Bart's cup. "Let me tell you about Tommy Yao." She filled her own cup.

"Tommy's family goes back a long way. Maybe a hundred fifty years, to the 1800s. Back to the days when Chinese laborers were building the railroads through the west. They had food cars especially for the Chinese workers—dried abalone and oysters and rice and specially imported tea—and they paid the Chinese cooks extra to cook for the Chinese workers. One of them was one of Tommy's ancestors. And after the railroad workers moved on, he stayed on and his little chuck wagon became a little restaurant, right near the train station. And it's still there, only it's not a little place anymore; it's a very good and well-established enterprise. And ever since then, the Yao family has been bringing their relatives over from China. The Yao family are magicians in the kitchen. What's more, Tommy does wonderful things with game. The local hunters around Laramie bring Tommy their venison and pheasant and their chukar partridge. Bear, even, and elk, and he cooks it up for them. Have you ever had a good bear stew? It's fabulous!"

She'd been waving her napkin around as she talked as she had warmed to her subject, which was, let's face it, to put Bart Hardin in his place, with his notion that nothing west of his precious New York is worth knowing. She was really revved up and now she slapped the napkin down on the table.

"So just don't tell me about chopsticks!"

There was silence at the table now. Annie stared into her plate, a little embarrassed by her outburst. And Bart just sat immobile, taking it all in.

Finally, he spoke.

"I guess I was kind of out of line there. I just figured—"

"I know what you figured," she said, a little petulantly.

"I'm sorry. I'll try not to do it again." They sat silently for a bit.

He drank off his cup of tea. She filled it up again.

And then the ribs arrived.

And, as no one can be angry with a plate of ribs in front of them, they each relaxed a little, and they each smiled a little—

"Friends?" he said.

"Of course." She started in on the ribs. "But you have to stop being such a horse's ass."

"I'm *not* a horse's ass!"

"You are, too." She licked the sauce from her fingers. "Sometimes."

They ate in silence. Bart thought things over. And she wondered if she'd gone too far.

When the ribs were done, the apprentice waiter arrived with a tiny tray of hot, moist terry cloths, which he handed to them, one by one, with small tongs. They cleaned up, they handed the little towels back, and he disappeared. The next course hadn't arrived yet.

"Annie?"

He was looking at her so seriously.

She tilted her head, attentive.

"Annie, I don't want to be a horse's ass with you."

She felt a thump in her heart, touched by this sudden exposure of his very honest vulnerability, and she had to take a couple of breaths. She was glad that their dinner arrived just then, because she needed a little diversion.

And what a diversion it was. There were sea scallops served in their own shells, and a chicken soong. A plate of dumplings, light and savory. And a platter of dried, steamed green beans, bright and aromatic. With her chopsticks, she lifted a scallop from its shell where it seemed to float in a light-as-air creamy sauce. One taste and she thought it must have been whipped up by culinary wizards.

How are they able to make them so delicate and so rich at the same time?

"These are wonderful," she said.

"I knew you'd like them," he said. He beamed as though he'd prepared them himself. "And how about that soong dish? You've got to try that." The bowl of finely diced vegetables and chicken between them was surrounded by a fan of a romaine lettuce leaves, fresh and crisp and just waiting to be filled with the chopped mix.

The exotic food, the perfect service, and the elegant ambience cast a seductive spell over them, and by the time they were ready to leave, there was no longer a shred of tension between them.

It must have rained a little while they were having dinner; it seemed everything had been washed clean and the light mist that hung in the air seemed scented with flowers. The rain had stopped but the pavements were still wet; vehicles made a soft swishing sound, like brushstrokes on a snare drum, and the street was all activity, people coming and going all around them, the nighttime traffic different from the daytime, a rush of taxis, black town cars everywhere, no delivery trucks, and the dark obliterated by the illuminated storefronts, the street lamps above, and the light from thousands of windows looking down at them. If the skies had cleared and if there were stars above, it would not have been possible to see them, and if, by chance, the moon should ride by, high above the skyscrapers, it would have been indistinguishable from the surrounding multitude of lights that made daytime of all hours in this city that never sleeps.

Bart took Annie's hand and, in the manner of an old-fashioned gentleman, slipped it through his arm so that, with her hand on his arm, he was truly escorting her, in a formal manner, through the lively clatter and bustle, back to her hotel. The Riesling had left her with a little buzz, the pavement was a bit uneven, and she seldom wore really high heels, so she was glad of his steadying presence, glad to rely on him to get her safely back home. Glad to relax and allow herself to be unaware of her surroundings, to let Bart guide her. No surprise then, that she didn't notice that Bart was alert to something—to an unnameable something that his instinct told him to pay attention to—that same instinct that had alerted him in the park, when he knew they were being watched, that something in his environment was not right.

Careful not to alarm her, Bart checked his surroundings, checked the throngs of people moving around them, the dog walkers, the doormen, ordinary pedestrians on their way here and there, folks getting into and out of taxis, diners eating at outdoor tables, but he couldn't find the source of his concern. They arrived at her hotel with no danger surfacing, and he allowed himself to let his guard down.

He brought her into the lobby and it was time to say good night. Time, perhaps, for a good night kiss? But in such a public place, right there, in the midst of strangers?

They were both quiet. The unasked questions lay between them. Bart said nothing, waiting, as though trying to read her mind. Waiting until she did make up her mind.

"If you'd like to come up—"

No more words were needed between them.

They rode up silently in the elevator. People got on. People got off. Annie saw their reflection in the elevator's mirrored wall. Bart was watching her intently, as though he was memorizing every feature, every curve and plane of her face, every wave of her hair.

In the room, she turned on a light. She slipped off her light jacket. She turned toward him, and he was waiting for her. She moved right into his arms. His hand was in her hair, and she felt his intake of breath, as though his pleasure was too much. She glanced toward the door.

"My sister—"she whispered.

"It's only nine. The show won't end for another hour." His hand stroked through her hair. He held her still closer. "They'll go out for a drink after. We have time—"

And now, in the quiet, he kissed her. And yes, they had time. He kissed her again. She felt his heart beating. She felt her own heart beating.

Annie knew. This man was different. There'd never been this sense of comfort and completeness, this sense of safety.

He held her a little bit away from him, as though he wanted to study her.

"We have time," he repeated. "And I've got to catch my breath." He shook his head, as though to clear it. "You take my breath away."

Annie laughed. "That's supposed to be the girl's line."

"Whatever."

She was glad he wasn't rushing things.

"How about a drink," she said. "There's a mini bar—" She pointed toward it.

"Good idea."

He went with her.

"There's vodka," she said. "And some juice."

"That'll do it."

Together, they took out a couple of mini bottles and mixed a couple of drinks.

"And pretzels?" she asked.

He nodded. He loosened his tie. He took off his jacket and dropped it on a chair. He took the glasses from her hand and put them on the coffee table. "Come here," he whispered. He led her to the sofa. Again, he pulled her gently into his arms.

"You do, Annie. You take my breath away."

In the light from the entryway—the only light there was—his eyes were darker, his face was shadowed and so serious. As he drew her closer still, she forgot all those others, from another time in her life, and she forgot why she was here, and what she'd been doing these last days, and—

—and just then, in that very moment, Bart's cell phone rang.

"God *dammit!*"

His jacket was across the room, on the chair where he dropped it. He left Annie, who was suddenly thrown back into reality, abruptly trying to remember where she was.

Bart crossed the room, in a fury, and he fished the damned phone out of his jacket pocket. He looked at the screen.

"I have to take this."

He glared at the phone's screen.

"Hardin here."

She saw his eyes widen, all focused attention now. His face turned grim.

"I'm on my way!" And to Annie, almost as though she'd disappeared from his world, he said, "I have to go."

Reflexively, he pulled on his jacket. And without another word, he was up and gone and she was alone. Staring at the door—which he had not fully closed. Thoughtfully, she got up, went to the door. Closed it.

"So what happened?" Liz said. "He just suddenly left? Without a word, not even a good-bye?"

"Exactly. Not even a word."

"Do you know who called?"

"I just saw his face go all fierce and he said, 'I'm on my way,' like it was obviously some sort of emergency, and then he said, 'I have to go,' and he was out of here like a shot. Didn't even close the door."

"Well, at least you know it wasn't anything you did."

"Of course not. We were getting along just fine." She paused and her expression turned sort of dreamy. "Just fine—"

"Oh?" Liz's expression said it all. "I'll just bet you were."

Annie chose to change the subject quickly.

"So how was the show?"

Liz let Annie off the hook. She knew she'd get the whole story eventually.

"The show was wonderful," she said. "Great music, great dancing. And hilariously funny. The whole audience was screaming with laughter. I see what they mean about a Broadway musical. Such incredible talent. It surely is not the Laramie High School drama club."

"Oh, Liz, not you, too. If I hear one more word about how wonderful this city is, I'm going to chuck everything and get the next plane out of here."

Liz was unimpressed by Annie's outburst. She took a handful of pretzels.

"You can't. You signed a contract."

"I know. I know. But honestly. I'm just so tired of the way this city toots its own horn."

"I thought you were having a good time."

"I'm having a wonderful time. And everyone's been very nice to me. But dammit, this city is *not* the center of the whole universe."

'Well, *something's* bugging you. Did that cop do something to upset you?"

"No, Liz. He really didn't. Not at all." Her eyes went dreamy. "Not at all," she repeated softly.

Liz gave her sister one sharp look.

"Hmm," she said. She took another couple of pretzels. "Well, I'm going to bed. This has been a full day."

Chapter Twenty

The Morning News

Thursday – Early

The morning newspaper lay on the carpet outside the door. Liz, still sleepy and bleary-eyed, barely awake, pulled her robe close around her, glanced up and down the hall to be sure no one could see her.

Before she could pick up the paper, she saw the headline. She paused, she bent down, and she read:

Lindy Hopped?
A Times Square Favorite Is Missing

"Lindy?" She whispered the question into the empty hallway. "I recognize that name."

She carried the paper into Annie's bedroom, reading as she went.

"Wake up, honey." She poked a bump in the blanket that was probably Annie's shoulder. "There's something here in the morning paper you should see."

A muffled voice came from the folds of the pillow.

"What time is it?"

"Seven. You said to wake you at seven. And there's something here you should see."

Annie rolled out of bed and staggered to the bathroom.

Through the door, Liz read to her:

The mounted police unit on New York's West Side was broken into last night, and Lindy, a Times Square favorite among New Yorkers and tourists alike for almost fifteen years, was taken from the stables at Troop B Headquarters. The officer on duty, Jess Yardley, reports that he was held at gunpoint by two masked men while a third man, also masked, mounted Lindy bareback and rode him out of the building and up 12th Avenue.

Annie came out of the bathroom. She was wide awake. "Let me see that," she said. She took the paper out of Liz's hand.

"Isn't that your guy's horse?" Liz said.

Annie nodded and kept reading.

Officer Antony Biello, who arrived to take over the next shift, found the officer in the stable, handcuffed to one of the steel posts that enclose Lindy's stall. No other horse was taken and a source close to the investigation says a printed leaflet associated with a dissident group was found in Lindy's stall. It is believed that the horse-napping may be the work of this group, which has been conducting protests outside the United Nations building. The group's leader was arrested on Sunday and the police are not discounting the possibility that the horse is being held for ransom.

Annie looked up from the paper. "For ransom!"

"Is it your bunch? From Sunday?"

Annie nodded. "Probably. Wait. There's more."

On Sunday, Lindy was part of the mounted unit that conducted crowd control at the demonstration at the UN and was identified by name in TV coverage of the event. "We'll find those men," said Sergeant Bartlett Hardin, who is Lindy's assigned rider. "But if they hurt that horse, if they do any harm to him at all, they're going to be very, very sorry."

Sergeant Hardin has a special attachment to Lindy. The horse's previous rider was the sergeant's father, Lieutenant Des Hardin, who was killed five years ago when gunfire broke out during a street demonstration, similar to the one last Sunday at the UN.

Police horses must meet very special specifications and are therefore generally acquired by Police Department purchase, but Lindy had originally belonged to the Hardin family, which owns the ranch in Wyoming that bred the Lindy strain. Although title to Lindy was transferred to the department, Lindy has always been regarded as the property of the Hardin family. Lieutenant Hardin's son, Bartlett, had just completed training at the police academy at the time of his father's death, so the department allowed Sergeant Hardin to replace his father as Lindy's rider.

Annie folded the paper and put it on the bed.

"What time is it?"

"You just asked me. Now it's 7:06."

"Call room service. I need some coffee." She went back into the bathroom. She called back to Liz as she turned on the shower, "Maybe there's something I can do—I don't know—something. I have to think." She closed the door behind her.

By the time she came out of the bathroom, wrapped in a huge bath towel, with her wet hair turbaned in a smaller one, room service had already rolled in a cart with their breakfast.

"Lord, I could get used to this," Liz said. She poured a cup of coffee and handed it to Annie. "Any ideas?"

Annie shook her head.

"Still thinking. Bart must be out of his mind right now. No wonder he ran out of here like that last night."

"Will you call him?"

"I don't know. I'm sure he has enough to think about without my bothering him. But I feel so bad for him. I know how he's feeling right now." She sipped at her coffee, put it down absentmindedly. She walked to the window, and looked out for a minute, then came back and sat on the bed. "Remember when my Paddywhack turned up missing?"

"I remember. That sweet little filly. Took us two days to find her."

Annie was silent for a moment, staring at the floor. Then she said, "And all you found was what the cougar left."

"Yes, I remember that, too. You were only eight years old then, just a little kid, and you tried to take Daddy's rifle to go hunt down that animal yourself."

"That's how Bart is feeling now."

Liz sat next to Annie on the bed and put an arm around her.

"Oh, honey. I'm so sorry." Liz saw the beginning of tears in Annie's eyes and she hugged her more closely. "Don't cry, Annie, sweetie. Please don't cry. They'll find him. It's going to be all right. Here." She reached for the basket of hot muffins on the breakfast cart. "Have a muffin."

"I don't want a muffin. And I'm *not* crying." She blinked her eyes to clear them and straightened up defiantly. "And of course it's going to be all right. Bart will get those guys—whoever it was took Lindy. And I pity them when he does!" She picked up the paper and pointed to the story. "But think what this must mean to him? Lindy isn't just Bart's horse. He's Bart's *dad's* horse. The paper said Bart's dad was killed during a street demonstration, so he had to have been riding Lindy when he was killed. Bart didn't tell me any of that. He just said his dad had died a few years ago. And that's how Lindy came to be Bart's horse. Like he was entrusted with this special animal—and look what happened. Along with everything else, he must be feeling such guilt—that Lindy was stolen on his watch!"

She picked up the phone. "I won't call. I'll just text him. If he's too busy, he just won't answer." With thumbs working, Annie wrote:

I saw the paper. Is there anything I can do?

And an answer came back instantly.

I wish there were. It's probably that Buljornia crowd. Forensics is working on it. I'll call later. Too busy here.

"They think it's that Buljornia group. The ones that mobbed me on Sunday."

She walked to the window, drew the curtains aside, and looked out over the view, at the crowded mass of buildings, the tall stacks of human habitation jammed up against each other with the morning sun shining off the thousands of windows, and a separate life going on behind each window.

Eight million people out there. I wonder how many of them care that Sergeant Bart Hardin's horse has been stolen.

And I wonder why I care so much.

"Honey, there isn't anything you can do. This is a police problem. And we're supposed to be enjoying ourselves on this trip. So let's finish breakfast, get ourselves dressed, and let's go out and enjoy ourselves. We could do that sightseeing boat tour around Manhattan."

Annie said nothing for a minute or two—just kept staring out at the city.

She turned away from the window. "No, Liz. I've decided. I don't have to be totally helpless. There is something I can do."

"Uh oh." Liz made a face. "I know that look. Here comes that stubborn streak of yours."

"Number one. Only a few blocks from here is one of the greatest libraries in the world. A resource like no other. I'd planned to see it anyway during this trip—I wouldn't come here and miss that, of all things. So here's my perfect opportunity. I could find out something *not* forensic, something different from what the police would be looking for. I could make a different kind of search."

She was back in the bathroom, brushing her hair.

"I'm going to go to the library. I'm going to find out about these people. Who are they? What are they about? You can't fight an enemy if you don't know who they are."

"Couldn't you just Google them?" Liz came to stand at the bathroom door, watching Annie dab on a bit of lipstick, a breath of blush. "Wouldn't that be enough? Everything's on the Internet these days. Why do you have to make a trip to the library?"

Annie brushed past Liz, who followed her into her bedroom.

"I'm surprised you said that. Information on the Internet is not always reliable. Everyone knows that."

She got into her panties and pulled on a pair of skinny jeans. "Number two, I'm a librarian. I know how to use primary sources." She pulled on a loose-fitting tee—pale pink—over her lacy bra. She stepped into a pair of moccasins. "And number three, I've got to do something to help. I can't just sit here."

"So, no boat tour around Manhattan?"

"You do it without me. Oh, Liz. Don't be mad. I know I've been neglecting you. And I'm sorry. Really I am. But this trip is just not turning out the way we expected."

"Annie, I knew from the moment Bart Hardin appeared on the scene, this trip was not going to turn out the way we'd expected. So I'll just be a good big sister and try not to interfere with your adventure. For the time being. And don't worry about me. Actually, I'm getting used to this big, bad New York and I'm kind of enjoying not having to deal with the usual—kids, Craig, ranch work. Just enjoying my own self, being on my own. This is my first vacation in ten years and I'm beginning to get that this really is 'Fun City.' So you just go ahead and do what you have to. I'll be okay. But have your phone with you and keep in touch."

"You really are the best sister—when you're not being a watch-dog. I'll stay in touch and we'll meet for dinner or something."

"Or something. Don't worry. I'm going to have breakfast and take a nice long bath. I might go out and buy a bathing suit and take a swim in that fancy pool they have up here on the top floor." She took some toast off the breakfast tray. "Go. Go. Do what you have to." She waved the toast at Annie. "I'll be fine."

Chapter Twenty-one

Front Moving In

Thursday Morning - Later

The taxi crawled through the morning rush hour traffic and Annie was a mass of impatience and frustration by the time it pulled up in front of the library. She handed the driver a ten-dollar bill, waved off the two singles he was counting out in change, stepped out onto Fifth Avenue—and was stopped short, momentarily transfixed by the massive edifice that confronted her.

The place was enormous, with a broad expanse of stone steps rising up to the entrance doors. And all was guarded by those two famous lions, Patience and Fortitude, who were just like their pictures, as supercilious as she'd imagined them, so terribly above it all. Here they were, the real thing (with a pigeon perched on Fortitude's head), looking down at the passing scene as though through a monocle. And the passing scene was looking right back, with smiles and nods of greeting and cameras flashing. She was torn between getting out her own cell phone to grab a photo, and her eagerness to begin her research.

"These lions are made of stone," she reminded herself. "They'll wait." And she ran up the broad steps—all thirty-plus of them.

Alas! The library didn't open until ten a.m.! And it was now barely nine o'clock.

Oh, damn! I should have checked. This city doesn't keep college hours.

What to do now?

Okay. The gods are telling me to slow down. Collect my thoughts. Plan how to approach this project.

And maybe savor the moment.

She'd have to kill an hour, maybe take a walk around the block, find a place to get some breakfast—the gulp of coffee an hour ago would hardly be enough for the full day that lay ahead of her—reread the article in the paper and think things through.

She went back down the steps, more slowly now, took one last look back at the library's imposing façade, walked down toward the corner to take a long shot of Patience and Fortitude with her phone's camera, bought some coffee, a croissant, and a banana from a street cart at the corner and brought them back to the steps where she sat for the remains of the hour and studied the steady flow of traffic and of people.

Maybe these people aren't really all crazy living in this madhouse. And it isn't really a madhouse. They seem to get along well enough; they leave each other alone. They get to sit on the steps of this fabulous place as though it were their own front porch. And I'm eating my breakfast out of a paper bag and I'm all alone and no one thinks anything of it. No one comes over to ask if I'm all right. And I am all right. Like everyone else here, totally anonymous and minding my own business and everyone else minds theirs. There's something to be said for that. And by the way, this is not bad coffee. From a street vendor!

And now that she had killed an hour, it was time to get to work.

She ran up the steps again and passed through the great iron doors. The grandeur of the ornate, beaux-arts rotunda, and the wide marble stairs at either side that wound up to higher floors, the great arched passageways and, on the distant ceiling, too high above her to be seen clearly, the mural of Prometheus—it all demanded at least a moment's recognition and an appreciation that, though the rotunda was busy with people moving about, the enormous space that rose up above them seemed to absorb their sound. The result was a quiet that was utterly appropriate to one of the world's great libraries.

She paused. She took it all in, made a promise to herself to come back someday and visit properly, and then went to the information desk and made some inquiries. She was directed to the appropriate rooms, to her left down a long hall, and others upstairs. And after several hours digging through microfiche and well-chosen archival material, she had a cache of some interesting data, about Buljornia, its people, its culture, its history—and particularly the history of its present protest.

It would be up to Bart to work out how useful it would all be.

It was midafternoon when she walked out of the library; the wind had shifted. A few clouds had drifted over Fifth Avenue's skyscrapers. Scattered randomly along the steps, people relaxed, unmindful of the weather, and she picked her way among them as they took pictures, read their books, ate their late lunches out of plastic containers and paper bags and snacked on the hot dogs and pizza slices and ice creams they'd bought from the vendors along the sidewalk's edge in front of the library. It reminded her of Central Park. The pace was leisurely. A group of street performers was doing its ragged thing, and the folks sitting on the steps cheered and applauded. A couple of youngsters were drawn into their show, pulled at random out of the audience, making them a part of the performance, all so good natured, so easily enjoyed. Off to one side, there were small tables set out for the public's use, and she found one far enough away from the show's spectators to give her a little privacy.

She'd had her phone off while she was working in the library, but now, as soon as she reset it, she saw a text message from Bart.

They're shoving me out of here. I'm making them crazy. I've got to get calmed down. I've been told to go home. Can I see you first?

She called immediately—and he answered immediately. She heard the stress in his voice as he answered.

"Annie. Where have you been?"

"I'm at the library. Want to get away?"

"The library? When all hell is breaking loose? What are you doing at the library?"

"I'll tell you when I see you."

"Okay. Okay." He sounded impatient. "Go to the outdoor cafe in the park right behind the library. I'll meet you there. Fifteen minutes."

When he arrived, she was already waiting at a table under an enormous patio umbrella. He looked as though he'd been caught in a threshing machine. Obviously he'd had no sleep, his hair was wild, and he was still in the blazer and jeans he'd been wearing when he left her last night, which seemed to have been in a fight with an angry rhinoceros. He fell into a chair, propped his elbows on the table, and buried his head in his hands.

"Oh, God, Annie. When I get those guys——" A waiter materialized next to him. "Get me some coffee," Bart said, without looking up.

Annie smiled at the waiter. "He'll have a turkey burger with sweet potato fries, please. He's had a hard night."

"Boy, you didn't have to tell me," the waiter said. "I think he needs a margarita."

"No, that's okay," Annie said. "Just the food and some coffee, thanks."

The waiter smiled at her. "Whatever. And for you?"

She glanced at the menu. "The same for me. And a fruit salad, too."

"You got it, luv," he said. And he was off with the order.

Annie opened her bag and put some papers on the table between them.

"Maybe some of this will help. I've been doing some research here at the library."

Bart looked up between his spread fingers. With a gesture, he dismissed her papers.

"Our guys know what they're doing, Annie. They've got the best resources. Canines, trackers, high-tech electronics. All units are on it." He sat up, put his head back, rubbed his eyes. "We figure by now they've gotten Lindy out of Manhattan, probably up to Westchester or out on the Island, like Great Neck or someplace."

"The paper said they left one of their protest leaflets."

"We've got our guys processing that now—for prints, for whatever it can tell us. They're certain it was that Buljornia bunch. Crazy sons of bitches! If they hurt that horse, if they do him any harm——"

"I don't think they will, Bart." He looked at her as though she'd interrupted his train of thought with some trivial notion. "I've been doing some research on their history. On their culture."

He peered at her in wonder.

"On their culture? Excuse me, Annie, but are you nuts? Their culture? Who cares about these guys' culture? They stole Lindy, for God's sake. They're criminals. They took my dad's horse!"

Annie understood his stress and she forgave the rudeness.

"I think my research may be helpful. Don't discount it till you've seen it."

"Annie, I'm sure you're a great librarian and all that, but why are you messing with stuff you don't know anything about? This is police business. Just leave it to the guys who know what they're doing." He ran his hands through his hair, as though trying to settle the turmoil inside his head. "They even sent me away. I'm getting in everyone's way."

"Bart, I'm cutting you a lot of slack here, because you're exhausted and suffering. But the stuff you need is exactly the stuff I *do* know about. My stuff is information. That's my work. And information is what you need now. So have your food." The waiter had just put it down in front of him. "Be quiet for a minute, and listen to me without automatically discounting what I tell you."

Bart looked at the soup as though it had mysteriously materialized out of thin air. He looked at Annie as though she, too, had appeared out of nowhere.

"I'm sorry, Annie. I'm a wreck and I don't mean to be rude."

"I know." She set her soup to the side, not the least bit interested in it. She opened the pack of papers she'd put together.

"Now, here's what you need to know about Buljornia and about those guys." She leaned toward him across the table, to be sure she had his attention. "About Buljornia, first of all. Right now, it's a tiny breakaway state with a very sad history. Ever since the fifteenth century, it's been under the control of one Eastern European nation or another, with a long history of wars raging all around so it was always under the control of one country after another. For the last couple of generations a segment of the population has been trying to establish Buljornia as an autonomous state, to become a sovereign state all on its own. And that's your guys. Nobody has paid much attention to them and they've mostly been treated as a joke by the great nations.

"However, Buljornia was once a great nation itself, back in ancient times. I'm talking about thousands of years ago. I won't bore you with the details, but much of what we call civilization started in Buljornia, and that's the argument these protesters make. It's a lost cause, I suppose but that's not our concern. There's plenty of scholarly material about them, if you're ever interested."

Bart waved a hand in dismissal.

"Not interested," he said.

"You don't need to be. But now here's what you do need to be interested in. The Buljornian culture that you're dismissing so casually is rooted in their history as—now get this—the 'horse people.'"

That got Bart's attention.

"Yes," Annie said. "Some horse cultures go back as much as six thousand years, and stretch all the way from Eastern Europe, Ukraine, through the Caucasus and across Siberia and Mongolia. Their people are nomadic and their lives are—or were—totally built around their horses! Their philosophy, their religion, their technology, all was built around their horses. They lived in the saddle. They drank their mares' milk, they ate the flesh of their horses, they wore their horses' hides and made their tents from their horses' skins. When they died, their horses were buried with them. They were apparently the first humans to get up on a horse and use the horse for transportation, bareback, at first—note that, Bart, bareback!—and they were the first to create saddles. They practically lived in their saddles. They played games on their horses. And most famously of all, they used their horses as instruments of warfare. They were the first cavalry in the history of warfare. On horseback, they conquered vast territories. The chariot warfare of the ancient Romans and Greeks was no match for them." She paused to let that sink in. "The point is, these people who took Lindy—they know horses."

"But that was all long ago."

"No. These are still a nomadic people. That's why they've not yet become successful as a settled culture. They still keep and ride and value their horses. Think about this, Bart. The report in the paper said Lindy was ridden bareback out of the stable. Have you ever ridden bareback?"

"Well, yeah. Back on my granddad's ranch. When I was a kid."

"So you know it's not easy. Takes training and practice. And experience. Especially at a gallop. And even more so if you're *stealing* the horse—and maybe you're being chased. By the whole damn NYPD!"

She hadn't touched her food, and suddenly Annie realized she was hungry. It had been hours since she'd eaten. She looked at her lunch and decided it was time. She took a bite of the now-cold slider.

"So here's what I think," she said, through a mouthful of turkey. "First of all, these people respect horses. And they know better than to run him to the ground for thirty or forty miles. What good would he be as a hostage if they've wrecked him?"

She took another bite.

"What's more, if those people were going to take a horse, and hold him for ransom, or for any other reason, I'd bet anything they wouldn't take just any horse. Not these people. It would be contrary to their culture. They would naturally choose to take a special horse. Here's the thing. They wouldn't have known Lindy from any other horse, but something must have made them decide he was the one to take."

"Okay. Why Lindy?"

"Right. Why Lindy? They must have seen that TV report, the day of the protest. He was named. His history was described. They learned that he was beloved and brave and had been ridden by a warrior and the warrior's son. Just their kind of horse. Now, here's what I'm thinking: the protests had just started that day, on Sunday. The chances are good that they were new to the city, arrived here specifically to make their cause public, at the United Nations and before the cameras. My guess is they are holed up somewhere not far from here. My guess is they wouldn't have taken Lindy far from the stables. After all, you can't go riding a horse around New York City just like that, especially if you're riding bareback, without being noticed. The only horses on the streets here are either dragging a hansom cab behind them or they've got a cop up on top. Do you think they would have ridden Lindy from here to Westchester or to Great Neck without leaving a trail of cell phone photos a mile wide? Thousands of people would have been taking pictures."

She finished off the sliders and started on the fruit.

"No," she said. "Lindy is somewhere close by. And I think you and I can find him."

"You really are nuts, Annie. Do you think you can do police work better than the NYPD? You haven't the resources. You haven't the training." He put his hand out and rested it on her arm. "And it could be dangerous. Do you think I'd let you be in danger? You said it yourself. These are a violent people."

"I said the horsemen of ancient times were violent. These people today are clumsy oafs. I'm not in any danger from them."

"You don't know what you're doing. I'm not letting you go out chasing criminals."

"Oh, Bart. Don't be silly. I'll be careful."

They sat silently for a while, squared off against each other.

The clouds had thickened and a new wind was slapping at the umbrella above them. The temperature was dropping and the London plane trees in the park were showing the bright undersides of their leaves, a sign of the storm coming. Papers and plastic bags were beginning to fly about, and people were gathering their papers and belongings and heading for shelter.

Bart looked around, suddenly aware of the world around them.

"It's going to rain," he said. "Let's get you back to your hotel."

She looked up. Of course. In Laramie, you'd have seen the approaching weather across the valley an hour before it arrived. Here, the front appeared over the nearest skyscraper before you had a chance to prepare for it, and this storm was already declaring its arrival.

They made it back to the hotel in five minutes, minutes ahead of the downpour and in two more minutes, they were opening the door to room number 4420.

"I'll just get a jacket," Annie said. She went into the bedroom.

Bart headed for the sofa.

"Take your time," he said. "This won't blow over for a while."

In the bedroom, she stripped off the T-shirt and put on her favorite shirt, a long-sleeved pink and yellow paisley print from Lands End. She added her rodeo belt and her silver-and-turquoise earrings. She dabbed on some fresh lipstick. She pulled the elastic off her ponytail, and she brushed out her hair, and again enjoyed seeing in the mirror the humidity's lovely effect and wished she could take it back to Laramie with her.

She got a denim jacket out of the closet.

She went back into the living room, where she found Bart sound asleep, sitting up.

She stood over him for a full minute. He never moved.

With a smile, she thought, *For this I put on my prettiest blouse?*

Her next thought was, *Poor guy. He's exhausted.*

She pushed at his chest lightly, with one finger, and he went right over, facedown, like a fallen tree. She hoisted his legs onto the sofa where he settled in comfortably and nestled into the cushions, still deeply asleep.

She smiled again. She scribbled something on a piece of note paper. She slipped on the jacket. And she left him there.

Chapter Twenty-two

Tracking in the Asphalt Jungle

Thursday Late Afternoon

It was like swimming up from the bottom of the ocean. The surface seemed so far away, he'd just as soon sink down to the bottom again. He was still desperately in need of rest.

But he knew he was awake and would have to open his eyes. Especially since he could feel someone was watching him.

And when he did, he saw that the room was now dim, the subdued light telling him it was late afternoon, and he knew that hours must have passed. A woman was standing there, watching him. Same blond hair, same general build, but not the same girl.

"You must be Bart," Liz said. She held up a piece of paper. "She left a note."

Let him sleep. He's had a bad night.

He blinked a couple of times and got himself upright. He rubbed his face and felt the stubble that had grown there since yesterday morning's shave. He ran his hands through his hair.

"I fell asleep," he said.

Liz laughed. "I guess you did."

"You must be the sister."

"Yes. I'm the sister. I'm Liz Cameron."

"Where's Annie?"

"I haven't the foggiest. Last I saw her, this morning, she was headed to the library."

He nodded. "The library. Yeah. I met her there. At about two o'clock. We had lunch and then we came here. I didn't mean to fall asleep."

"You don't know where she was going?"

He was still groggy from sleep, and he needed a minute to get clear. Then he remembered. How was he to tell Liz that her sister was off—on her own—to rescue a kidnapped horse from some very dangerous criminals? There was nothing she could do—and he figured she might freak.

So he punted.

"Has it stopped raining?"

"It has now. I got caught in it. On that tour boat that goes around Manhattan. Too bad Annie didn't get to go. It was a great view of the whole island. And it was kind of pretty, being on the water in the rain."

Bart was not really listening. He was fully awake now and his priorities were getting sorted out. Number one, he needed to find Annie before she got herself into something she couldn't handle.

He raked his hands through his hair again and made a pass at straightening his jacket.

"I've got to go," he said. "I'll give you my cell phone number. If Annie calls—"

And just then, as if on cue, his phone rang. They both smiled at the coincidence, and he pulled it out of his pocket.

But it wasn't Annie. It was Max, at headquarters.

"Bart. You okay?"

"Yeah, I'm fine. What's up? Is there any news?"

"Where's that girlfriend of yours?"

Bart frowned. He didn't like the sound of that.

"She's not my girlfriend. Not really." He made a face at Liz, embarrassed. "And I don't know where she is."

"Yeah. Well, whatever she is, you better find her. We've had a message from that crowd that took Lindy."

Bart looked at Liz. He didn't want her overhearing this conversation. He walked into the bedroom with the phone and closed the door behind him.

"What is it, Max? What's the message?" Now he really was fully awake.

"A kid brought it into the precinct. He said some fat guy on the street gave him a buck to deliver it. Wait a minute. I'll read it to you." There was a pause. Then Max read, "You have our leader. We have your horse. If you do not release our leader, the pretty blond lady with Sergeant Hardin will be next."

Bart sat down on the bed. He'd felt a blow right to his chest.

"You there, Bart?"

"Yeah. I'm here." He was taking a couple of deep breaths. "That's all it said?"

"That's it. We have forensics on the note now. You better get back here so we can put together some information on this girl. What's her name?"

"Annie. Annika. Annika Cornell." He felt the words strangling in his throat. "It'll take me maybe ten minutes. I'll be right there." He never heard Max's answer. He was already on his way to the door.

"That was headquarters," he said, keeping his voice as neutral as possible. "If Annie calls, tell her to call me. Right away. It's really important. Here's my number." He was jotting it onto a notepad. "And call me if you hear from her. Please!"

He'd hoped to keep the alarm out of his voice, but Liz knew something was up. As the door closed behind him, Liz thought, *Oh, Annie. What have you gotten yourself into now?*

Riding down to the lobby, Bart was convinced he was trapped in the only slow motion elevator in New York. People got on. People got off. It was forever before he reached the street level. And across town, as he sped his motorcycle in and out of the evening's rush hour traffic, he was thinking, *Oh, God! Don't let them get to her. Don't let them hurt her.*

And also, *Annie, you damned fool!*

But Annie was no fool. She knew just what she was doing. She was looking for a horse and she was thinking like a horse person. The place to start would be at Troop B headquarters down by the river, where Lindy left the building, so that's where she was. Not easy, she thought, to track a horse in this terrain. All pavement and concrete, no trees to show a broken twig, no brush for a thread of fabric or a strand of horsehair to catch on, and so much traffic—pedestrian *and* vehicular—any trail would be obliterated by now. But still, she'd had a look at those protesters the other day, and they looked pretty dimwitted to her. She suspected their plan must be fairly simple. Maybe, if she could think simple-minded, she could pick up something.

The news report had said the rider went out of the stables and *up* Twelfth Avenue. So she looked *up* the avenue.

Two-way traffic, several lanes each way and a broad median divider between. Heavy traffic during the day, but probably almost empty in the wee hours. But Lindy wasn't taken in the wee hours. Bart got the call in the hotel room. It was after dinner at Charlie Wu's. Must have been around ten o'clock. Why then?

She started to walk along the route the rider must have taken.

There must be surveillance cameras all along here, and of course the police will have studied the tapes carefully. Be nice if I could see them, too, but there's no chance of that. Traffic would have been lighter at that time, but still, the rider would have wanted to get out of sight. I think these people know something about stealth in moving a horse. He'd have wanted to get some cover.

Across the avenue, a convention center stretched for several long blocks. Its blank rear wall ran along the opposite side of the avenue and cast a long shadow over the street. Annie crossed over at the intersection—just as Lindy's kidnapper must have done—and continued walking under the cover of that shadow. A rider—or someone leading a horse—would not be easily observed. But he'd also want to get off this broad thoroughfare as quickly as possible. He'd want to turn into the first available side street off the avenue, and when Annie reached it, she knew in her bones the ransomer would have turned up this street, the first one that would have taken him away from any observer. She saw immediately that her intuition had led her in the right direction. This was neither a residential nor a shopping area, nothing to keep things active after business hours. Not surprisingly, in this out-of-the-way part of the city, at the waterfront, there were only warehouses and parking lots, a large storage rental building, a couple of empty construction sites—a busy scene during the day with workmen coming and going, operating track hoes and graders, raising great cranes high into the sky, food carts on the streets and office trailers on the job site. But after five, after business hours, all would be shuttered for the night. These streets would be deserted.

She picked her way along the edge of one of the building sites. Scaffolding extended over her head, out beyond the sidewalk, and under her feet, concrete slabs had been torn up, exposing raw, clayey earth beneath. The rain last night had turned it muddy. And there, as though to confirm her intuition (her *horse sense*?) under the shadow of protective scaffolding above, on a path not conducive to ordinary pedestrian use, she spotted unmistakable imprints of a horse's hooves. She smiled to herself. She recognized the print of the high-traction shoes made especially for the NYPD horses. But that trail of hoofprints was not made by a police horse on his daily patrol. No legitimate rider would have taken his horse across this stretch of torn-up, unstable, irregular sidewalk. Only someone keeping to the shadows would have brought a horse through here. And by the spacing between the imprints, she knew she'd been right. The horse *was* keeping to a slow walk. Staying unobtrusive.

Some thirty feet farther along, scaffolding jutted out across the street, low enough that if the kidnapper had been riding, he'd have been forced to climb down from Lindy's back and walk. Like all of the scaffolding Annie had seen in the city, this looked as if it had been rather hastily assembled. There were bolts and crossbeams and protuberances aplenty, and there, sure enough, Annie found the telltale bit of light brown horsehair looped around an exposed bolt. A couple of strands of Lindy's tail.

"Thank you, Lindy," she said to herself. "Were you deliberately leaving a trail? Could you be that smart?" She laughed to herself at the idea.

She'd known horses that seemed pretty smart. Horses that knew how to get you off their backs if they didn't want to be ridden. Horses that seemed sensitive to all sorts of human stuff, like music, and perfumes, even people's moods. Horses that understood what you wanted as soon as you showed them. Some horses could learn any trick you tried to teach them. Look at how easily Lindy had learned the Cowboy Joe song. And there were the dumb ones, too. Horses that never seemed to figure out what they were supposed to be doing. Horses so dumb they could make you crazy, wasting your time while you tried to teach them stuff.

But Lindy was definitely one of the smart ones. She figured he couldn't be a police horse if he wasn't. So maybe he really was helping her to find him.

With her cell phone camera, she began to record the evidence of a horse's passing along this street, a horse that most likely was Lindy.

The shadows were beginning to lengthen as the sun moved closer to New Jersey across the river, and she didn't want to lose the available light. Those hoofprints in the damp earth and the bits of hair in the scaffolding might well be obliterated by morning, and it would be useful to have photos of them.

When she was done taking pictures, she decided to take a break, think things through, try to come up with a creative idea. At a street cart at the corner, she bought a coffee and a donut, and studied the terrain again, trying to imagine herself into the kidnappers' heads. Nothing helpful presented itself. She was at a broad intersection, where the side street met a wide avenue. Little storefronts, seedy looking tenement buildings, a couple of corner diners, a small grocery store with banks of fruit and flowers along its front—this was a neighborhood far from the glamor she'd been treated to since her arrival, a part of the city the tourists never see. Down the street, a couple of young men, ragged looking, lounged in a doorway. A homeless man dug for empty cans in a waste bin. At the corner, an older man eyed her up and down, his gaze resting on her face. She turned away and concentrated on her coffee. She wondered if she was safe.

Bart wouldn't want her to be here. For sure. There were plenty of people around. She was probably safe, she decided. For the time being.

Maybe I ought to call Bart.

But no. Bart is sleeping soundly back at the hotel. Poor guy. He really needed it.

Still, I'd feel a little better if he were with me here.

She finished her coffee. She brushed the crumbs of her doughnut off her fingers and crossed the avenue. She considered checking in with Liz, but decided Liz would only worry about her. Instead, she spent the next half hour crisscrossing the streets of the neighborhood, up and down the avenues, and back and forth along the side streets. She wasn't turning up anything new, and the neighborhood was getting increasingly seedy. Her bravery was beginning to wear thin and she began to think she was very much alone in a city she didn't know at all.

What have I gotten myself into?

"My God, Hardin! What happened to you?" Captain Simon looked up from the file of papers spread out on his desk as Bart opened the door to the office. "I thought I sent you home to clean up. You're a mess!"

Bart rubbed his hand over his jaw. The morning's stubble was turning into a beard.

"Yeah. I guess. Sorry about that, sir."

"I'm not going to have my men walking around like that, out in public. After I fill you in on what's happening here, I want you to go upstairs and get cleaned up. Shave. And get into uniform."

"Yes, sir."

"And you're going to have to find that girl and get her in here."

"Can I see that note?"

It had been placed in a plastic sheet protector to preserve it as evidence. The captain handed it over and Bart confirmed that the handwriting matched the earlier note.

"They must have been following us. I don't like it, sir. She's out there somewhere, looking for Lindy. She thinks he's somewhere nearby." He was a lot more worried than he'd let the captain see.

"I don't know why she'd think that. We've had sightings as far away as Yonkers. We have all units alerted—all units within a forty-mile radius. And now, just what we need," his face registered his irritation, "is some amateur civilian sleuth getting in our way." He opened the file in front of him. "Of course, those sightings we've had can be pretty unreliable." He flipped through reports in the file. "We've also had reports coming in from all over the map, from Hyde Park upstate and Kingston across the river and from Setauket out on the Island and Englewood in New Jersey. Guy on a horse. Two guys on a horse. A guy and a girl on a horse." He waved a paper at Bart. "This one is two guys on a camel." He took back the note from Bart and added it to a file. "You need to be in touch with her, Bart. Get ahold of her—call her—find out where she is and we'll send someone out to bring her in. We need to put some protection on her."

"I'm calling her now," Bart said. "But I'd like to be the one to get her. I don't like her being out there somewhere, unprotected. I'd feel better if I were with her."

"Can you shower, shave, and change in fifteen minutes?"

"Yes, sir! And thank you, sir!"

"Close the door behind you."

And Bart was taking the stairs two at a time, phone in hand, trying to reach Annie.

Five o'clock had come and gone and the streets were turning quieter as offices emptied and people headed for home. With activity all around her, she was stopped in her tracks, feeling lost and trying to decide on a next move. Annie was beginning to understand how people could feel very much alone in the midst of the multitudes.

Her cell phone rang, and she felt a wash of relief when she saw it was Bart calling.

"Where are you?"

"I'm hunting for your horse."

"Oh, that's just fine." His sarcasm—and irritation—were clear, even over the phone. "I need to know where you are."

His bossiness got her back up. "Oh, you are, are you? Young Lochinvar, riding out of the west to rescue me again?"

"I don't know what you're talking about, but I need to know where you are."

"Lochinvar. It's a poem. Look it up. In the meantime, it's your horse I'm looking for. You could at least say thank you."

"Annie, don't mess with me. You may be in danger and—"

With a glance around her, she realized he could be right. There were plenty of unsavory looking types all around. "I think I'm just fine," she added stubbornly, "and I don't think I need saving."

"I want you to stay right where you are. Just tell me—"

"You could at least say please."

"Jesus *Christ,* Annie. You're impossible!"

"If you're going to yell at me, I'm not going to tell you anything."

"Annie! Stop it right now! Lindy is miles away from here by now. We've got reports of sightings as far north as Yonkers and New Rochelle. So just tell me where you are."

She knew she was being childish, so she gave in and read the address of the nearest shop. "In front of a pawn broker."

"Don't move. And don't talk to anyone. I'll be right there."

Mentally, she gave him a snappy salute.

Yes, sir!

"Did you hear me, Annie? Don't talk to *anyone!* I'm taking a squad car. I'll be right there."

"I heard you. I won't move."

Chapter Twenty-three

Simon Says

Thursday Evening

The blare of the siren reached her before the squad car turned down her street. It appeared with its light bar flashing and screeched to a stop in front of her. He was out the door and around the front of the car before she took a step. And he was looking fierce.

"Are you okay?" He made a quick scan in all directions as though checking for possible danger.

"Of course I'm okay. Why shouldn't I be?"

"You'll need to come with me right now."

He was in full uniform, boots and all. The scruffy, unwashed vagrant hobo look was gone and he was back to his tall, sandy-haired self.

"You sure cleaned up nicely," she said. She touched his newly shaved cheek—and was surprised that he drew back. His eyes shifted away from her, and she realized that people were glancing at them.

Of course. He's in uniform now. He can't be seen smooching right out in public.

But she also realized that no one stopped, no one stared. Back home, a crowd would have gathered, but here people kept on walking, as though she and Bart and the flashing lights had been quickly sized up and found not interesting enough to break their stride.

"We'll talk later. At headquarters." He led her to the car and was holding the rear door open for her.

And she looked questioningly at him.

"Can't I sit up front with you?"

"Nope. No front-seat passengers in a squad car. I'm afraid it's not real comfortable back there, but it's only a short ride."

He was right. It wasn't comfortable. Molded plastic seat, covered with a kind of gray flocking to add a little texture to the hard surface, and a screen of metal mesh dividing front from back, a reminder that this backseat was a cagelike form of confinement. No, definitely not comfortable.

"Come to New York and ride in a police car."

She added this ride in an NYPD cop car to all the unexpected twists her trip to New York had taken. One more "who'd have expected . . ." to add to her scrapbook.

And she felt odd, riding through the streets of Manhattan in the back of a squad car, to be seen, perhaps, as a criminal. She was torn between feeling like an impostor—which was kind of fun—and wanting to shout out, "I'm only riding here; I haven't done anything wrong. Honestly!" Mostly, she wanted to scrunch down in the seat until they pulled up into the headquarters parking lot.

Bart held the door for her.

"Captain Simon wants to talk to you," he said.

Being sent to the principal's office must feel like this, she thought, as Bart led her into headquarters.

The nameplate on the door read: "Captain Anthony Simon."

Bart opened the office door for her and they walked into the captain's cluttered office. The captain looked up from the papers he was studying, put down his pen, and sat back in his chair. He was not smiling.

"Please take a seat, Miss Cornell."

His voice was quiet because he had learned how to give orders and have them obeyed and he knew that quiet worked best. Captain Simon loved his work, he loved his horses, and he loved his men. In that order. But today, he was not a happy man.

"It seems you've been out there, doing a little unauthorized police work on your own." Before Annie could register any protest or explanation, the captain stopped her with a look. "Miss Cornell, we don't appreciate civilians adding to our workload." He waited a couple of beats to let that sink in. She didn't like the feeling that she was being scolded—which was exactly the feeling Captain Simon was going for. He watched while she straightened her back, got herself a little less comfortable in her chair. He knew, by the set of her chin and the little lift of her head that she was feeling defiant, but not prepared to mouth off at him. She wasn't the type. He recognized her as a solid citizen and he knew she'd understand and cooperate. Now he softened his approach a little. He let his face show his concern for her.

"Miss Cornell, I'm afraid we've received some information that we need to share with you." He pulled a file from the drawer and put it between them on the desk. "It seems there are some bad guys out there who've been trailing you and Sergeant Hardin. We're not yet sure of their motives, but we're afraid you may be in some danger."

He watched her attitude shift while she took that news in. It took her a couple of moments.

"I don't understand. Why would anyone be trailing us? Why me? Why would I be in any danger? Why would anyone be interested in me?"

This was not the kind of adventure she'd counted on. Here she was, sitting in a police precinct, being advised that she'd been caught up in some kind of serious trouble that involved the police. And now, just because she'd been trying to find Lindy, everyone seemed to be mad at her.

Captain Simon took the warning notes from the file and handed them to her one at a time.

"Here, in the order we received them, are notes that have been anonymously delivered here at headquarters. You'll see that the most recent one refers to 'the pretty blond lady with Sergeant Hardin.' The sergeant assures me that refers to you, Miss Cornell." He noted that Annie glanced up at Bart, embarrassed. "The notes appear to have been sent by the same group that you encountered on Sunday in front of the UN building. We think they saw the TV coverage and did some checking on Lindy and Bart and decided to take the horse and hold him as a hostage."

"For what? What do they want?" She glanced over at Bart, who was standing back against a cabinet, his arms folded, being professionally impassive.

"Two things. One, we're holding their leader and they want us to release him. And two, they want attention for their cause. There's nothing we can do about their fight for independence. We don't even care about that. But they hope they'll get media coverage, and maybe an opportunity to present their case to the public. As far as we're concerned, they're criminals, they've broken the law, and we'll bring them to justice." He took the notes back from Annie and put them into the folder.

He swiveled his chair around and gave a few moments to the contemplation of the view through the window. Nothing much there—just the vehicles parked outside, the chain-link fence, the street traffic beyond. Wet pavement and a misty threat of more rain to come. He swiveled back to his desk, drummed his fingertips on the desk, and gave Annie a bit of time to digest the fact that the kidnappers had targeted her, and that she was actually in danger.

"But why me?" She repeated the question. "Nothing in that TV report on Sunday's protest identified me. I was just an anonymous person caught up in the crowd."

The captain pulled some photos out of the file and placed them on the desk in front of Annie.

"After we got the last note, we made some inquiries. Sergeant Hardin told us about your contest and about the opening of the new store. He was there and, of course, so were you. These are from the security cameras at the store's front. I'd like you to look at these pictures."

Annie saw several photos of what appeared to be a gathering of spectators at the ribbon-cutting on Tuesday. They included enlargements of a detail from one of the photos, showing a cluster of three men standing at the edge of the small crowd.

"Do you remember seeing these men?"

She thought back. "I think so, yes. Maybe. I was a little overwhelmed that day. It was all so strange, the cameras, the attention—"

"Of course." He put the photos on top of the file. "But they were paying attention to you." He took more photos from the file. "And these show both you and the sergeant. I understand that you and Bart had spent some time together the evening before, when you came here to headquarters to pick up your bag." He noted Annie's embarrassment and Bart rolling his eyes. "So I understand why these photos show there were smiles and eye contact between the two of you. Perfectly natural, of course. I gather the two of you made a cordial connection the night before. None of my business, of course."

His finger pointed at the men in the photo.

"However, you'll notice that the three men in the photo seem to be conferring." He spread out the pictures, sorting them as he spoke.

"And this photo here shows them studying you, Miss Cornell. Here, in this one, the tall one—the bald guy—is writing notes on a pad that appears to be similar to the kind on which the threatening notes were written. The notepad isn't clear in this picture, but our lab guys will work on a clearer enlargement."

He put the group of photos aside and took some more from the file.

"After Lindy was taken, we went back and looked at our records from security cameras here at headquarters. And we see"—he put some more pictures in front of her—"that same man, the tall, bald one, among a group of tourists, again taking notes. Obviously planning the kidnapping."

His face registered irritation and impatience.

"I refuse to call it a horse-napping. I can just see the tabloids: 'New York Mounted police caught napping.' Or some other 'funny' headline." He knew the media, typically unhelpful, would have fun at the unit's expense.

"We're pretty sure we'll find those same men in the photos taken on Sunday. So we know who we're looking for, and we'll be able to locate other members of the group who may, if we're lucky, be willing to work with us. Taking Lindy is a serious matter to us here in this unit. But the thing is escalating to more serious danger, now that they're targeting you, Miss Cornell.

"You're going to need protection till we get these guys," he continued. "I want someone with you twenty-four hours a day—at least until you return to Wyoming. I'm pretty sure they'll lose interest in you if you're gone—and I'm hoping we'll have them in custody by then.

"The odd thing is," he said, studying the photos again, "we had several reports from drivers saying they saw a man on a horse riding out of here—odd enough on Twelfth Avenue—but what's even odder, no one got a video. Same thing for the many reports of sightings from distant locations—upstate, out on the Island, New Jersey, Connecticut—but no one thought to get a video. Or even a still shot. Must be a first in the history of cell phone cameras."

Annie sat there silently. She was trying to take it all in. It was all too preposterous. When she'd been practically stampeded at the street protest, she thought the men, with their silly "cause," were a bunch of clods. But now, they'd become a genuine danger to her, personally.

"I don't know what to say," she said. "I'm baffled. I can't imagine that I actually need protection. The whole thing is so ridiculous."

"We don't think it's ridiculous, Miss Cornell." The captain was frowning at her. "We take threats seriously and, as I said, we're going to see that you're protected for as long as you're here in the city. Ordinarily, we'd have Sergeant Hardin out there looking for Lindy—but it turns out the man is utterly useless, getting in everyone's way and driving us all crazy." Bart made a gesture to object but the captain cut him off. "No, Bart. You know it's true. You and that horse are too close and you're too wound up to be much help. No discredit to you, son. Totally understandable." He paused, and his expression was almost tender as he turned to face Bart. "Don't forget, I rode with your dad, and I know all the history."

He paused again, seemed to be thoughtful for a moment. Then he turned back to the file, made some entries, and put it away.

"So, Bart, we can spare you here for the time being. And I'm assigning you to guard Miss Cornell—eight hours on, eight hours off, starting right now. Max will be your relief. I don't think this will be an unpleasant assignment for you." His smile was almost conspiratorial. "As long as you don't forget you are on duty. And keep your eyes open."

He remained seated as he ended the interview.

"You can leave now, Miss Cornell. I hope the rest of your stay will be uneventful. And if you see any sign of these men or anything else that disturbs you, be sure Bart is made aware, and if you need to, contact us here." He handed her a card with the headquarters' number. He turned to Bart. "And your surveillance assignment begins right now, Sergeant. You're dismissed."

But Annie remained in her seat.

"Captain Simon, I've done some research and I have some information that may be—"

He cut her off instantly. "I thought I made myself very clear." He was giving her a look that strong men had trouble standing up to. "We'd like you to go back to your hotel with Sergeant Hardin. Or have dinner with him. Or go to a movie. But do not play detective. We have professionals who are trained to do that."

"But I have information—"

She got no further. Bart had her arm and with unmistakable irritation—and an embarrassed glance at the captain—pulled her up from the seat and steered her to the door.

"Annie, let's go. The captain is busy and we're finished here."

"But—"

"Come on, Annie. We're out of here. *Now!*"

"Oh, and Bart," the captain called after them. "Take the squad car. You're on duty. And I don't want you and the lady exposed on that motorcycle of yours."

Chapter Twenty-four

Interlude

Bart kept a grip on Annie's arm as he led her out to the parking lot. He didn't speak till they were outside, and when he did, he was looking straight ahead, not at her. His jaw was clenched and his voice was low.

"I can't believe you would talk back to Captain Simon like that!"

Annie pulled her arm loose.

"What do you mean? I wasn't talking back to him." She stopped walking and faced him.

Bart stopped, too, and confronted her.

"When the captain says it's time to go, you go. You don't argue with him."

"I wasn't arguing with him. I just wanted a chance to tell him—"

"There was nothing to tell him. He'd dismissed you and it was time to go."

He took her arm again and was steering her toward the squad car. She stopped by the rear door. He didn't open it. She remained facing the car, not wanting to look at him. They were both silent, unmoving. The cool mist was giving way to the first few drops of the coming rain. Neither of them noticed.

"Annie—"

"I'm feeling bullied." Her voice was quiet, almost a whisper.

He reached around her, with a hand on her shoulder, and turned her to face him.

"I don't mean to push you around. Please don't be mad."

Her head was down, avoiding his eyes.

"Annie, I don't want you to be mad at me. But don't you understand? You can't disrespect the captain."

She looked up at him. His head was bare and a few raindrops glittered on his hair. He looked so sincere and so innocent. And so committed in his loyalty to the force. How could she stay mad? Slowly, reluctantly, *very* reluctantly, she gave up any hope that her information and her opinions would be listened to.

"Okay. Let's forget about it."

His whole body relaxed. His smile spread slowly.

"Okay," he said. "Okay! That's good!" He opened the door for her. "So, what do you want to do? We've got a car, the whole city and no program."

"I'm not sure—"

"You can't get rid of me, you know. I have my orders."

She laughed. "I know. Should I feel sorry for you?"

He stopped smiling and was looking most seriously into her eyes. He said nothing for a long moment. Then, thoughtfully, he spoke.

"Annie. We could go to my place."

There was a question behind the suggestion and he waited for her answer.

Her answer came very slowly.

"I don't know. I'm just not . . ."

Was it only Sunday that they'd met? So much had happened. Still, she knew how she felt. She felt safe with him. He was marvelously attractive—and she felt very attractive herself with him. Not every man made her feel like that. And the pages of her imaginary scrapbook had already turned into a collection of surprises. Maybe this one ought to be added. But still—

"We have only a few days, Annie. You'll be leaving soon."

"I'll tell you what," she said. "Let's go back to my hotel. I'll check in with Liz. I have completely neglected her this week. We can have dinner there—maybe have room service bring it up—and then, I don't know—we'll see—"

"I'm not a hatchet murderer, you know. You'll be safe with me."

She laughed. "That's one thing I feel absolutely sure of." She got into the car's backseat. "But first, there's something not far from here that I want to show you."

Bart closed her door got and behind the wheel. "Okay, ma'am. What do you want to show me?"

"Just drive up Twelfth Avenue. Drive slowly. Then turn onto 40th Street. Don't go far."

"You're the boss," he said, and he drove out of the lot.

"But first, stop right here, at the gate."

He stopped.

"Look up the street," she said, pointing uptown. "It was reported that the rider took Lindy *up* the avenue. But there's a median strip with a railing along here with uptown traffic going north on the other side of the median. Your man would have been totally exposed to view riding up this side of the road. And you can see there's no way to get over to the other side when you're just coming out of the building. So he must have ridden up on this side, against the traffic only because he *had* to—because there was some specific place he had to get to. But he'd be looking for an opening to get to the other side. Because," she pointed to the rear of the building opposite, "the back of the convention center runs for a couple of blocks and the shadow from that long wall would give him the cover he needs. So, you see the opening across the median about a block up from here? My guess is that's where he crossed. And then he would have walked Lindy very slowly, staying close to the wall, blending into the nighttime shadow to avoid being seen by the passing cars. Now," she pointed in the opposite direction, "if you go down to the next corner and make a U-turn, we can follow the path he took. But drive slowly."

Bart looked thoughtful. He didn't argue. He followed her directions.

"You can see," she said, as they moved slowly up Twelfth Avenue, "he could have been almost invisible along here. But still, he'd want to get off the avenue as soon as possible. And the first turn would be up there at 40th Street. So turn right when you get there, and drive slowly. I have something to show you."

"You're the boss," he said, and drove to 40th and made the turn. "Where do you want me to stop?"

"Pull up here. We have to get out. And bring your flashlight."

They picked their way through the construction debris until they came to the muddy patch that had stopped Annie earlier.

"There," she said. He flashed his light where she pointed. "I was afraid this mist might have washed it out, but it's still dry enough so you can see it."

And he saw the hoofprint.

"That's Lindy's print!"

"Yes. And what other horse would be coming through here? A carriage horse? They're all over at the park. And you'd see evidence of wheels—which couldn't get through all this mess of concrete and stuff, anyway. And your police horses wouldn't be ridden through this muck—your men wouldn't ride a horse through this, you'd take him out on the street where the surface is smoother. No, he wants cover." She pointed at the scaffolding above. "So he's avoiding the street."

"We should get a picture," Bart said.

"I got pictures. On my cell phone. And there's more." She led him farther along. "Here are the next hoofprints. You can see Lindy's pace. Moving slowly in the dark. No wonder no one spotted him, in all this construction mess and on a deserted street at night." Bart was paying attention to her now. "But wait. There's more." She led him onward. "Lindy left a trail. Look here."

He shined the flashlight's beam where she pointed. He reached out and touched the strands of horsehair caught in the scaffolding. "That horse is a wonder," he said. "Lindy knew we'd be looking for him. He managed to catch a bit of his tail here, in that exposed metal."

"That's just what I thought." She smiled at him. "And I took pictures of this, too. And that's what I wanted to tell Captain Simon. The people who took Lindy are horse people like I told you. They know how to hide a horse. And I couldn't find any trail beyond here. I'm positive they loaded him into something and have him parked somewhere not so far away. What I'm thinking is, they're foreigners. They probably don't know their way around this city. They wouldn't venture upstate or out to Long Island or Connecticut. I think they're holed up somewhere around here, and they're keeping Lindy nearby. Not in a horse trailer—that would be too obvious. And anyway, where would they get one? I can't imagine there's much call for livestock equipment in this city. I'd bet one of their group has some sort of ordinary-looking, unobtrusive, commercial box truck sort of thing that would hold a horse. I'm sure they plan to keep him fed and watered until they can negotiate a release of their leader. And I thought the police ought to know."

Bart had taken a single strand of Lindy's hair and was looking at it thoughtfully.

"I don't know, Annie. We have some pretty smart people working on this—"

"I know. And if no one wants to hear me, I'll let it go. Anyway, I'm supposed to be enjoying the prize I've won, the whole thing at *Lady Fair* and Galliard, and the clothes and the fuss and the attention—not doing police work for the NYPD. So let's forget the whole thing and let's go back to the hotel and have dinner."

"Now you're mad."

"No. Yes. A little. Mostly I'm just frustrated. But I'll get over it."

He gave her a big smile.

"Maybe I can help you get over it."

"Okay, then, driver. Take me home."

They walked into a darkened suite.

"Liz?"

No answer.

"You said she was here when you left."

"She was."

Annie turned on the light.

"She left a note." She took it off the coffee table and read it aloud.

Don't worry about me. I'm having a great time by myself. First time ever without a mess of family and house and the ranch hanging on to me. Don't even miss the kids - much. Getting used to crowds - everyone leaves you alone. I might go to a movie.

There was a long silence. They didn't move. Just looked at each other.

"She might go to a movie," Bart said.

He took off his duty belt and laid it on the coffee table.

"She might not."

They continued to stare at each other.

"Let's order dinner," she said.

"Are you sure?" He took a step toward her.

She turned away.

"Yes, Bart. I'm sure. For now." She picked up the phone. There was a menu on the desk and she handed it to him. "Hamburger and fries okay?"

He glanced at the menu, not caring.

"Sure, that's fine."

She placed the order.

"Would you like a drink?" She pointed to the mini bar.

"I'm on duty." His eyes never left her.

The silence was awkward.

"I'll turn on some music." She took a step toward the player. Only one step.

"No," he said. He had his hand on her arm and turned her to face him.

"Annie, you're going to be leaving in a couple of days." His hands went to her face, cupping it gently, his fingertips buried in her hair, holding her as tenderly as one would hold a baby bird, as though he feared she might slip away. He was looking intently into her eyes. "I know I can't ask you to stay, but maybe we can find some way to—I don't know—maybe stay in touch, have something in the future for us."

The depth of his feeling, the surprise of his suggestion startled her, left her confused.

"I feel as though I should say, 'This is so sudden.'"

"No, not sudden. Not since last Sunday, when Lindy and I pulled you out of that mob. I didn't know it then—but I know it now. Not sudden. It's been four whole days. That's not sudden."

They both laughed.

Then he was serious again.

"Annie, I want us to be more than a chance encounter. A vacation fling for you, a quickie romance for me. I want it to be more than that."

"Bart." And she was serious, too. "We hardly know each other."

"How can you say that?" A wisp of mischievousness slipped into his eyes. The beginnings of a smile softened his lips. "How can you say that? Didn't I show you where I grew up? And the school I went to? For God's sake, I took you to meet my mother! What else do you need to know?"

"Now you're being ridiculous."

"It wouldn't be the first time." His smile broadened and his eyes were actually twinkling. "Listen," he said. "Come over here." He took her hand and drew her to the sofa. "Let's sit down and talk about us. You tell me all about you, and I'll tell you about me. I'll answer any questions and we can get to know each other." Over her head, he glanced toward her bedroom. "As for anything beyond that," he said, almost to himself, "well, I'm a big boy. I can wait." He sat into the corner of the sofa and pulled her down close to him, with his arm around her and her head fitting neatly against his chest. "There," he said. "That's perfect. Comfortable?"

"Mmmhmmm."

"Good." He squeezed her a little, companionably. "Now tell me about little Annika."

She snuggled against him.

"Wouldn't know where to begin." She thought for a moment. "You know about ranch life—plenty of work, plenty of fresh air, plenty of chances for a kid to play and explore and learn things. Learn about life and death. Learn how to make things, learn how things work. You live around animals, you learn early how babies are made. You learn to ride, and to drive—I was driving the pickup around the ranch by the time I was twelve. Not out on the road, of course, but sometimes someone needs to get something to someone and they send you. And there's no 911 around the corner when you're up on the summer range, and you carry a rifle in your scabbard to protect the herd from cougar and wolves, and maybe a sidearm on your hip because there can be other kinds of predators around. And that's about it."

"And what about your parents? I get the feeling Liz is more than a big sister—more like a watchdog."

A moment or two passed before she answered.

"There's seven years between us. She was thirteen when our mom died and I think it helped her handle the loss to become a sort of substitute mom for me."

"I thought maybe your mom was gone, because you never said anything about her. Even when you met my mom. Is it okay to talk about it? About how she died?"

"Oh, yeah. I'm okay talking about it. I was awfully young, just six years old. I'd just started first grade."

"How did it happen?"

"Very sudden. She was doing the wash, just carrying a basket of laundry out to the yard to hang it out to dry in the sun. My aunt Velma was with her and she said they were just talking and hanging the clothes and Mom just suddenly clutched real tight to a blouse she was holding, looked up the road like she heard someone calling her, and collapsed on the ground. Just sudden like that." She was quiet for a moment. Then she smiled. "My memories of her are all good ones. She had the prettiest yellow hair—so pale it was almost white, and she wore it in a braid down her back."

"Hair like yours?"

"Oh, much prettier. I loved watching her comb it out first thing every morning. It always made me think of fairy wings. And then she'd braid it up again, with a twist of a rubber band at the bottom and then she was ready for another busy day." Annie smiled at the memory. "She was always on the go, not rushing or anything, just never stopping, always busy. But at night, when it was time for me to go to bed, she'd come in and sit with me, and we'd talk about the day I'd had, and what I was going to be doing the next day. And I'd pick out a book and she'd read to me till I fell asleep. I guess that was nice for her, too, to have a quiet time of the day. And a chance for her to read a little bit. She loved to read and she taught me to read long before I started school. Actually, I was in the school library the day she died. I remember I was at one of those little schoolroom tables, reading an Uncle Wiggly story, and Miss Prime, the librarian, came over to me and she said, 'Annika, honey'—everyone at school called me Annika—'I need you to come with me, dear. Miss Barth wants to see us.' I remember that so clearly, like my life took a big turn in the road in that minute. I even remember what she was wearing—a long-sleeved white blouse with a green striped vest over it and a skirt with white and green flowers. And she said, 'You can bring the book if you like.' I guess that's how I knew I wasn't in trouble. Because she let me take the book. And she took my hand and she walked with me down the hall to Miss Barth's office. Jacqueline Barth was our principal. And in the principal's office, Liz was already there, with Aunt Velma, and I could see they'd both been crying, and I think I knew right away. And Miss Barth left me alone with them and they told me, and then they took me home. And after that, Aunt Velma became our 'mom' and Liz appointed herself my 'also-Mom' and that's how I grew up. End of story." She snuggled up against Bart's chest. "Well, not really, of course. But enough for now."

"And what about your dad?"

"My dad was killed in a plane crash. He and some friends were flying up to Montana to do some fishing and there was engine trouble. Up by Kalispell. That's all I know. I was very young, just barely three. I remember him carrying me. I remember snuggling into his chest. His shirt was soft against my face and he smelled of soap and leather." She ran her fingertips around the snaps on his uniform shirt. "And I remember his hands. They seemed so big to me when I put mine up against his. They were hard hands because ranch work is hard, but also soft, at the same time. Somehow."

She took Bart's hand in hers and matched her smaller one up against his much bigger one.

"Like yours," she said. And she turned his hand over and examined it. "You have nice hands."

His fingers closed around hers and she could feel an urgency in the gesture. And she looked up and saw that his eyes were closed.

"Annika. That's such a pretty name," he said. He brought her hand to his lips and kissed her fingertips. "Annika. Sweet Annika." He was breathing deeply. "You do know how I'm feeling, don't you?"

"I do know, Bart. But we're not really alone here."

He opened his eyes and smiled at her.

"I know. Liz might walk in any time."

"Right. So now it's your turn. Tell me about your dad."

Bart kind of puffed his chest, almost as though he were saluting, and he said, "My dad was my hero. He was an honest cop, brave, and he died doing his job. You'd have liked him, Annie. And he'd have liked you, too."

"I read in the paper that he died in a gunfight. Five years ago, in a street demonstration like the one last Sunday."

"Yes, it was in Times Square—maybe you read about it, even way off in Laramie. And the part about a demonstration, that part is true—a local political outfit was protesting a new civil ordinance. But what happened was, a couple of guys decided to use the demonstration as cover for a robbery and while everyone's attention was on the protest, they broke into a jewelry store down the street. My dad and Captain Simon—he hadn't made captain yet—were patrolling together, on crowd control. I was just out of the academy, and I was on duty there in Times Square, so I saw what happened. It was all over in just a couple of minutes. Lindy gave Dad the danger signal and they were on the scene immediately. My dad had his gun out, the robbers came out of the store, running and shooting, the owner had a gun and he was running after them, yelling and shooting, and people were dropping for cover all over the place. I was running toward them and I saw one of the men targeting my dad. Lindy wheeled around to protect my dad and a bullet caught his right flank, and right at the same time, my dad took a hit. I saw him slump forward and then slide off the saddle. As I ran toward him, I saw his gun fall out of his hand. By the time I got to him, he was on the ground. I called for a bus—an ambulance—and for backup. Then I saw one of the robbers head down a side street with everyone after him, but the one who shot my dad, Lindy had him up against the wall of one of the theaters there. That man wasn't going anywhere with Lindy jamming him up, so I stayed with my dad till help came—but he was gone by then."

He was still holding Annie's hand, and he held it to his face, using the palm of her hand to rest his cheek on, as though he found comfort in it. He was speaking so softly now.

"Lindy tried to save my dad that day. So did I. But neither one of us could do it. I made my report, and later on I told my mom what I just told you. And that was the last time I talked about it—till now. They fixed Lindy up and then assigned him to me. And that's what happened." His hand was still holding hers against his face, and he turned it and kissed the palm and then moved her hand to his shoulder so she could reach around him, to hold him close, and he buried his head against her neck. His voice was muffled when he said, "And I'm glad you know about it."

Annie knew that strong men do cry—but not if they can help it. And mostly, they do help it. She also understood that Bart had long ago buried the tears that went with this story. So she said nothing, and together they were close to each other and knew each other a little bit better.

A knock on the door startled both of them.

"Room service," she said. "I forgot all about the hamburgers."

He looked at her blankly, as though coming out of a dream. Then he stood up quickly.

Back to the present. His head was clear now. And he remembered he was on duty. And why.

His Glock was in its holster snapped to his duty belt. He removed the gun, and said to Annie, "Wait in the other room."

"Oh, Bart. Don't be silly. It's just our hamburgers."

He gave her a look—and she went quickly into the bedroom.

"Room service," a voice said from the hallway.

Bart checked to be sure Annie was out of sight. But as soon as he turned away, she was peeking around the corner, and saw him open the door, wait while the waiter wheeled the cart to the table, and hand him a tip, all while keeping the gun concealed. When he closed the door and made sure it was locked, he said, "You can come out now."

"I'd forgotten all about the food."

"Just once," he said as she began to turn on a couple of table lamps, "I'd like to be alone with you with no interruptions."

"You might have to travel to Laramie. It's real quiet out there, and there's space enough to get away from everyone."

"Do we need so much light?"

She smiled at him.

"Absolutely."

She lifted the metal cover off one of the plates. The hamburgers looked gorgeous. There was a platter with an assortment of hamburger toppings. She sat down, ready to be the hostess.

"Raw onions?" she asked.

"Only if you have 'em, too."

"Always, if no one minds."

"I like my hamburgers traditional," he said. "Medium rare. Raw onions. Ketchup. Plenty of black pepper. Nothing else."

She looked at him with surprise and approval.

"Me, too. I thought I was the only one. No special dressing. No mayo. No pickles. No bacon or mushrooms or anything else. Sometimes maybe with cheese."

"Exactly!" he said.

They both broke out laughing. They both were suddenly, together, very hungry.

They were slogging their fries through the ketchup when they heard the entry card in the slot and Liz came in. They looked at each other. Annie giggled. Bart smiled guiltily.

"Hey, you two," Liz said. "Have you been here long?"

"Should we have ordered dinner for you? Your note said you might go to a movie."

"No movie. And I've had dinner. Never knew a chicken sandwich could cost eighteen dollars. How do people manage to live here?" Her hair was wet and so were her shoes. "And I got caught in the rain." She stepped out of her shoes. "Anyway, I can't believe what just happened." She ate a French fry off Annie's plate. "I decided to just walk around. It wasn't really raining yet, and I thought I'd just explore a little. Did you know—the stores here are open all hours? Some of them all night."

She pulled a small chair up to the table and joined them.

"And, big surprise—a Home Depot right here in Manhattan? I'm just walking along and I see this Home Depot sign but it's just a little storefront, which made me curious because you know how enormous those places usually are. So I went in, and there's nothing there but a couple of escalators going *down*! I got on and actually went way down a couple of flights under the street. And there, deep underground, a full Home Depot, big as anything I've seen in Cheyenne. All under the street. I can't get over how these people live—way up in the sky, and way down inside the earth. And that must be how they get millions of people onto this little island. Stack 'em up. Pack 'em down. Fantastic.

"Anyway. I decided not to go to a movie and was coming back to the hotel. So I was just walking along, looking in store windows, just down the street here, about a block away from the hotel. And I saw this truck, a sort of white box van, like a U-Haul but with no markings, kind of moving along slowly in the same direction as I was going."

She was busy eating Annie's fries and didn't notice how Annie and Bart were suddenly all ears, all eyes, all attention.

"And as I got near the corner, these two guys got out—a scruffy looking pair—and came right up to me. I'll tell you, I was wishing I had my Colt in my bag. And very quietly, one of them steps right up in my face and says, 'Lady, you must to come with us.' Well I wasn't going anywhere with those two, but before I could say anything, the short guy grabs the other one's arm and says, 'Wait! Hugo! Wrong lady!' And the skinny one stops, looks me all over, top to bottom, but especially my hair, and he thinks for a second. Then he steps back and says, 'Oh. Excuse please. You are wrong lady. Right hair, wrong lady.' And he gives the other one a push and says, 'Let's go quickly, Leon,' and they're back in the truck before I can do a thing."

"You said there were two men?" Bart was getting his notebook out of his back pocket.

Liz was surprised by the sudden interest.

"Three, actually. One was driving the truck—a bald guy—and like I said, the two that approached me, one was short and fat and the other taller and skinny. They all had these big fat mustaches."

She looked from Bart to Annie and back again to Bart, who was writing in his notepad.

"Why? What's up?"

Bart said, "Annie, where are those photos the captain gave you?"

"In my bag. I'll get them."

When Bart had them, he pushed the food tray to one side and spread the pictures out on the table.

"Do you recognize these men?"

"Omigod! That's them! I couldn't forget those faces. Even the guy driving. That's them." She looked up wide-eyed. "What's this about?"

"They're the ones who took Lindy," Annie said. "I'm sure of it. They probably had him in that truck. Just driving around town with a stolen horse. Was the truck big enough for a big quarter horse?"

Liz thought for a moment. "Yeah. I'd say you could get a horse in there. Not a lot of room, but enough."

Annie turned to Bart. "I *told* you they have him here. Not upstate somewhere or forty miles away. He's right here in Manhattan. I knew it!" She was getting into her sandals. "Let's go. Let's find him."

"Annie, I don't think—"

"If you don't want to go, I'll do it alone. I'll find him for you."

"Don't be stupid. Of course I won't let you go alone. Those guys could be dangerous. What am I saying? They *are* dangerous. Honestly, Annie, you need a keeper!" He was putting his notebook away. "I never saw such a stubborn woman."

She paid no attention to his complaining. She took her driver's license, a credit card and a few twenties from her wallet, and put them in her pocket. She set her phone on vibrate and put that in another pocket.

"Liz, can I take your Colt?"

"No, you don't!" Bart had her arm and was pulling back from the door. "You think I'd let you run around Manhattan packing? We've got laws here. If there's any shooting, I'll be the one doing it."

Liz chimed in. "Don't be silly. Annie's just messing with you. She knows I didn't really bring my revolver. Not to New York. She knows better."

"Of course I was joking. For goodness' sake. You guys are so touchy. And I wasn't really going to go alone. I can't go anywhere alone now. Bart is assigned to guard me."

"Guard you?" Liz stopped nibbling on the French fry. "What are you talking about?"

"It's a long story," Bart said. He was strapping on his duty belt and his helmet, preparing to leave. "Before Annie goes charging off to save the world, you two are going to have to come back to headquarters with me. Liz, we'll need a full report from you about the men who approached you. So don't get too comfortable. We'll take the squad car and bring you back. It won't take long. And then our intrepid sleuth here can go larking about all she wants. But if she does, I'll be going with her."

Chapter Twenty-five

Interrogation

Thursday Night - Late

It was a fifteen-minute ride back to headquarters, with Annie sulking in the backseat and Liz taking cell phone photos like mad.

"Wait till I tell the boys about this." Liz was beaming. "They'll be telling everyone, 'My mom got to ride in an NYPD squad car.' With photos for show and tell. I'll score a million points."

"You're such a tourist," Annie muttered under her breath.

Liz poked her with her elbow. "Well, aren't *you* Miss Sophisticated!"

When they entered Captain Simon's office, they found him as they had left him, at his desk and still poring over paperwork.

"You're back," he said. "What's up?"

"You know Annie Cornell, sir. And this is her sister, Liz Cameron. Ms. Cameron is accompanying her sister on her visit to New York. She is also visiting from Wyoming. She has some information that may be useful. About the Buljornia protesters."

The captain peered at Liz.

To Bart, he said, "This is going to help us find Lindy?"

Bart stood up even straighter and avoided Annie's eyes.

"Perhaps, sir. But it's more about the threat to Ms. Cornell."

The captain frowned. He looked skeptical. What could the sister possibly have to contribute?

"Take a seat, Ms. Cameron. I'll be interested in hearing your contribution." To Bart he said, "Sergeant, bring over a chair for Miss Cornell."

When Annie and Liz were settled and Bart took up his position, standing near the door, the captain invited Liz to begin.

"Well," she said, a little nervous at first but soon settling into her account, "Annie had been out—we're staying in a hotel—Annie won this contest—"

"Yes, I know about that."

Liz took a breath and settled down.

"Well, I was alone in the hotel room and I decided to take a walk. Just see a bit of the city, you know. I was sort of nervous the first few days—we don't have such crowds of people back home, except maybe at a football game—but I was kind of getting used to it and thought I'd give it a shot. So I walked around, looked in some stores, had dinner. And I was going back to the hotel, just about a block away, and I noticed this ratty old white box truck that was riding along, but it was sort of keeping pace with me. Which seemed sort of funny. But before I could think about it much, the truck stopped and these two guys came out and they came right up to me, a short, fat guy and a taller one, skinny, and the skinny one was right in my face and he says, 'Lady, you must to come with us.' I noticed his funny way of talking. Foreign, you know? And like I told these two"— she gestured at Annie and Bart—"I had no intention of going anywhere with them and I was thinking of all those things I'd heard about how dangerous it is here and I wished I had brought my Colt revolver even if concealed carry isn't legal here, but before I could do anything, the fat guy tells the other one to stop, they got the wrong lady. And the tall one looks me over like I'm a statue or something, and says, 'Right hair, wrong lady.' And they run right back to the truck and they take off. Fast. And when I got back to the hotel, Annie and Bart were there and I told them what had just happened and they got all excited and showed me some pictures and it was the same guys—there was a third one in the pictures and I'd seen him in the truck, behind the wheel. And I said, 'Yes, those are the same men,' and they said I had to come here and tell you. And that's the whole thing. And I have no idea what this is all about."

She sat back in her seat, ready to be illuminated.

"And that's everything?" Captain Simon was still frowning, but also now more interested.

"Well, yes. Except that nothing about this trip to New York has turned out the way we expected. I feel like I'm in a multiplex movie, trying to watch two shows at once. We came for the whole contest thing and *Lady Fair* and Annie's shopping spree—and there's this whole other thing happening, with Annie meeting Bart, and his horse being stolen, and kidnappers, and here I am sitting in a police station reporting—I don't know what—reporting that two goofy men with big mustaches stopped me on the street and then ran away. I'll be glad to get back to Laramie where life moves a little more slowly and it's easier to keep up."

While she talked, Captain Simon was studying her carefully.

"Yes," he said, finally. "I can see it. Same general build, same long, very light blond hair. It was dark. And raining. They could have mistaken you for your sister."

Liz looked at Annie, sitting next to her, and then to Bart, standing behind them, and then back to Annie.

"I don't understand."

"Ms. Cameron, I think your sister hasn't explained everything to you."

She laughed. "It wouldn't be the first time."

"You know about the theft of one of our horses?"

"Yes. I saw it in the paper this morning. And Annie went rushing off, saying she had to find him—the horse, that is. I knew she'd gotten to know the horse's rider—Bart, here, I guess—and I know how she is about the livestock back home. She's very protective of all the animals. But I didn't think she'd come to New York and get involved with finding a lost police horse."

"Not lost, Ms. Cameron. Stolen. And we take our animals seriously, too. These horses are very valuable, highly trained, and a very important part of our effort to protect the public."

"Well, yes. Of course." Liz felt a little scolded. "Anyway, I think she said she was going to the library. I just figured she'd be busy researching something or other. She likes to do that. It could be all day, so I just went on with my own plans."

Captain Simon nodded. He'd heard enough for now. He pulled out the file and placed it in front of him.

"Now, Ms. Cameron," he said, "I need to share some information with you. First of all, we believe the horse was taken to be held as a hostage by the same people your sister got caught up with in that demonstration on Sunday, at the UN."

Liz glanced briefly at Annie. *I told you to stay out of trouble, didn't I?*

"Yes, I saw that on the TV. Was that Bart—Sergeant Hardin—I saw in the news report?"

"Yes, it was. And we think these people also saw that report, realized Lindy's publicity value, and got the idea to steal him. We think they've been following Sergeant Hardin since Sunday. And I'm afraid they've seen him with your sister. Not her fault, of course. She couldn't have known." He opened the file and took out the latest note. "We've had several notes delivered here, threatening Sergeant Hardin and Lindy. But I think you should see this one that arrived just this afternoon." He handed it across the desk.

She read it.

> *You have our leader*
> *We have your horse*
> *If you do not release our leader*
> *the pretty blond lady with*
> *Sergeant Hardin will be next.*

Several heartbeats passed while she took it in. Her face paled. Then she looked at her sister.

"Oh, Annie! What have you gotten yourself into?"

"It's not her fault," the captain said. "She had no idea, of course. But she is in some danger. Apparently these men have figured out where she's staying and were waiting for her to arrive. You do have a strong family resemblance—same general build, same long blond hair. They didn't see their mistake until they got close. And as soon as they did, they ran off."

Annie burst in here—she couldn't help herself. "And I'm sure they had Lindy in that truck. Liz, you said it was a ratty old white truck, dirty with patches of rust—a lot like Walt Jeppsen's old box truck back home that he uses for hauling feed and tack and stuff like that. A horse could be hauled in a truck like that. I'm sure those men are holed up somewhere in the area, and all we have to do is find that truck."

Captain Simon looked at Annie and it was not a friendly look. His lips compressed and his impatience was apparent.

"Miss Cornell. I've tried to make it clear that while we welcome citizen eyes, ears, and support, and we value useful information, we have the very best technical and forensic resources in the country, and we are hindered in our work if amateurs get in our way."

"But you'll admit those men are at least good candidates for the kidnappers?"

"Yes, I think they are. And we'll be looking for them. But I do not believe they had a horse in that truck. I do not believe anyone is riding around Midtown Manhattan with a valuable horse inside a ratty old vehicle like Walt Jetson's box truck back home."

"Jeppsen," Annie muttered under her breath.

"Now I'm going to show Ms. Cameron some pictures for her to identify, and Bart—Sergeant Hardin—will write up a full report. And then he's going to take Ms. Cameron back to the hotel, and in the meantime, you, Miss Cornell, are going to wait here at headquarters and stay out of everyone's way. If you'd like to go into the stables, and visit the horses, I'm sure you won't get into any trouble there. And then the sergeant can come back and resume his guard duty. The two of you can go off and amuse yourselves however you like, but please—do you hear me, Miss Cornell—*please* stay out of everyone's way."

Annie was very much offended. Captain Simon did not care the least little bit.

"You may go now, Miss Cornell."

She stood up. She said to Bart, "I'll wait for you in the stables. Take good care of my sister. She's the only one I have." She turned to the captain. "But I *know* that horse is in that truck!"

Captain Simon leaned back in his chair. He smiled at her.

"Miss Cornell, if you find Lindy in a ratty old truck on a street here in this city, it'll be a miracle. And I do not believe in miracles. I'd be willing to bet that you will find nothing. And then, if you're wise, you will go back to your fashion magazine and your contest and your pretty clothes. And when you're finished with that, you will go back to Wyoming, where you belong, and you will not bother us here anymore."

"And what do I get if I'm right?" Bart rolled his eyes and pulled at her arm. *Stop it, Annie. Don't talk to the captain like that.* She shook him off. "You're betting I'll fail. What do I get if I succeed?"

Captain Simon's irritation was visible. This girl was close to being in trouble with him. Insubordinate is what she was. "Miss Cornell, if you pull that off, I'll have the Police Pipe Band perform for you. Kilts and all."

Annie smiled sweetly at him. "Great. I look forward to hearing them."

And she walked out and went into the stables

What is it about horses? Why is it that people find comfort around them? Annie's mood mellowed as soon as she was walking among the stalls. The horses came to greet her, to examine her, to see if she had something for them. She didn't, of course, but she could stroke a face and pat a mane as she said hello. And she could talk quietly to them.

"They're all mad at me," she told them. "Your captain thinks I'm a fool and a nuisance. Bart thinks I'm a silly, innocent, cute little librarian from a small western town, so dumb I need a keeper. And Liz is mad at me for getting into trouble. They all think I've taken on more than I can handle."

Annie's pride was pricked. But she was a tenacious sort and she knew what she meant to do. She continued discussing her plans with the horses. "Lindy was taken from his stall during the night. Probably he had no halter. I'm going to need a halter. You guys keep any rope around here?"

They waited while she hunted around the stables until she found a coil of rope that had been dropped on top of one of the feed bins. Probably left there by a hostler. She checked it out. Length was okay and flexible enough for her needs.

She got comfortable on the floor. This would take about twenty minutes.

"Thank you, Jimmy Ray," she whispered.

Way back when she was little, maybe nine or ten, one of the ranch hands, Jimmy Ray Tyson, had set about teaching little Annie how to tie a rope halter. Jimmy Ray said anyone who worked around horses should know how to manage with just a good length of rope, and he spent hours teaching her how to make a halter out of a twenty-five-foot piece of double-braid polyester. She'd been fascinated by the intricacies of the task, learning to tie the knots, the ins and outs and overs and unders, the complexity of making the fiador and getting the nose piece and the cheek pieces lined up just right. How many hours she'd practiced that skill, sitting in the porch swing, and at night in her bedroom, until she had it down perfectly and could whip up a rope halter blindfolded, in fifteen, maybe twenty minutes. Grandpa Cornell had been so pleased, he added another hundred dollars to her college fund and told her she was a good little rancher and he was proud of her. He'd also slipped Jimmy Ray a little something extra.

"That's all I need," she said, standing up and brushing off the seat of her pants. She draped the halter around her neck to leave her hands free. She stepped to the front of the stalls and addressed the whole group.

"Now," she explained to them, "as soon as I'm sure the captain's finished with Liz and she and Bart are gone, I'm slipping out of here. I don't think Bart will get in trouble. The captain ordered him to go with Liz. And I really do know what I'm doing."

None of the horses disagreed with her.

Chapter Twenty-six

Larking About

Thursday Night - Late

The side streets were dark, empty, and creepy. The rain had stopped but the air was still misty. Fog horns made their mournful call from the river and from time to time, if a car drove by, it seemed to come out of nowhere, and then disappear again into the gray mist, leaving only the *swish-swish* of its tires on the wet pavement. An occasional light gleamed from an apartment window, but the buildings on these streets were old tenements, many unoccupied and run down; sad, seedy places, so little sign of life. Perfect for plotters and their nefarious schemes. Somewhere here, she was sure, the men who took Lindy were sitting together working out their next move.

There were some cars parked along the street. A couple of commercial vans, several rusty, battered vehicles. No white box truck. But at the corner, a small, covered pickup. This was her chance to try out her plan.

When she got close to the pickup, she whistled the tune she'd taught Lindy. Loud enough for a horse to hear but not loud enough to wake the neighbors. "Ragtime Cowboy Joe" seemed a funny tune to be whistling on this sad, slummy street in this sad, slummy part of the big city, but she was betting if Lindy heard it, he'd know what to do.

There was no sound from inside the truck—and she hadn't expected any. It was a good try, but this truck didn't match the one she was looking for.

She kept going. Another creepy street. And another. A couple of possible vehicles, but none with a smart horse inside.

And then, of course, she saw it. Parked near a hydrant in the shadows under a non-working street light, on a street of rickety buildings, in front of a house with a stoop of seven steps leading up to a rotting door, there it was. It couldn't be any other than the one Liz had described. Annie agreed—it did resemble Walt Jeppsen's old box truck. Dirty white, patches of rust, no markings, and a sagging license plate. Yes, a horse could fit in there. Tight, but possible.

She thought she'd be cool when she found it. But now her heart jumped and it was like fireworks inside her head.

I knew it! I knew I was right!

She crept up to the truck. A light went on upstairs. She kept her head down.

Quietly, she whistled, just loudly enough. And her heart pounded even harder when she heard the hoofbeats on the wood floor inside the truck.

"Oh, you wonderful horse!" she whispered. "I knew it. I knew you'd be here. I knew they didn't take you to Yonkers or Great Neck or any of those places."

She was at the back of the truck figuring out how to unlatch the back—

Omigod!

There were people coming around the corner, turning into the street. She could hear their voices.

She scooted fast as she could into the shadows of a basement doorway, away from the approaching men. She peeked around the corner and saw them—five men—approaching the house with the seven steps. They climbed up to the door, knocked, and the door was immediately opened, as though someone inside was expecting them. There was some conversation among the men in a language Annie couldn't understand, and then two of the men—one fat and one skinny—came back downstairs and went to the truck.

Oh, please! No! No! No! Don't drive away!

But they didn't. They leaned against the lamppost, lit cigarettes, and apparently prepared to stay there.

With Liz safely returned to the hotel, with assurances there would be no future efforts to abduct her, Bart U-turned the squad car around and zipped back to headquarters. He was afraid Annie had turned into a loose cannon.

That girl looks like an angel but she is sure a handful. Some "innocent" little librarian she turned out to be! "Headstrong. Stubborn." He whispered his complaints into the wind as he drove. "Never heard anyone talk to the captain like that. Like she knows better than everyone."

At headquarters, he went directly into the stable and found no Annie.

"Uh oh!" he said to the horses. "Now where is she?" But there was no response and there was also no trace that she'd been there, though he looked around quickly.

"Maybe the captain has her back in his office." He crossed the big lobby, knocked on the captain's door, and went in.

"Sir. Where is she?"

"Who?"

"Annie. Miss Cornell."

"In the stable."

"No she's not."

"Oh, damn!" from both of them.

The captain tossed his pen onto the papers, thinking, *That girl is a nuisance. Cute, but a nuisance.* He shook his head, fully irritated now. "Call her!" he ordered.

She answered the instant it vibrated. Her voice was tiny.

"Bart! Thank God it's you. You've got to get here *fast!*"

"Why are you whispering?"

"I'm hiding in a doorway. I found him, Bart! I found Lindy. But I see those men. They're outside the truck. They're talking—I can't let them see me. Oh, Bart, now I'm scared."

"Where are you?" He didn't waste breath or time scolding her. Now she was really in trouble. He felt his own adrenaline rush.

"Not far away. On 37th Street. There's a white box truck, just like Liz described."

"Stay where you are. Don't move. I'll be right there."

"Wait, Bart. Listen. Lindy is in that truck. Don't come where I am. I don't want them to see me. There are two guys standing under a lamppost next to the truck. I think they're guarding it. If you can lure them away somehow, I can get Lindy out the back."

"Oh, Annie. You are too much. Okay. Don't move. I'll be there in a minute."

"And Bart. There are a bunch of these guys upstairs, too. I think they're having a meeting. Please hurry. They could come down any minute."

"Stop talking. Hang up."

She did and he did.

"Sir," he said to the captain, "she says she found Lindy. I may need backup. I'll assess the situation first." And shaking his head, he added, "That girl—"

The captain agreed.

That girl!

Chapter Twenty-seven

Chaos!

"That girl" was crouching in a doorway, trying to be as invisible as possible.

Oh, Bart. Hurry up. Please get here. Please, right away.

It was damp in the shadowy doorway, damp from the recent rain with an acrid smell of wet concrete. She tried not to think of rats. She tried not to think of spiders, and of the more urban vermin, of which she'd read but not yet encountered. She tried to concentrate on the two men lounging at the truck, the gathering of men upstairs, and the wish that Bart would get there *soon*! She also concentrated on the back of the truck, only about fifteen feet away, to work out at this distance its opening mechanism so that when the time came she'd be able to get Lindy out of there quickly. She checked the rope halter, still draped around her neck, and made sure it would come to her hand as quickly as she'd need it. Between being scared and being ready to jump into action, her heart was pounding so hard it seemed to be in her ears.

And then she saw the squad car come around the far corner. Very slowly, it cruised up the street, passing her, passing the two men—who turned away from it and tried to make themselves unobtrusive—and continuing on almost to the next corner.

She watched as Bart got out of the car. He had some papers in his hand. She watched him walk slowly down the street, pausing at each vehicle, as though to examine it, looking at license plates, looking at taillights, and referring always to the papers in his hand, as though comparing numbers. Till he arrived at the white truck. The two men stopped talking and watched him. He looked the truck over. He shuffled the papers, removed one, placed it on top of the others as though he'd found what he wanted. Then he turned to the two men.

"Is this your vehicle?"

"Is problem, officer, sir?" The taller man definitely looked nervous. His companion, the shorter, fatter one, clearly wanted to disappear. He glanced up at the lighted windows above, as though hoping for help.

"No. No problem. I just need to verify some information. If you gentlemen could come with me up the street, where the light is better, I have some questions." He indicated the paper in his hand, a very innocent-looking paper.

The men looked at each other. Again, there was a glance up at the window to see if the watchman who had been posted to keep an eye on them and on the truck was seeing what was happening on the street below.

"Of course, officer, sir. We come. Of course." The taller one gave the other a look, and they both went with Bart up the street.

Annie waited till they were far enough away. She ran to the little drop step that trailed off below the tailgate. She was on it in a minute and was lifting the rusty old side latches, scraping her fingers and ruining the fancy *Lady Fair* manicure that was only three days old. She jumped down from the truck and pulled the gate after her. And there, big and bold and presenting his big rear end, was Lindy. She clucked at him a couple of time, a universal signal to a well-trained horse, especially a horse who was accustomed to being transported, that he was to back up out of the vehicle.

But in that moment, as Lindy was stepping down the lowered gate onto the street—*oh, God!*—the door to the house opened, light flooded the steps and sidewalk, and seven men scattered toward her. They were an uncoordinated mass, as though none of them was sure where he was to go, but she was close to panic herself.

"Bart!" she shouted up the street, but she needn't have. Bart was already on his way, at top running speed, his hand to his holster. And God bless the horse, Lindy was shielding her with his big body, keeping everyone away from her.

In the chaos, short-and-fat and tall-and-skinny had jumped into the truck's cab. She heard the aged engine trying to get started. The men were scattering in all directions. Police backup was arriving behind them, sirens blaring, lights flashing. The truck was in bumpy motion. Bart had the driver's door open and was wrestling for the wheel as the truck weaved down the street caroming off cars, tailgate flapping.

Annie saw the tall bald man with the big mustache, the one Captain Simon thought was the leader. He was running fast, almost up to the corner by the time she spotted him. She slipped the halter from her neck and slid it up over Lindy's muzzle and fitted it quickly onto his head.

In a moment, she was on his back and was yee-hawing down the street at a high-speed gallop. Her quarry got to the corner and turned up the avenue, going as fast as he could, pushing people aside, knocking over trash bins and little old ladies. But he wasn't a young man and he wasn't going to outrun Lindy. Only a couple of blocks away, Lindy had caught up with him and blocked him with a solid wall of horseflesh. The man wasn't going anywhere.

Squad cars reached the truck. Police were racing in all directions, chasing the fleeing men into basements and stairways, dragging them out of their hiding places. Bart brought the truck to a stop and had the two men under control. He'd seen Lindy go by with Annie up top, and he signaled a couple of cars to follow her. When they reached her, Lindy still had the leader of the plotters pinned against the brick wall of a tall apartment building. A few locals, coming out of a bar, stopped to watch. Lindy was blocking the man's efforts to run, with Annie using him like the good quarter horse she knew he was, effectively cutting the targeted one out of the herd.

The police took over and had the man cuffed and into a squad car in a matter of moments. And Annie rode Lindy back to where they'd started. Lights were going on in windows up and down the street. The sound of hoofbeats on pavement was most unusual, and residents all along the way ran to windows to watch.

By the time Annie reached the truck, her excitement had settled down to pure pleasure. She'd been right all along and no one could discount her any longer. She'd found Lindy, she'd led the police to the bad guys, and she'd captured their leader. Bart would be proud of her. Liz would be proud of her. She was proud of herself.

There was a knot of uniforms gathered in the middle of the street, surrounded by an excited horde of arriving media people. News teams from the local TV stations, newspaper reporters, and neighbors with their cell cameras, including a scrum of curious kids. Squad cars in all directions, their headlights lighting up the street, with light bars making the whole scene brilliantly colorful. And there was Bart in the middle, talking on his radio, reporting to Captain Simon back at headquarters.

Annie clip-clopped up to him with people falling back to give her room. She dismounted, grasped her handmade halter by the fiador knot and, with a big Wyoming smile, led Lindy back to his owner.

"I've brought you your horse," she said to Bart.

She waited for Bart's big, grateful smile, maybe a handshake, and a hearty thank you. The warm kiss of gratitude could come later.

But they didn't come. Bart's expression was ice-cold. He signed off his report and turned to her. Silent for a moment. Then he pointed to the halter.

"Where'd you get that thing?"

"I made it."

The air was going out of her elation. What could be wrong? Why is he being like this?

"You made it?"

"Yes. I made it. And I found your horse. And I brought him back to you. I thought you'd be glad."

He nodded slightly. He looked at her thoughtfully and there was something painful in his expression, something Annie couldn't understand.

"I am glad. Of course. Thank you."

Lindy bent his head toward Bart and Bart took the halter from Annie.

"I am glad," he whispered, to the horse, not to her. He rested his forehead on Lindy's and had a moment of thankful reunion with the animal. Once more, he whispered, "I am glad."

Then he turned and gave Annie one more inscrutable look.

"That was a terrific performance," he said to Annie, ice-cold. "You look terrific riding bareback, so very wild west. But I don't get to play cowboys and Indians and I don't have his saddle with me, so I'm just going to call headquarters for a trailer to come and take him back to the stable."

And he walked Lindy off to the side with a noisy trail of media people running after them.

Annie stared after him. The freeze in his remark was stuck like an icicle in her chest.

But reporters with mics and cameras were gathering around her and she had no chance to figure it out.

Someone from *Extra* put a mic in her face and as soon as she got Annie's name, it clicked in her reporter's brain and she connected it to the *Lady Fair* contest winner who, she remembered, was from a ranch somewhere out west. She'd seen Annie's bareback ride up the street on Lindy, she put two and three together and came up with a whole new human interest and entertainment dimension to the story. *Pray God,* she thought, *I hope our camera guy got a shot of that ride.*

Other reporters were catching on, too, and they were trying to crowd each other out. Annie was feeling suffocated and almost blinded by the camera flashes. She made no effort to answer their questions and was looking frantically for someone to get her out of this crush of bodies. When Max Wozinski pushed his way through the crowd to reach her, it was as though the cavalry had arrived.

"Sergeant! Max! Can you get me out of here?"

"That's what I'm here for." He got a protective arm around her and used the other to clear away the reporters.

"Okay, folks," he was saying. "A little air, if you don't mind. Let's get this lady out of here. We need her back at headquarters. You'll all get your story. Press conference at ten o'clock tomorrow morning."

The media mass followed her right up to the squad car and kept the mics in her face till she was in the rear seat and the door was closed. As Max turned the car around and headed back up the street, she looked back and saw the blue-and-white police trailer arrive, and Bart waiting with Lindy to go back to the stable.

Chapter Twenty-eight

The Morning After

Friday Morning

She didn't sleep well that night. Too much excitement, perhaps. Or, more likely, it was the cold shoulder from Bart that had nagged at her through the wee hours. There'd been no chance to talk to him at headquarters, what with the gaggle of reporters outside, yelling questions at her, and the activity inside—the booking of the kidnappers, the recording of her account of events, the department veterinarian checking Lindy's condition. She'd had barely a glimpse of Bart in the stable, working with the vet and getting Lindy settled in, and it was Max who brought her back to her hotel. His comment, as he held the rear door open for her to get into the car, was the only clue she had.

"Imagine a sweet young girl like you doing what all of us couldn't."

He'd given her a big, admiring smile when he said it and she knew it was a compliment but somehow, she felt a chill run through her, like a warning.

For the rest of the ride, he talked only about the super evening they'd had at the theater, he and Chloe and Liz, and he said he felt like he knew a real celebrity, what with Annie's contest and all the evening's excitement, and as he left her off at the hotel, he asked to be remembered to Liz. Then he U-turned the squad car around and headed back to headquarters.

So it was almost five a.m. when she finally fell asleep, and it was seven when the phone started ringing.

"I know it's early!" Mitzi was already on fast forward. "I had to get to you before everyone else does. You're going to be swamped and *Lady Fair* and Galliard's need to keep things under control."

"Hmmpf???"

"Aren't you awake yet? Don't you know what's happening?"

"Who is this?"

"Omigod! Wake up, Annie! *The Today Show* wants an interview. So does *Vista from New York*. CNN already has the video of you chasing that bald guy. And remember, we already had you scheduled for the *GMA* taping later today. Wake up, Annie. We have a busy day, busy, busy, it's going to be crazy, totally slammed. And we have to get you ready."

Annie stared at the telephone in her hand, as though it was sprouting lollipops. What in the world was going on?

"Call me back in ten minutes. I'm not awake."

"Ten minutes. That's all you get."

She was still staring at the phone when Liz walked in, holding the morning newspaper. Without a word she dropped it onto the bed, rolled her eyes, gave a huge sigh, and turned and walked out of the room, leaving Annie to contemplate the latest news.

LINDY FOUND

CONTEST WINNER
UNLIKELY HEROINE

Wyoming Cowgirl Rounds Up
Fleeing Horse-nap Suspect

"What's going on?" she asked the empty room. "This is crazy." She set the paper aside. "I need a shower. I need to wake up."

Ten minutes later, as she stepped out of the shower, she heard her cell phone ringing. She heard the hotel phone ringing. She heard Liz's cell phone ringing. She was brushing her hair when Liz walked in, cell phone in hand.

"The Zimmers, from Laramie, are calling." Ranch people get up early, and Carl and Jennie Zimmer, from the next ranch over, were calling to tease Annie about "showing them city folk a thing or two."

Annie shook her head. "I'll try to call them later. I can't think."

Liz turned and left the room. Annie heard her saying, "She's just hardly awake, Jennie. Can she call you later?"

She set her phone on silent. She asked the hotel operator to hold all calls to the room. She picked up the paper and read the hyped-up account of last night's events—with photos—that made her sound like something out of a western movie. It also made the NYPD sound like Keystone Kops, razzing the "highly trained professionals in blue" for needing to rely on a "pretty young tourist" to get them out of trouble. It was all written in good fun, and wound up taking a more serious tone, praising the department for its good work in controlling unruly street demonstrators like the Buljornia group that was responsible for the events at the United Nations the previous Sunday.

A second column was devoted to Annie herself, highlighting the unlikely coincidence of her being the very lucky winner of the *Lady Fair* contest, and also being the "damsel in distress" seen in the filmed coverage of the demonstration at the UN. Some biographical information was included, so now the whole world would know Annie Cornell, 26, of Laramie, Wyoming, college librarian, lives on a ranch, etc., etc., with *Lady Fair* photos that show her looking more glamorous and professionally beautiful than any ordinary woman can possibly be.

"Oh, this is awful!"

She tossed the paper aside and stuck her head under the pillows.

And stayed there until Liz came into the room a few minutes later.

"Annie, don't be ridiculous. You wanted an adventure. Now you've had one. A real adventure. So cheer up, honey. This is the price of fame. You should enjoy it. And someday, you'll be glad when you can tell your children all about it."

Annie sat up. Took a couple of deep breaths.

"I know. You're right. We can go home in a couple of days, and be done with all this craziness." She started to get dressed.

While the thought slipped through her head:

And be done with Bart Hardin?

But not a word about that to Liz.

And Liz thought it best not to tell her at this time that going home to Laramie was probably not going to be the end of "all this." Her phone hadn't stopped all morning and there was already talk of welcoming festivities, including brass bands and parades.

"Okay, Liz." Annie got the phones turned back on. "Let the whirlwind begin."

And, indeed, it was a whirlwind. She was whisked off to *Lady Fair*'s offices where she was informed that her stay in New York would be extended through Sunday—all expenses paid, of course, for her and Liz. There would be TV appearances in addition to the one already scheduled for *Good Morning America*, including a full fifteen-minute segment on *Vista from New York*, and a crew was already on its way to Laramie to get some local reaction and shots of the ranch, the college library, the campus. *Lady Fair* would do a much longer article, maybe a full profile (they'd already assigned a writer) and Galliard's was preparing festivities of its own, which would include some sort of lifetime gift—maybe the sable coat she'd admired *(what in the world would I do with a sable coat back home?)* or a Galliard charge card with a monthly credit, or some such. They were working on it. The mayor's office was going to award her a citizen's medal for bravery, honor, and general wonderfulness.

And the NYPD had arranged for a special presentation by the Police Pipe Band in full regalia, kilts and all.

Through all the rush and attention, while she tried to keep track of everything and at the same time remember to be appropriately excited and gracious while feeling totally upended, there was the dark undertone that ran beneath everything: *Why haven't I heard from Bart?*

She wasn't altogether surprised to realize his silence mattered to her more than all the attention. Not after the night she'd had, kept awake by his all too apparent rejection, wondering why she cared, wondering what his behavior meant, telling herself it was of no concern to her, seesawing back and forth between "he's just a cute guy I met on a trip to New York" and "I thought we had something special happening," back and forth between scolding herself and feeling sorry for herself, and either way, unable to put it all aside and just, for goodness' sake, go to sleep!

It was late afternoon before they were all done preparing her, and she was still asking herself the same question.

"Where is he?"

Bart had spent a miserable day at headquarters. Like Annie, he'd hardly slept that night, and from the time he reported in that morning, the guys had been ribbing him. He knew it was all in good fun and he'd never let them know they were really getting to him, so he swallowed his pride and went along with the banter.

"Yeah, she really is something, that girl. I'm going to have to take some roping lessons from her."

"And tracking, too. Bet some Arapaho friend must have taught her."

"Maybe she's part Arapaho herself."

"Not with that hair."

"Yeah. If that girl belonged to any tribe, it would be the Golden Angels. Right, Bart?"

"Right." Bart kept up the big smile. "Angels is right. Just a sweet little angel brought Lindy back home safe and sound."

Then he went into Captain Simon's office and begged off any duty assignment for a couple of days. Claimed Lindy needed a rest and reacclimation after all the excitement and stress.

"Yeah, sure. Take a couple of days." And after Bart had closed the door behind him, the captain added, "And just a wee little slip of a thing she was, too. Who'd a thought."

Hours later, while the squad was out on assignment, Bart was still sitting with Lindy.

"Dammit. It's not like I wouldn't have found you myself, without her help."

Lindy apparently didn't buy that.

"We were getting close to finding those guys. And that would have been the end of it."

Lindy chose to eat some of his special feed.

"And the nerve of them, putting you in a box like that. Those clowns. Who'd have thought they'd do such a thing."

Lindy snuffled a little.

"Well, yeah. Okay. Annie did."

Lindy was no comfort and Bart was feeling that everyone was against him.

He was still there at three thirty in the afternoon when the morning shift returned and the evening squad went out. He busied himself with currying Lindy, as though Lindy needed any more attention than he'd already had, and he allowed the bantering of his buddies to swirl around him, knowing they'd all be gone soon and he could go back to his ruminations about Annie, her fearless exploit, her courage, her skill in figuring it all out, her sudden fame, and trying unsuccessfully to figure out how to get out of the hole of humiliation he'd fallen into. Not that the guys really seemed to think less of him; it was just the usual kidding, no malice. And as for the media, well, that would all be yesterday's news soon.

"It's just that I thought I was going to be the one to take care of her. Protect her. Show her around, see that she was safe. I felt like such a—well, I don't know—I guess I felt like a big shot. Yeah, like she was such an innocent, helpless little thing. Where did I ever get such an idea? I know, Lindy. I should call her and apologize. But I just can't. I can't do it."

Lindy stepped to the other side of the stall and turned his head away from him. He felt sure Lindy was disgusted with him. He really was being a jerk, and he knew it. And he couldn't stop himself.

So when his phone alerted him to an incoming message, and when the ID showed it was Annie texting him, he closed his eyes for about twenty heartbeats, bracing himself for—for what? Some more razzing? Maybe some gloating about how she told him so? How he should have listened to her? How big city, street savvy, macho guys don't really have all the answers? How a "little librarian" from a small western town could show up the whole NYPD?

Well, he had to have *some* backbone. So he took a couple of deep breaths and read her text.

Are we still friends?

That was her whole message.

He felt his heart bang around in his chest. He was ashamed of how his thinking had turned so poisonous. Of course. That's the kind of thing she *would* say. She wasn't a girl to rub a guy's nose in his own foolishness. How do you stay mad at someone you want desperately to be with? But still—

Yeah. Sure.

He managed to get that much out. He felt like a ten-year-old, being coaxed to smile when he didn't feel like it. He didn't like the feeling. He didn't seem to be liking any of his feelings since yesterday.

A minute or two went by, and then her answer came back.

It's been a crazy day. Hoped I'd hear from you. Quieter now. I'll be here till Sun nite. Lindy ok? I miss him.

He thought long and hard, deciding on his response and composing his message carefully.

Off duty for a couple days. See u tmrw? 2 p.m.? If ur not 2 busy. Same place, the cafe behind the library?

No answer came for about half an hour and he started to imagine—what?—what does a guy start imagining when he thinks a girl is preparing to reject him? He found a thousand explanations for her silence. And another thousand for why he didn't care. Plus some more for why he was being a fool to think she'd be interested in him. And then he swung back the other way.

"But she texted me first," he told Lindy.

If a horse could roll his eyes, Lindy would have been rolling his.

And when her message finally came back, Bart's heart jumped again.

Prfect. I'm on Vista at 11 and done by noon. Time Magazine wanted an interview, but I canceled them. Enough, already! C u 2 pm tmrw, behind the library.

He knew he was headed for another sleepless night. But what the hell.

And Annie, for her part, was still trying to catch her breath, after a day of being on the edge of a cyclone and trying to find her way to a quiet center. And somehow, she imagined Bart waiting in that quiet center. And she couldn't imagine why it mattered so much to her, because he could be such a horse's ass!

Chapter Twenty-nine

In Margaritaville

"You're looking good," he said.

He'd been standing there for a long minute, watching her reading her book, waiting for her to realize he was there. She had her hair loose and in the bright sunlight it was pure platinum. She was wearing reading glasses, and he found that charming.

She'd arrived early and taken the same table they'd had on Thursday, prepared to read quietly for a few minutes. Now she looked up to see him silhouetted, tall and dark, against the bright light. And she had to laugh. "We match," she said. They were both in jeans and black tops.

She realized he didn't understand. Guys tend not to notice such things. But when he sat down, she looked more closely at him, and knew he hadn't paid any attention to what he'd put on that day. She saw how tired he was.

"Lindy is all right?" she asked.

"Yeah. Lindy's doing just great." She sensed some reticence.

"You look tired," she said. "This has been hard on you, I know."

"Yeah. Hard."

Their waiter—the same one from Thursday—arrived at the table.

"Well, welcome back, you two. I've been reading in the papers about you. And the TV, too, you and your horse. It's famous, you both are." He put a couple of menus in front of them. "What can I get you?" He looked at Bart. "Ready for that margarita now?"

"Good idea," Bart said. "You, too, Annie?"

"Sure. I'm not driving today. I'm not driving for another few days. Bring it on."

"Anything else?" The waiter put a glass full of tall, skinny bread-sticks between them.

"Not me. I had lunch," she said.

"Me, neither." He handed the menus back to the waiter. "Not hungry," he said.

She looked at him closely.

"You look as though you ought to eat something."

"I know when I need to eat something. Don't need you to tell me."

The waiter raised his eyebrows. He knew the signs of trouble. "Then if that's all, folks—" and removed himself from the scene.

"I didn't mean—"

"I know what you meant. I haven't had much sleep. Lots to think about."

"What does that mean?"

"I'll tell you when I figure it out."

"About us?" she said.

"Yeah. About us."

"Well, I have some things to figure out, too."

She knew, by his expression, that that hadn't occurred to him.

"So why are we here?" he asked.

"I don't know. You suggested it."

"I don't remember. I thought you did."

"Doesn't matter."

Now they were both silent. For many long minutes.

The waiter arrived with their drinks. He surveyed the two of them. "You guys sure you don't want some food?"

They both looked up at him silently.

"Suit yourselves," he said, and he made a quick getaway.

Some more long, silent minutes.

Finally Bart spoke. "We can't just sit here."

"You go first. You're the one who's mad."

"I'm not mad."

"Then what are you?"

He stared into his glass. Drank it all off. Stared a little more.

"I'm not sure. That's what I'm trying to figure out."

"Well, you be sure and let me know when you do." *That sounded mean,* she thought. *What made me say that?* She looked into her glass. Also empty now.

"Yeah. I'll just do that." He looked up, caught the waiter's eye and signaled for two more margaritas. The waiter rolled his eyes and went off to get them. He hoped this wouldn't turn nasty.

Silence again until the drinks came.

"Those breadsticks are a specialty of the chef," the waiter said, hoping they'd eat something. "Really good. Baked with cheese in them."

Bart glared at him and he disappeared.

Annie took one of the breadsticks and nibbled at one end.

"Why are we fighting?" she asked. She took a hefty gulp of her drink.

"Are we fighting?"

"Feels like it to me."

He drained half the drink in his glass. He looked up into the trees, avoiding her eyes.

"I've been taking a lot of razzing."

She was astonished.

"Why?"

"Why?" he repeated. "Because it's not every day some girl comes along—some 'little slip of a thing,' as the captain says—comes along and shows me up."

"Well, I never heard anything so stupid."

"So now I'm stupid?"

"And that's even stupider. I didn't say *you're* stupid. I said it's stupid to say I showed you up just because I was able to find your dumb old horse. Anyone with an ounce of horse sense could have done it."

"Yeah, well, we had the whole force out looking for him—and you did it right in our own neighborhood without any training or anything. Made us all look dumb. Made *me* look dumb!" He finished his drink and signaled for another. "And my horse is definitely not dumb."

"I'm sorry I called him dumb. I didn't mean it that way. He's a very smart horse." She finished her drink, too. "Very smart horse. Smarter than some people I know."

The waiter set Bart's third drink in front of him and Annie pointed to it.

"Me, too," she said.

"The kitchen stops serving lunch at three," he said. "Sure you don't—" But he didn't bother to finish. They weren't listening to him at all. Funny about that. They'd seemed to be getting along so well the other day.

"And the press was ragging us, saying we were incompetent."

"They were not. It was just a cute human interest story—and they said nice things about the mayor's office and the NYPD generally. I thought it was all pretty friendly. And they really wanted you to find Lindy—and get those jerks who took him." Her third drink arrived and she started on it right away. "By the way, whatever happened to those guys?"

"Oh, they'll be charged. The whole bunch of them were operating out of that house you found. They'll probably all get deported."

"They didn't really hurt anyone, did they?"

"But we didn't know they wouldn't. And they threatened to kidnap you, too. But come to think of it, if they had, I suppose you'd have been okay. You'd have just gone ahead and rescued yourself, too, if they had kidnapped you. Probably would have chewed through the ropes or something. We'd have found them all tied up to a telephone pole or something. The whole bunch of them."

Now it was her turn to roll her eyes.

"No," he said, "don't make a face. You're just full of little surprises to make a guy look dumb. Full of li'l trisks. Tricks." His tongue seemed to be getting thicker. Li'l feminine wiles."

"I don't know why I bothered to see you today." She wasn't feeling too clear herself. "I could have gone to a movie. A western. Full of ropin' and tyin' and shootin.' By guys who pretend to know how to do it. Or just stayed in the hotel and watched TV. Watched myself on TV."

"Right. You could have spent the whole day watching sweet, innocent, gorgeous, wonderful Annie Cornell on the TV while the whole world goes gaga over you. And makes fun of the men who try to take care of you."

"That's it!" She stood up abruptly. "I've had enough, Mr. Caped Crusader. Like I need anyone to take care of me!" She grabbed her bag and fled.

"Annie!" Bart also got out of his chair, but too fast, and over it went, while he made an effort to grab at it and instead got his feet tangled up in its legs. She was well away by the time he got clear. He grabbed a handful of twenties out of his wallet and tossed them onto the table—too much, but he didn't care—and ran after her, but too late, for she had already hailed a cab and was gone. He stood there on the sidewalk, knocked over by what had just happened.

And the waiter, picking up a hundred and twenty bucks, said to himself for the thousandth time, "Some people just can't hold their liquor. At least she didn't throw her margarita in his face."

In the taxi, Annie rested her head back, closed her eyes, and said to herself, *I can't believe the nerve of that man. You'd think he'd be so pleased, he got his precious horse back, all safe and sound. And they got all the bad guys, too. You'd think he'd be happy. You'd think he might have said thank you. If he were a gentleman. A gentleman would have given me a little credit. Praised me a little. I think I deserve at least that much. He's no gentleman. That's your problem, Bart Hardin,* Sergeant *Bartlett Hardin, you're no gentleman. No gentleman at all.* She opened her eyes. She was sure she could see the four gargoyles at the top of the Chrysler Building, ahead of her on 42nd Street, and she imagined one of them stuck his tongue out at her as her taxi approached. So she stuck her tongue out, too, right back at it. "So there!" she said. She closed her eyes again.

"What did they put in those drinks?" she muttered hazily.

And sitting on the stone steps at the edge of the park, Bart closed his eyes and rubbed his forehead. *The nerve of her!* he said to himself. *Riding into town like the cavalry and no respect for anyone. With her fancy research and her showing off like that, with cameras and reporters all chasing after her like she's a miracle worker or something. And her TV shows and her interviews, and lah-di-dah, I've got to meet with the press, and everyone loves me, and winning contests and all. And so what if she rides bareback, anyone can ride bareback. Just leave off the saddle.* That seemed funny to him, so he laughed.

He opened his eyes and looked up, way up—and there, high in the blue, blue sky, he could have sworn he saw a peregrine falcon at dizzying speed, chasing a pigeon. "Go get her," he whispered. "You're the fastest thing in the sky, buddy. Show her what you can do." His head started to spin and he closed his eyes again.

"They must have put something in those drinks."

Chapter Thirty

The Wobbles

S he needed to put a steadying hand on the wall of the elevator as it sped her up to the forty-fourth floor. When she wobbled into their suite, she found Liz curled up on the sofa, watching *Vista from New York.*

"I recorded it," Liz said. "I called Craig and told him to record it too, so we can see it again when we get back home."

Then she looked at Annie.

"Are you okay?"

"The nerve of that man. He's no gentleman, Liz. He just is no gentleman. No gentleman at all."

Annie seemed to be having trouble holding her head up and trying to focus.

"Omigod. Have you been drinking? You look so funny."

"Funny, ha ha?"

"Well, yeah, funny, ha ha. That, too." She already had a hand on Annie's arm and steered her to the sofa. "Here. Sit down." She took Annie's handbag and put it on the coffee table. "What have you been up to?"

"It's been a long day, Liz. A very long day. I was on that show this morning."

"I know, dear. I was there."

"And they wanted me to tie a halter. They had some rope and they gave me the rope and wanted me to show all the viewers out there in

TV land how easy it is to tie a halter for a horse out of a piece of rope." She peered somberly at Liz. "It's not easy to tie a halter for a horse out of a piece of rope. You know that, Liz. You know how hard I worked to learn that. I must have spent a hundred hours practicing. What's the matter with those people, Liz? It's not easy at all. A thousand hours Jimmy Ray must have spent a thousand afternoons teaching me how to do that. Said it would come in handy someday. And see? He was right." She kicked off her shoes. "He was a very wise man, Liz. He said it would come in handy someday, and it did."

"I'm going to get you some coffee."

"The nerve of that man. You'd think he'd be happy. You'd think he'd say thank you, at least. What's the matter with people here?"

Liz was calling room service. "I know, honey. I know." To room service she said, "Make it extra strong—and hurry!"

She hung up and to Annie she said, "It's been a long couple of days and you need a rest."

"Yes, long days. And those women on the show, they kept talking about the contest, and the Buljornia crowd, and the library in Laramie, and showing that damn video of me on Lindy, running down that bald man, and there I am, in my jeans and the yellow paisley—that shirt is silk, Liz, and you know I would never wear that shirt riding. Galloping Lindy down a city street, past grocery stores and dry cleaners and I felt so ridiclorus. Rilicolus." She paused. Focused. "Ri-*dic*-u-lous. And I didn't do anything that you or a hundred other folks we know wouldn't have done. I don't know what's the matter with these people, Liz. They make such a fuss over everything. And they talk so fast. And all in explanation points." Another deep breath. "Ex-clam-*a*-tion points." She closed her eyes. "I seem to be having some trouble talking."

Liz hadn't seen Annie like this since she was fourteen years old and someone spiked the punch at homecoming.

"I can't wait to hear about your meeting with Bart today," she said. "Must have been interesting. Later on, after you've had some coffee and a little rest, you can tell me all about it."

"Oh, Liz, don't even say that man's name to me. I don't want to ever think of him again."

"Yes, dear. We'll talk about it later."

"He hates me."

"I don't think he hates you."

"Yes, he does. He thinks I ruined his life."

"Why don't you lie down, Annie. Take a little nap. You'll feel much better after you sleep it off. Then we can go out and have dinner, maybe go to a movie, and you can tell me all about it."

"And I thought I was doing him a big favor." She was getting wobblier by the minute. Her eyelids were already drifting shut. "It just shows to go you."

A knock on the door announced the arrival of the coffee.

"Just in time," Liz said. She let them in, tipped them, showed them out, quickly poured the coffee, and brought it to Annie.

But it was too late. Annie was sound asleep on the sofa.

Chapter Thirty-one

In the Neigh-borhood?

Saturday Evening

A couple of hours' rest, a shower, and a change of clothes, and Annie was restored to her usual, sober self. Sober enough to remember that Bart's feelings were hurt and somehow he thought it was her fault, and they hadn't parted on friendly terms. Again.

Facing the bathroom mirror, she had a little talk with herself.

"You've known him for only a few days. You're making too much of this. He's just another guy, with an ego that gets in the way of—oh, I don't know—whatever it is."

She had to pause and try to figure out what she was trying to tell herself.

"Okay," she said finally. "Okay, he's cute, and strong, and protective. And every man looks good in a uniform. And even more so on a horse. And for a while there, you thought maybe you'd found someone you had a special feeling for."

The mirror looked back at her. She felt as though she didn't even know herself anymore. She decided to leave off the makeup. She'd had enough of that, after all the gussying up of the last week. She looked deep into her reflection, deep into her own eyes.

"Maybe it's like those shipboard romances in old movies. Fun while it lasts, but then you come home to reality. No more magic. That's probably what this was. Like a fever. A cold shower, a little penicillin, and you'll be fine. Go home to Laramie, get back to work, put all the craziness and fuss of this last week behind you, and be a normal human being again."

She took a deep breath. Then a second one. And went into the living room to join Liz, who was waiting to leave for dinner.

"I'm ready," she said. "Feeling fine. What do you want to do this evening?"

"Dinner and a movie. There's a new George Clooney movie out. You know how I am about George Clooney."

"Who isn't?" Annie said. "Okay. Whatever you want. You've been such a sweetie, Liz. This whole trip, you've let me hog the spotlight. Tonight is all for you. "

"Much appreciated. I'll just get my bag."

On the way down to the lobby, she said, "The concierge told me about a good place for dinner. Not far from here."

"Lead on," Annie said. But when Liz led her to Charlie Wu's, she said, "Oh, no!"

"What's the matter?"

"Nothing. Nothing at all. This is your evening. This will be fine. Looks very nice."

They were led to a table in the middle of the room, so Annie was at least spared the grief of winding up at the same spot she and Bart had shared. But she wasn't spared the embarrassing arrival of Charlie Wu himself, who came to the table, told her how glad he was to see her, and to tell her he was honored that New York's heroine chose his restaurant for dinner. She introduced Liz, he said their dinner would be comped, of course, and he sent over a bottle of wine.

"That's for you, Liz. I think I've had my quota for the day." *That's all I need, after my performance this afternoon.* "But nice of him to do that."

"Might as well face it, Annie. You're the toast of the town and you ought to enjoy it."

"Right. Until the next 'toast of the town' shows up. Good thing we're leaving soon."

"Plenty of girls would give a lot to have the adventure you're having here."

"I know it. Of course I know it. It's just—well, I guess this whole thing now with Bart has made it sort of like ashes in the wine. Know what I mean?"

"So what did happen? Do you want to talk about it?"

"Not really. We'd had a couple of drinks. He got mad. I got mad. He feels I showed him up and I guess his male ego can't take it. I felt unappreciated, and I guess my ego can't take it. I said he was stupid. Well, not that, exactly, but I guess it sort of came out that way." She picked up her menu. "I'll just add the whole episode as a postscript to my New York adventure. You win some, you lose some. I won a contest, I lost a guy. No big deal. Just think of all the clothes I'm going home with."

Liz gave her a funny look but said nothing. They ordered. They ate. They left. With Charlie himself escorting them to the door and saying he hoped he'd see them again soon—any time they were in New York. A great honor to his restaurant.

Liz had the movie theater's address in her bag and she gave it to the cab driver.

"The movie starts at 8:30, so we have time. But I can't get over how everything stays open so late. Did you know the movies are still going after midnight? Don't people sleep here?"

Annie laughed. She was getting used to New York's round-the-clock pace. But she stopped laughing when the cab stopped and she saw that they were in Times Square.

Why here? He could be patrolling here.

"I have to leave you off here," the driver said. "The street is closed. Some work crews down there." He pointed to a couple of temporary sawhorses. "You can walk it, easy. Just down the street here."

So Annie paid the driver ("It's your night, my treat," she said), they got out—and to Annie's dismay, a couple of mounted cops were not more than a hundred feet away, in the midst of a bunch of tourists who were taking their pictures and stroking the horses. And of course, Lindy was one of them, and of course, it was Bart riding him. She hoped, in the midst of Times Square's crowd, he wouldn't see her, and she hurried Liz around the corner toward the movie theater down the street.

But of course Bart had seen her. Maybe a hundred times, he'd imagined he'd seen her, and now, when she actually appeared and he saw that flash of bright blond hair out of the corner of his eye, he knew he'd seen the real thing. He signaled to Max, who was up on Hip Hop, that he was going to move on down to the corner, and when he got there, he saw Annie and Liz going into the movie theater.

* * *

The interior of the theater was like a mall. There was a food court and escalators in all directions. And the aroma of popcorn and hot dogs and nachos.

"Twenty-five screens!" Liz marveled.

"I can't get over it," Annie said. "I remember when they opened the Fox Theater in Laramie and five screens was such a big deal."

"We are such country hicks," Liz said.

"I know," Annie agreed. "Thank God. I couldn't live in these crowds. I mean, it's fun for a few days, but the noise and the speed of everything and all the people. I'll be so glad to get back to big sky country."

"Me, too."

"On the other hand, look at all the movies here. And all the restaurants and the museums and the concerts and even on the street—it's like theater wherever you go. That's something we don't see back home."

"True. No way to have everything."

And with those words of wisdom, they arrived at the top of the escalator, several stories up, and went into the dark to spend a couple of hours with George Clooney.

It was almost eleven o'clock when the movie ended and there were streams of people arriving for the next show. In the midst of the human swirl, they paused on the sidewalk outside to study Liz's map and to get their bearings. There was plenty of street light to see by, and the crews that had been working earlier were gone. The two blond heads were bent over the map, concentrating.

And Annie felt something against her neck. Something soft and familiar. Lindy had his muzzle up against her cheek, giving her a warm greeting.

She turned and looked up into Bart's blue, blue eyes.

"Sorry about that," Bart said. "He wanted to say hello. I didn't mean to bother you."

A little crowd was gathering around them. Annie was so tired of crowds. What devil turned her pleasure in Bart's—and Lindy's—appearance into a stubbornly contrary need to make a sarcastic jab?

"You sure you aren't afraid I'll upstage you? I mean, you put on such a great show out here, with your glamorous uniform and your gorgeous animal."

Even Lindy look startled.

And Bart's face went grim. His jaw clenched and his eyes went cold.

"Well, folks," he said, addressing the tourist onlookers, "we have a real celebrity here. Meet Annie Cornell, New York City's current heroine of the week. You can ask her all the questions you want. Take a bunch of selfies with her. She just loves the attention."

And he wheeled Lindy away and they disappeared into Times Square's nighttime crowd.

Liz pulled her quickly out of the crush of descending gawkers and into the street, where she quickly hailed a passing cab and stuffed the stunned Annie into it.

"What in the world got into you? That was so rude."

"Well, he was rude, too."

"Annie, you two are acting like twelve-year-olds."

"I know."

And she began to cry.

"I don't know what's the matter with me." She dropped her head and covered her face with her hands. "I'm so confused. Everything had been so fabulous, and I was feeling so lucky. I thought the whole world was smiling at me. There was the shopping spree and being on TV and oh, just all the fun of being here in this great city. And then, out of the blue, along came Bart—"

Just saying his name produced a new flow of tears, and Liz dug a tissue out of her bag and handed it to her.

"I know," Liz said. She was stroking Annie's hair. "I know. I never thought it would turn out this way. Not at all. I really didn't."

"Oh, Liz, I thought he was someone special. Someone really special. And I thought, maybe, together, we *had* something special. We were having fun together—in the park and eating hot dogs, and—and—shepherd's pie—I even met his mother and I walked around the neighborhood where he grew up." With the memory of Bart's mother, the home he grew up in, his willingness to share that with her, she cried still more. "And when Lindy went missing, I felt I knew him well enough, and knew enough about his family, what Lindy meant to them, that I thought I did, really truly understand what he was going through, how he was suffering. So I tried to do whatever I could to help. And I thought it was a precious gift I was giving him when I actually found Lindy. I thought he'd be so pleased. And I thought my good luck that had been with me every minute of this trip, was still with me. Like a good angel was dancing me along every step of this fabulous week. I expected he'd be so happy, and so pleased."

Liz handed her another tissue and she blew her nose, hard. "And instead, he was mad at you." Liz picked the wet tissues out of Annie's hand and stuck them deep into a corner of her bag. "Sometimes, I think the male of the species makes no sense at all."

"Where did it all go so dreadfully—so *disastrously*—wrong?" Annie wasn't really talking to Liz. She was her own audience. "How could he get it all so—so—*unbalanced!?*" Liz handed her another tissue. "I did him this great favor, I was practically a hero, and he acts like he just can't stand the sight of me. Oh, Liz, what a terrible way to end this adventure. All the air has gone out of my bubble and now I just want to go home."

"Oh, my poor Annie. It's all the excitement. This city and the excitement. It's good we're leaving tomorrow. We'll get you back to the real world and everything will settle into its proper place. You just have to make it through tonight."

"I know. I know." She raked her hands through her hair. "But oh, Liz, I'm so miserable."

Chapter Thirty-two

A Word from Mom

A Month Later

The smell of gingerbread baking reached him even before he went up the front steps. It was the first bit of comfort he'd felt for weeks.

There was mail in the mailbox and he took it out as he opened the door.

"Mom? You home?"

Mrs. Hardin came out of the kitchen, stood in the doorway and took a good look at her son.

"You look like hell. What's going on?"

"I need to talk to someone about—well, about something."

"Are you in trouble?"

"In a way."

She looked at him in that brisk way she had, sizing everything up in a single piercing glance.

"Sit down," she said. "I'll make coffee." She went back into the kitchen.

In the living room, Bart dropped into the blue wing chair. His mom was right. He did look like hell. There were dark circles under his eyes and he had lost some weight. He hadn't shaved for a couple of days, his face was stubbled, his hair was shaggy around his shirt collar and he seemed to have slept in his jeans and white shirt. A half-dead animal washed up on the beach looked in better shape.

His mom came back into the room. A tall-backed Chippendale

chair was close to the wing chair, and she sat there, where she could see Bart's face clearly, lit by the afternoon sun.

"Now tell me. What's wrong?"

"It's so stupid, Mom. It's just so stupid. You remember that girl that came here with me, a few weeks ago?"

"Of course I remember her. Annie. Annie Cornell." With all the trouble a police officer could get into, girl trouble was probably not so serious. Unless—

"The news was full of her for a few days," she said. "I'd hoped to see her again before she left. I liked her."

"I liked her, too."

"So? So far, I don't see a problem."

"Yeah. Well, it didn't work out."

"What happened?"

"You *saw* what happened. She made me look like a jerk!"

"She did? How? I didn't see how you looked like a jerk."

"Oh, Mom, not you, too." Bart's face flashed his impatience. "Lindy was Dad's horse. If Lindy had been stolen while Dad was alive, wouldn't Dad have been the first one to track down the kidnappers? Do you think he'd have let some little slip of a thing—that's what the captain keeps calling her, a 'little slip of a thing'—come along and do his job for him? A job he was supposed to be doing?"

"And that's what this is about?" She was relieved; it could have been something much more serious. "That's what has you looking like an unmade bed?"

"I can't help it, Mom. The guys were all razzing me. And the press was all over the unit, like somehow we weren't doing our job—saying some out-of-town tourist who can't weigh more than a hundred and ten pounds came along and solved the case and captured the bad guys single-handed."

"And what did she say about all this?"

"Oh, I don't know." He looked away, unwilling to meet his mother's eyes.

"Did you talk about it?"

"I tried to."

"And?"

"She called me stupid."

"She didn't strike me as the kind of girl who calls people stupid."

"I was trying to get her to understand."

"And she didn't?"

"No. She didn't understand at all. I tried. But she's impossible."

Mrs. Hardin sat quietly for maybe a full minute while Bart glowered at the carpet. She studied him closely. Then she spoke, in that quiet, centered way she had that he'd learned to listen to.

"Bart. I didn't raise my boy to be a fool. And you never gave me any reason to think you were a fool. Well,"—she smiled, a little indulgently—"maybe there were a few days here and there in your teens—every teenager has some pretty foolish days—but those days don't count." Then, more seriously, she said, "No, Bart, I've had every reason to be proud of you. Proud when you joined the force. Proud of how you've conducted yourself as an officer—and I don't mean only the special commendations, I mean your behavior day in and day out. I was proud when you made sergeant. I was proud of how you helped me when Dad died, helped me get through those black days, when I felt as though I'd died, too.

"But if ever I saw a man behaving like a fool, I'm seeing it now, Bart. Here, you bring home this really nice girl, a girl who's smart, sane, well brought up, well educated, independent, and lovely, and I thought, the minute I met her, now here's a girl who's good enough for my Bart.

"And then, on top of all that, what does this impossible girl do? She performs an act of bravery and skill that not one person in maybe a million could do, and not only that, she does the entire city of New York a big favor, not to mention the New York Police Department, its mounted unit—and by the way, a huge personal favor for you, too, Bart.

"And how do you say thank you to this very special girl who's done so much for us all? You get all bent out of shape because *she's* the one who did it instead of you. Is that how they trained you? Is that how your dad and I trained you? I'm ashamed of you, Bart. You've earned plenty of points for bravery and honorable behavior. Surely you can acknowledge it when someone else earns a few of their own. Surely bravery and skill can be shared. It's not like you're the only one who's supposed to be wonderful. Des Hardin was never like that. And Bart Hardin shouldn't be, either."

Bart was silent, his eyes fixed on the photo of his father.

"Well," his mother said. "I've said my piece. You think about it, dear. I have a cake in the oven." And she stood up and left the room.

He did think about it. "A girl good enough for my Bart." That's what she said.

But maybe I'm not good enough for her.

And with that thought, he remembered Annie's words: "I don't know why I bothered to see you today." And she called him stupid.

Well, not really. She said what I said was stupid. Not the same thing. I don't even remember what I said. Probably it was stupid. I said a lot of stupid things that day.

He went into the kitchen where his mom was sticking a cake tester into the pan of gingerbread. It needed another five minutes.

"She called me a Caped Crusader, like I was someone in a comic book."

"Oh, Bart, honey. I think that's your nicest quality. And I think Annie thinks so, too. She was probably mad. What did you say that made her mad?"

"I can't remember. Something about her thinking she didn't need me to take care of her." He no sooner said that than he realized how condescending that would have been. "Maybe I shouldn't have said that."

"You think?"

He turned a chair around and straddled it. He watched his mom as she got out a cake rack. He watched her preparing a frosting for the gingerbread. He watched how she wiped her hands on her apron, took a couple of pot holders off a hook on the wall and got the gingerbread out of the oven. He loved watching his mom in the kitchen.

"I said a lot of dumb stuff that day."

"A man in love usually does say a lot of dumb stuff."

Leave it to Mom to put it plain like that. With a single word. That's all it was. One word. But he couldn't say it right off. He needed to let it sink in.

And when it did, he gave his mom a straight look, eye to eye. He felt a huge space open up in his chest. About three hundred pounds of misery slid off him, dissolved, melted, disappeared, vanished. He looked at his mother as though beams of light were radiating off her head.

"You're right, Mom. I am in love with that girl. And I let her get away."

The look from his mom was like a slow drill, right into his heart. He'd been brought up well and he understood what that look meant.

"I know, Mom. I will make this right." He stood up. "It's going to take some work, but I'll make this right. Beginning right now."

"Sit down," she said. "The coffee's ready. And I'll cut you a piece of cake."

Chapter Thirty-three

Home Sweet Home?

Mid-August

It had been an unusually hot summer, and dry. Everyone was being careful about the water supply and by mid-August the predominant color scheme of the terrain was brown and beige. A few summer classes were in session, but mostly things were quiet on campus and there wasn't much going on in the library. Annie had been moping all summer, and her friends and family assumed that the excitement of the contest, her New York adventure, and the tumultuous festivities that had greeted her return had left her wrung out. There'd been the high school band waiting at the regional airport, with streams of cars and pickups strung out along Brees Road, and horns honking, and invitations to make speeches, and the exhaustion and the culture shock. After the dizzy verticalness of New York, she felt as though she'd landed on a different planet when they descended the steps from the plane onto the unremittingly flat horizon of Laramie's high plain, thousands of feet above sea level with only an enormous sky above that was empty of everything but clouds and wind.

Only Liz knew the truth, and that meant Craig knew, too, so at home they tiptoed around her misery and offered her only as much comfort as she was willing to accept. In time, they knew, she'd recover and life would go on—not quite as before, but it would go on.

At work, because of the light summer load, she was able to keep up appearances, and now that she was a celebrity, she was kept busy learning how to be gracious even though she wanted to be left alone. With the contest behind her, the gifts handed round, the clothes from Galliard hung in the closet, all the lotions and potions stashed away in various drawers and cabinets or presented to pleased colleagues, friends, and relatives, and the obligations of work at the college and on the ranch enough to fill her days and leave her tired in the evening, she had every reason to put New York and all it meant well behind her.

Which made it hard, perhaps, to understand why she often, quietly, when no one was around, got out the maps of the city and retraced the places she'd been, reviewed the memories that went with each, relived the details of those extraordinary few days. There were people whose names she knew now, people she'd never heard of that spring morning she and Liz had stepped on the plane to Denver. Mitzi, and Marge Webster, Damien and Louis and all the editors around the conference table at *Lady Fair*, the perfume saleslady at Galliard's, the mayor at the ribbon-cutting, and even the concierge at the hotel. Though she would never see any of them again, they would remain part of her big adventure.

But there were those other memories, the ones that came with a pang of remorse and loss. There was the jolly guard out in front of Troop B headquarters, and the taxi driver who first drove her there. And Captain Simon and Max and the other officers. And the silly Buljornia plotters. The Irish restaurant and its shepherd's pie and Katie, the waitress. Even Charlie Wu and Sergei and his hot dog cart in front of the Boathouse. And of course, there was Mrs. Hardin and the clapboard house on Windsor Terrace. Each of these memories, like the thread of a spider's web, circled around the one person at their center, the one person associated with each, and it was still so painful to think about him. And sometimes, though she'd fight off the urge, though she tried hard to resist, she'd get out her cell phone to look at the pictures they'd taken on their motorcycle tour around the city and her heart would break again.

It was on one of those occasions, an evening when Liz and Craig had gone to a movie with the Zimmers and she had stayed home on the ranch to babysit the boys, after she had Buck and Bran down for the night and she had curled up on the sofa in the front room, alone with a book—and her memories—she gave in once again. She slipped her phone out of her pocket and scrolled to the "New York" album.

There they were again, the photos of Bart and her. Pictures at the marina, at Gracie Mansion, at the Dyckman House, photos from Harlem and the Brooklyn Bridge.

But her favorite was the one in Central Park, that Tuesday when she'd gone to meet him at Tavern on the Green. The kids in the playground had been all around him, and he had just slipped off his helmet for a moment and brushed his hand through his hair. The sun highlighted its reddish sandy color that she'd found so appealing and she'd snapped the photo just as he'd started to walk toward her, with the beginning of a welcoming smile. She could stare at that photo for long minutes, for it caught all his easy, virile grace as he came to meet her, and as deeply as it hurt, she was never able to scroll quickly past it. She would have long make-believe conversations with his silent photo and make them come out in various ways—self-serving, self-punishing, even sometimes self-aware. Sometimes his part was angry. Sometimes he was sorry. Sometimes he was silent.

Oh, Bart. Where did we go wrong? I thought we had something good between us, something special.

Tonight, alone in the house, with the boys asleep and nothing to distract her attention, she allowed herself a long, long time with that photo. And she was silent, too.

She wondered if she'd ever get over him. Liz assured her she would. She didn't think so.

She put the phone back in her pocket.

There was a pile of magazines on the coffee table, copies of *Feed-Lot* and PRCA's *Pro Rodeo*, a *People* magazine and *Good House-keeping* and *Lady Fair* (of course), a Globex printout of yesterday's futures quotes on cattle, a couple of promos from Nutrena and Purina Mills, a newsletter from the Drovers' Association, and a copy of *Beef Magazine*. She picked the *People* magazine out of the pile and leafed through it absentmindedly. She paused at a story about Britain's royal family. There was a feature on Prince Harry, William's younger brother, playing polo. A close-up of his face. She decided he looked like Bart—the same crinkly, reddish-sandy-colored hair, the same tall athletic build. The same sweet boyish face—with a little mischief in his smile.

"Oh, damn!"

She was seeing Bart everywhere.

"I'm obsessed with that man. And you know, Annie," she said aloud to herself and to the empty room, "you *know* he's long since forgotten you. How can you be so stupid?"

She tossed the magazine back onto the coffee table.

She silenced her phone.

She went to bed and cried herself to sleep.

But of course Bart hadn't forgotten her. How could he? He was a man in love—and he was a man with a plan. For a couple of months, ever since that visit to his mom, he'd been busy making arrangements. And tomorrow morning he'd be ready to take the last step.

He was smiling when he turned out the light and went to sleep.

With summer's end, classes would be starting soon and Annie took advantage of a quiet Saturday to be alone in the library to get things ready for the onslaught. A certain amount of lifting and hauling would be needed, so she'd dressed grungy and had snagged her hair up into a pile on top of her head with a pencil twisted through it to hold it in place. She'd had nothing but a Pop-Tart for breakfast; the library cafe would be closed until classes started and she was thinking of having a pizza brought in. Or maybe a sandwich. When the phone rang, she was in the middle of deciding. Sandwich? Or pizza?

"Hey, Annie." It was Liz. "Whatcha doin'?"

"Just working. Thinking of getting something to eat."

"Oh." Liz said nothing for a moment.

"Liz. Why are you calling?"

"Nothing special. Just felt like saying hello. Can't a sister call and just say hello?"

"You're up to something. You never call just to chat. What's up?"

"Nothing at all. Just wondered if you'd be there at the library all afternoon. It's such a gorgeous day, I thought maybe you'd have gone out, gone for a ride or something."

"Well, I'm not coming home for lunch, if that's what you mean. I'll be here at least till about four."

"Oh, good." She seemed to catch herself. "I mean, good that I'll know not to fix lunch for you."

"Liz, you're being weird."

"No. Just a little bit overworked. You know how it can be. But that's fine. I'll see you tonight. When you get home. Bye."

And Annie was left standing there, looking at the silent phone in her hand and shaking her head.

"Well, whatever."

And she forgot all about Liz's call.

She ordered a pizza and went back to work.

A half hour passed. The pizza was half eaten. She gave no more thought to the gorgeous day. A box full of *Horse Sense* binders had been donated to the library, and she was concentrating on cataloguing them. She took a minute to leaf through some of the pages. It was a nice little local newspaper out of Salt Lake. Too bad it folded. But someone had liked it enough to collect a full set. And thank goodness for libraries, where such treasures could be preserved.

Another half hour passed. The sun had moved on and the room was in half shadow. She was finishing up the donated papers, and considering packing up for the day. She could go back to the ranch for dinner, but there were days when it was hard to be with the family when she was feeling—well, almost like an outsider, when she felt so unnecessary to their busy activities that she'd actually prefer to be by herself. Being alone too much wasn't good for her, either. She knew that. But maybe she could think up some other project to keep her there for just another hour or two

So, what to do?

And the silent library gave her no answer.

She could almost listen to her own breathing.

Go home? Or more work?

And then a voice behind her said, "Do you have room for a new student here?"

Not the voice of a student. This was a man's voice.

She sat up straighter. She tried to breathe. She knew that voice. But it couldn't be.

"Annie?"

Her breath caught in her throat. She felt herself beginning to cry.

She turned and yes, it was Bart, and she was out of her chair and into his arms, all in one motion and yes, she was crying and he was saying, "Don't cry, honey. Don't cry. Everything's going to be okay. Really. I've fixed everything and it's all going to be okay. And I'm not going to be a horse's ass any more. Really!" And that made her laugh and cry at the same time, so when he kissed her, her tears were all salty in his mouth, and he was laughing, too, and he felt so good in her arms, she knew that yes, everything was going to be okay after all.

They were like that, like two idiots, for long, delicious minutes, and then they calmed down and he held her a little away from himself and looked at her with all the love he was feeling and he took the pencil out of her hair and let all that beautiful blond hair gather around her face and he buried his hands in her hair and was almost crying himself, he was so glad to have her back. And she thought, he really does look a little like Prince Harry, but she'd never tell him that and she loved his sweet smile and his crinkly hair and she loved that he was still bossy enough to have fixed everything—whatever that meant.

There were couches in the reading room, comfy enough for them to curl up close to each other. His arm held her close to his chest and he could brush the top of her hair with his cheek.

"You should have known I couldn't stay away from you. I was no good to anyone after you left and the captain told me I'd better get my head straight or he was going to send me to psych services. He told me to take some time off and get some rest and figure out what was going on. So I did something even better. I went and talked to my mom. She made me realize I'd let a lot of dumb stuff get in the way of what you and I had going for us. Male ego, or something, I guess. You did a spectacular job, finding Lindy when the rest of us couldn't, and I love you for it. I really do. And by the way, my mom thinks you're not only a super person. She said she knew you were the right girl for me the minute she met you."

"She did?"

"Her words were, 'I thought now here's a girl who's good enough for my Bart.' It was like she wished she could hand you to me like a present, all wrapped up in tissue paper and red ribbons. And here I'd gone and driven you away. So dumb."

"I really like your mom, too. Where would we be without her?"

"We'd be two very sorry people. And I couldn't let that happen."

"So?"

"So here's what I've done. Are you ready?"

She took a deep breath. A wary deep breath.

"I'm ready."

"Okay. Here it is. I made some inquiries, I wrote some letters, I jumped through a few hoops. And I got myself a job as the newest member of the Laramie police force!"

"You what!"

"Yep. I filled out a bunch of forms. I flew out to Cheyenne when you weren't looking and took some tests and got myself interviewed. And they thought I'd do just fine. I said I thought they might be able to use a big-city cop, a sergeant with five years' experience, and they said, 'Well, we're just a bunch of small-town country boys out here, but we might still have a few things to teach you,' and we all laughed. They had my number right away."

"I don't know what to say."

"Well, don't say anything yet. I'll tell you the rest."

He pulled her closer and kissed the top of her head. She closed her eyes.

"Go ahead," she said.

"After I got myself certified in Cheyenne, I came out here to Laramie. I managed to stay out of sight—from you, that is—and I did some quick research and rented a little house up at the edge of town. Just temporary, of course, till we work things out. Then I went back to New York. I'd already resigned from the New York force and I convinced them it was time for Lindy to retire. He's fifteen years old—and he's earned a rest. They agreed and I was able to buy him back. He was always sort of the Hardins' horse, anyway. I bought a horse trailer, and got a hitch for it, and I've brought him out here so he can smell the air of the place where he was born, and run free in the fields, and not have to be in danger any more. He won't have to pose for tourists and do tricks for theater people. Of course, you can whistle that song for him any time you like."

He kissed her hair again.

"God, I love the feel of your hair," he said.

"I still don't know what to say."

"There's more," he said. "I got here—with Lindy—this morning. I went to the ranch, thinking I'd surprise you, but you'd already left. So I talked to Liz and Craig—super people they are—and I met the boys, too, and they were a hoot, seemed to think I'm a big deal because I'm a cop. And Liz and Craig offered me a deal—they offered to board Lindy on your property, as long as I promised to marry you and take good care of you, and if ever I don't, they're both going to come and kill me. It was an offer I couldn't refuse."

She was staring at him wide-eyed. Stunned. With tears brimming up.

"Are you proposing to me?"

"I think I just did."

She was trying to catch hold of this whole whirlwind that had just descended on her.

"But Bart, all this summer, while you were making all these arrangements, without telling me, how could you be sure I hadn't already met someone else, gotten involved? Maybe even gotten married? I had no word from you at all. You had no way of knowing I hadn't found someone else."

He looked at her in amazement.

"How could you have found anyone else? You were already in love with me."

And now the tears were falling, and she burrowed into his chest to hide them.

"Oh, Bart, you are such a sweet, sweet, fool."

"But I'm not a horse's ass, am I?"

Still burrowing into his chest, she shook her head. "No, not at all."

"So is that a yes? You'll marry me?"

"Oh, you knew it all along, didn't you? You knew I would. Even when I didn't know it."

"So say yes."

She looked up at him and smiled at him through her tears and said:

"Yes, Bart. Yes. Of course. Of course I'll marry you."

Epilogue

Happily Ever After

Labor Day

The town wouldn't let them get away with a quiet, private wedding.

The hullaballoo over Annie's return from New York had finally settled down, but then it got started up all over again when news got around that the horse Annie Cornell had rescued, and the hero cop from New York who owned him, a fellow named Bart Hardin, had come to live in Laramie. Folks sniffed out the romance right away and fell in love with the whole story. Reporters came from all over the state to do a piece on them, local TV stations wanted them for interviews, school children were brought round to look at them, and every club wanted them to join. Poor Annie and Bart, they couldn't find a moment's peace. They tried to hide out at the cute little house Bart had rented, where they could plan a simple wedding—and spend what they called "quality time" together. But neighbors kept coming round to visit and people would stop their cars out front to take pictures of their home.

At first, Annie thought Bart couldn't possibly give up his beloved New York, but Bart was having so much fun, learning to be a westerner, pointy boots, cowboy hat and all, she finally stopped worrying. Between them, they agreed that any time he really needed to, they'd manage to find a way to go back for a visit, walk its streets, ride its subways, visit Sergei and eat a hot dog, cross the bridge to Brooklyn, and breathe in the city's special atmosphere, its mix of pollutants that ought to kill its residents but somehow doesn't.

"And will you love me even though there isn't enough humidity here to fluff up my hair," Annie said.

"Oh, honey, I'm going to love you when your hair is all gray and stringy. And mine is all gone. I do love your hair, Annie, but that's not why I love *you*. You better know that."

"And why do you love me, Bart? Tell me again."

"I love you because even though you look like an angel, you have a will and a backbone of iron, and even though you have an iron will and an iron backbone, you still need to be taken care of. And I love you because you're willing to let me be the one to take care of you."

Annie wore flowers in her hair and a lovely white gown from one of the local bridal shops in town. She'd had enough fussing over clothes to last a lifetime and she loved the traditional white dress she found at Miss Mae's Brides on Second Street. The town loved the romance of their story, what with her being such a celebrity and all, and Bart, following her all the way from New York City to marry her. There was no way Laramie would let them have the quiet, simple wedding they'd planned, so they gave up and made a big barbecue wedding on the Cornell ranch, with Craig giving her away, and Max coming out to be best man. Liz was her matron of honor and, because the boys made a fuss, each one wanting to be the ring bearer, they each got to carry a ring—Brandon for Bart and Buckley for Annie.

Bart's mom was there, crying a couple of tears of happiness, and the Malones came down from their ranch up by Sheridan, eager to meet Bart's bride, and delighted that the New York branch of the family was finding its way back to God's country.

Troop B sent a great framed photo portrait of the whole group with each rider mounted, signatures all over. Captain Simon sent a warning that Bart better learn to rope steers, because that little slip of a thing he was marrying had a mind of her own and he better not let himself be bullied. He also wrote that the local theater community was donating a plaque to be put up over Lindy's stall to honor a valiant and beloved horse.

Mitzi sent a gorgeous crystal bowl, and Sylvie Pilard, on behalf of Galliard's, sent a sterling silver Champagne cooler which, had Annie and Bart known its cost, would have been wrapped up and placed in a safe deposit box. Fortunately, they did not realize its cost, so it was destined to live permanently on the counter in their kitchen, right next to the toaster and the food processor. Marge Webster sent a full service of sterling flatware from *Lady Fair*. She also wrote that the magazine wanted to do a follow-up on their amazing story. Bart thought it might be fun, but Annie and Liz nixed that idea.

Lindy also had flowers in his hair—in his mane, that is. And, as the barbecue happened right there on the ranch, he was able to be close by as Annie and Bart said "I do" and exchanged rings. And afterwards, when the band played the Wyoming fight song, Lindy tossed his mane and danced all around the field, doing steps no one had ever taught him, a Lindy version of pure pleasure and gratitude, because he'd been brought back to the high country of his birth where he could breathe its sweet air and run free over its endless terrain. And, God willing, there'd be little ones again who'd teach him tricks and climb up on his back and ride him bareback just for fun.

And so they all lived happily ever after.

Please turn the page for an exciting sneak peek at
J.M. Bronston's next contemporary romance
SUMMER ON THE CAPE
coming in May 2016 wherever e-books are sold!

Chapter One

Damn Adam!
Allie's fury was almost audible.

How did I allow him to talk me into this!

The little plane dropped several feet, wobbling as the pilot righted it, and a weak cry escaped from Allie's lips. She leaned her head back and closed her eyes, her hands gripping the edge of her seat.

I should never have agreed! Adam knows perfectly well I have important projects coming up.

The tiny commuter plane pitched and slogged along its course, like a toy powered by rubber bands, and Allie's fingers dug deeper into the seat.

Two new commissions and a couple of possible new clients. And there's the show at the Whiscombe Gallery in July. I have no business being away from New York for the whole summer.

The bouncing plane bucked a heavy headwind, and it helped her steady her nerves to lay the blame on Adam. She had completely forgotten that the night before, when he set up this trip, she had been enthusiastic and eager to participate.

If he was right about it—and Adam was always right—it would be a real money maker. And it would be a big career move for her, too. That's what she'd thought last night. Now, the only thing she wanted was to get this awful flight over with and be safely on the ground again.

She took a couple of deep breaths, opened her eyes and forced herself to relax and let herself look around. She hadn't known commercial planes could be so small. The cramped cabin space wasn't any bigger than the kitchen of her little apartment back in Manhattan. The aisle running between the nine little bucket seats was so narrow that even a slim woman like Allie had to twist uncomfortably to get to her seat and, although she was only an inch or two above average height, she had to bend her head and hunch her shoulders as she walked through.

Right in front of her, the pilot and copilot were chatting comfortably with each other, apparently at home with the mysterious panel of switches, winking lights, and quivering dials spread out before them. Allie took little comfort from their breezy manner and wished they would just pay attention to flying this little crate all the way to Cape Cod without incident. She was willing to bet that the other two passengers were, like her, clutching silently at their seats and praying that the fates would deliver them safely back to solid ground.

She forced her mind back to this scheme of Adam's, wishing she knew more about it. Last night at dinner, he'd been pretty cagey about the details, saying that he wasn't yet "at liberty" to disclose more than the barest outline. He'd taken her to a fancy little bistro over on the East Side that was one of his favorite places for twisting her arm and talking her into doing things she didn't want to do. And just about all she could get out of him, over the perfectly chilled Taittinger and the exquisite caviar, was that some big-shot clients of his would need promotional artwork for a major development project. Instead of her usual portraits, he wanted her to spend the summer at his place on Cape Cod so she could put together a portfolio of seascapes.

And then he'd said an odd thing. He'd said, "You're a good American, Allie. This project should appeal to your patriotic spirit." And that was all she could find out.

"You sly devil," she'd said to him, as the waiter filled their glasses. "You've got something up that well-tailored sleeve of yours."

"Nothing nefarious, my dear, I can assure you," Adam had said in that patrician way he had, as he spooned caviar onto small points of toast. "And you can turn off that suspicious glint in your gaze," he said fondly. "Your eyes are much too gentle for such hard looks." Adam's cool smile always softened when he talked to Allie.

Allie brushed her bangs back. "So this scheme of yours is not at all improper?"

"No, Allie, this is straight business. The plan is still in a very pre-liminary stage, and all I can say at this point is that some clients of mine are interested in a land development project on Cape Cod." He sprinkled a drop or two of lemon juice over the caviar and handed her the toast. "Have you ever been to the Cape?"

"I'm a working girl, Adam, and Cape Cod is for the rich and fa-mous. And anyway," she nibbled at the caviar, savoring its nutty oili-ness, "I'm also a city person, born and bred. What would I do on those barren beaches and sandy, windswept shores? Without the city's traffic and racket around me, I'd probably shrivel up and blow away."

"You won't shrivel up. You'll get a little sun and some streaks in your hair." He contemplated her honey-colored hair, reaching just below her shoulders, the full, rich waves glowing in the soft light of the little restaurant, beautifully set off by her pale silk dress and the pearls he'd given her on her birthday. "With your coloring," he said approvingly, "you'll look wonderful. And you're wrong about the rich and famous. Plenty of ordinary folks live on the Cape, too. And Provincetown, up at the tip of the Cape, has been an artists' colony for many decades. A very famous one."

"Well, of course I know that, Adam."

How could she explain to Adam? Any place with even a whiff of wealth felt forbidding to her.

"All right, Allie. You know you can trust my judgment." He leaned back in his chair, sipping his wine and smiling expansively at her.

It was true. In the ten years that Adam Talmadge had been her agent—ever since he'd discovered her, a raw sixteen-year-old at the Art Students' League—he'd not been wrong once. That's a tough record to beat, she admitted to herself begrudgingly.

"If this works out as I anticipate," he continued, "it's going to be very good for you and, just incidentally of course, at fifteen percent of your fee, it's going to be good for me, too." Then he had sketched out his proposal: She was to spend the summer on the Cape, painting seascapes. She could return, as necessary, to the city, to keep up with prior commitments, commissions already agreed to, and for her show, coming up at the Whiscombe Gallery in a few weeks. It was only an hour's flight by commuter plane between Provincetown and the Westchester County airport, just north of New York City. She could prepare a portfolio of studies suitable for use in a Cape Cod development project, paintings full of the clear air, the sandy stretches of beach, the sea gulls, the sailboats.

"But, Adam—"

"You'll enjoy this scheme of mine," he said, in a placating tone. "And don't worry. I'll explain fully when it's jelled a bit more."

"But, Adam—" Allie was running out of objections.

"Allie, it's a great place, right on the beachfront. There's some space in the house where you can paint. The caretaker will meet you at the airport in Provincetown." Adam had been so sure she'd agree, he'd already made all the arrangements. "Here's a card with his name on it. And here's the plane ticket. You leave from Westchester airport at three o'clock tomorrow afternoon, so go home and pack a few things"—he smiled affectionately at her—"and you can stop being so obstinate!"

Obstinate, indeed.

Well, Allie knew it was true. She couldn't help it. She had a quick flash point and couldn't stand being bossed. But there were good reasons. And right from the beginning, Adam had understood. Adam Talmadge didn't get to be number one in his business without having a super-sharp sensitivity to people in general and to artists in particular, and he recognized, in Allie Randall, an unusual combination of fine artistic temperament and hard-nosed practicality.

And, because he always made it his business to know everything about his clients, he knew what no one else did. He knew how Allie had learned, much too early in her life, that she would not survive unless she had an absolute self-reliance, an utter assurance that she could rely on her own resources. And because he knew the terrible origin of Allie's fierce independence, he was always careful not to trample on it. With the smooth-talking skill that worked so well on patrons, dealers and gallery owners, he knew how to get around her stubborn spirit while still reassuring her that she wasn't giving up any of her hard-won self-reliance.

So, by the end of their dinner, Allie had agreed to spend the summer at Adam's place on Cape Cod; and by the time Adam's driver had dropped her off at her apartment in the Village, her mind was racing ahead, making plans for the summer.

She had run up the four flights to her apartment, stopping on her way down the hall to knock on her neighbor's door. She wanted someone with a sympathetic ear to keep her company while she packed her things, and Maria, her neighbor and best friend for the last seven years, had the most sympathetic ear in New York City.

"Come on, Maria. Come on." Allie barely waited to explain as Marie got all the bolts and locks on her door opened, and stuck her dark, curly-topped head out into the hall. "I need some help packing. Come on!" Allie was already down the hall, unlocking the door of her own apartment. "I'll tell you all about it." Maria dropped everything. She told her husband, Steve, to mind the baby and joined Allie in her apartment.

Allie packed her suitcase as though she were throwing darts at a board, scooping her clothes out of dresser drawers and closets and flinging them at the suitcase. Maria smiled indulgently as she retrieved the jeans and shirts and underthings that Allie tossed about, and she repacked them in neat stacks. She listened patiently while Allie told her what little she knew of the revised plans for the summer and complained about being bossed around. She made Allie a cup of tea and got her to sit down for a bit.

"You know, Allie," she said, reassuringly, "a summer in a house on one of America's most beautiful beaches is not exactly a bad thing."

"But all my plants. What about all my plants?" Allie was digging under her bed, searching for her old deck shoes.

"Leave me a key. I'll keep them watered."

"You're a doll." Allie sat up, brushing at her dusty hair and tossing the retrieved shoes into the suitcase on the bed. "And in an emergency, call Adam." She grabbed a scrap of paper and wrote on it. "Here's his number. He's got a key to the apartment, too. If there's any problem, call him. He'll know how to reach me."

Finally, the suitcase was packed. Allie's nervous excitement was a little bit soothed and Maria left, taking Allie's extra key and promising to be in touch with Adam, if necessary.

And now, as she clung nervously to her seat, Allie tried to think ahead, to the summer that lay before her. She wouldn't have to do a thing except work. The man who took care of the house when it was empty would meet her at the airport, and he'd keep an eye on things for her.

Allie pulled her bag out from the clutter she'd just created and rummaged around in it until she found the business card Adam had given her in the restaurant.

Zachariah Eliot. *Now that's a good name for a caretaker*, she thought. Nice and trustworthy. A good Yankee name. Sounds like he stepped right off the Mayflower. Allie leaned her head back and closed her eyes again. Well, that's all right. If he's got an interesting face, maybe I'll do his portrait sometime this summer, behind Adam's back. She told herself that it would be a welcome change from painting the rich and powerful.

On the ground, Zach Eliot waited for the flight from New York. Cindy, at the desk in the little terminal building, had told him the plane would be arriving soon, so he'd come outside to watch for it. Looking out over the silver tops of the scrub pine trees that surrounded the airfield, he narrowed his eyes against the sun, searching impatiently for some sign that the plane was arriving.

He looked at his watch. *Damn*, he said to himself. *I don't have time for this*. At this time of the year he was needed down at the harbor, and the plane had already been delayed a couple of hours, really messing up his plans for the day. He leaned his long frame back against the white-painted cinder block wall of the terminal and looked at his watch again, trying to control his irritation.

He knew, of course, what was really bothering him, and it wasn't that he had to get back to the boats. It was that he'd been sent to pick up this woman who was on the plane. Not that he cared who Adam had in his house. That was entirely Adam's affair, and if Adam wanted to have a girl there, it was all right with Zach.

But ever since this other thing, this damned project, Zach had been in no mood to accommodate anything or anyone associated with Adam Talmadge. When Adam's secretary had called to notify him that this woman—what was her name? Allie Randall—was going to be on the three o'clock plane, he'd been about to tell her that Adam could go screw himself.

But he'd held his tongue. There was going to be plenty of trouble over this development scheme of Adam's, and the time for the real fight between them was still down the road. When that time came, there would be many changes, and this old arrangement—providing transportation from the airport—would be ending. In the meantime, he would continue to honor it. The Talmadges had set it up with Zach's father when they first started to rent their house on beach, back when Zach was just a kid, and he didn't like to terminate an old custom.

He looked at his watch one more time. *Damn!* Well, he couldn't do anything at this minute to stop Adam and that bunch of barracudas he was representing. And there was also not a damn thing he could do to bring that plane in any sooner. Zach thrust his hands deep into the pockets of his jeans, rested his head back against the wall and closed his eyes, letting the sun warm his face.

Bad weather in the New York area had delayed their take-off from Westchester for more than two hours, and heavy winds still buffeted the plane as it made its way above Long Island Sound. Allie watched in fearful fascination as the plane's wings rocked on either side of her like a seesaw.

Pressing her forehead against the window, she stared down at the water, three thousand feet below her, the wind-whipped whitecaps visible on the surface even at this height. Through thick, swirling patches of cloud, she could see the little towns along the Connecticut coast, and, in their harbors, the bright clusters of sailboats, jerking at their moorings in the choppy water, the rough waves breaking up against the shoreline.

Abruptly, as though she'd been slapped, Allie recognized the real source of her anxiety. A wash of terrible memory clutched deep inside her body.

Of course. The recognition came with heart-wrenching clarity. Of course.

The bad weather, the rough waters below her. How could she not feel fearful? Inevitably, like cold hands over her face, it all came back.

It was down there, in one of those little seaside towns where rich people had their summer homes and where they kept their pretty sailboats in the town marinas, that she'd had to go to claim her father's body. The Coast Guard had been holding him in a horrible little local morgue, and a union representative had been sent to her home in the Bronx to tell her of her father's death. She was a few months short of her eighteenth birthday, barely old enough, they thought, to handle the details, so the Coast Guard officer told her only that the winds of a sudden winter storm had swept her father from the deck of the barge as it fought its way through the waves. What they didn't tell her, she already knew. Probably he'd been drinking. They thought a girl who was still in her teens should be shielded from such harsh realities. But it was too late for that. Allie Randall already had a firm grip on reality, in all its harshness.

Those men at the morgue had no way to know, but Allie had been handling "the details" ever since her mother's death, six years earlier. While Mike Randall, bereft, sank into ever-lengthening periods of bitter self-pity, raging against his fate, his daughter took on the care of their shabby little house on Etheridge Street, a sad little fringe of a decaying old neighborhood in the Bronx, only steps from the river, under a dirty network of railroad bridges and factory smokestacks. Young as she was, she quickly learned to manage the real demands of everyday life. She learned to manage the meager wages Mike earned working the barges along the Sound, and on the infrequent nights that he came home, she had a hot meal ready for him—and stayed clear of his helpless rages as he grew increasingly hard on himself and everyone else. He drank too much and, though he never struck her, she learned to be wary around him.

In time, the little girl became glad that her father was rarely home. Mike needed comfort far more than he could give it, and so the little girl mourned the loss of her mother alone.

Who can say why it was that Allie found her own comfort in the little sketches that began to fill her notebooks? What moved her to capture the radiant beauty of the color-filled sky and the shifting tints and hues of the trees and houses around her? In the evenings, when her schoolwork and her housework were done, the lonely little girl painted pictures of everything she had seen that day – the sky and the bridges and the people on the streets. It was almost enough to make up for the loss of a normal home and family. Almost. But she could never put aside her fantasies about the others, the girls at school who, she was sure, went home to ideal families, to warm kitchens and happy laughter and loving parents. Too proud to allow anyone to know the sad circumstances of her life, she learned to move unobtrusively among her classmates, drawing little attention to herself, making no close friends, and becoming an observer rather than observed.

Like so many lonely and neglected children, she watched from outside the circle of other girls' popularity. But for Allie, this was not the sad place of isolation and resentment that it might have been. With the clear eye and the exquisite sensitivity of the skilled artist she was becoming, it brought her profound pleasure to pay close attention to the ways emotion and character were revealed in faces and body language, to feel her talent and her art as they gathered strength inside her and built a force against the demons of envy and self-doubt that are so often the results of poverty and isolation. Gradually, the pages of her sketchbooks filled with drawings of people from the world around her, faces seen in the school's lunchroom, in home room, on the streets of her neighborhood, and in the shops where she bought her groceries: brilliant portraits, quickly captured.

Inevitably, her teachers recognized her talent and with their help, before her junior year, Allie was granted a full scholarship at an exclusive prep school where her talent would be properly developed. It was a prize plum, rarely awarded.

But there are no pure pleasures, and the price Allie paid for her scholarship was the ostracism by some of her new classmates; rich kids who, with their privilege and a meanness of spirit, tried their best to make her miserable. Their message was clear. She should understand that despite her scholarship and her presence in their midst, she was an intruder; there were doors that would never open for her, there were worlds that would never welcome her, there were places where she would never belong. Though they couldn't break her spirit and they couldn't take away her talent—for that became still more powerful as her sword and shield—they did make wounds that her later maturity and experience could only veil but never fully heal. The damage had been done.

The cool window of the plane felt good against Allie's forehead. She lifted her gaze from the water below, and stared straight out into the sky, empty except for misty clouds, empty except for the memories of that cold night, the cold morgue, her father's body cold on a gurney. Memories of her life after Mike Randall's death.

Her years of managing home and finances and her obvious independence and competence made it easy for the union staff to provide for her legal guardianship for the few months remaining until her eighteenth birthday, so she was able to stay at home and continue at her school. There'd been a small insurance policy, enough to get her through a year or two and, as she stood by her father's drowned body, Allie offered up a sort of truce to her many losses. She would not let self-pity hold her back. She was determined to use the grace period the insurance money provided to begin to build her own life on the twin pillars of her talent and her stubborn independence.

She rarely thought now about those hard times. Success was becoming a reality, and she was beginning to enjoy the fruits of her hard work. Adam had encouraged her to concentrate on portraits, and she was already being recognized as one of New York's most gifted young portrait painters. There were many blessings to count and she was grateful for each of them.

She sighed deeply once or twice, and closed the door again on the bad memories. With both hands, she brushed her ragged bangs back from her forehead and looked around her – and realized, as the plane continued on to Cape Cod, that her anxiety had disappeared..

The plane swung out over the ocean to make its approach to the windswept landing strip outside Provincetown. Allie watched, fascinated, through the front window, over the pilot's shoulder, as they flew low over the blue ocean, over white waves at the shore's edge and then over pale yellow beach fringed by green-tipped dunes. The runway lay straight ahead of them, flat and bare in the intermittent sunshine and a strong crosswind bounced the little Cessna up and down as it made its wobbling descent onto the field. To her amazement, the pilot looked totally unconcerned, making a perfectly smooth landing and taxiing the plane up to the terminal building as gently as a grandma wheeling a baby's stroller through the park. After the door opened, Allie let the other passengers leave ahead of her, and took a minute to catch her breath, glad to be on solid ground.

She had to scrunch down to step through the low doorway onto the steps that were suspended from the plane's door opening, and she grasped the frame to steady herself as she stepped onto the tarmac. Then she stood up straight and shifted her carry-on bag by its shoulder strap to be more comfortable. A shaft of sunlight broke through the cloud cover, and a light breeze sent a strand of hair across her brow. She lifted her hand to brush it back. She paused and looked around.

* * *

Zach heard the plane's engine as it taxied down the runway, coming to a stop not far from the terminal building. He opened his eyes and watched as Sonny Boardman, the mechanic, ran out to the plane and opened its little door, letting down the attached steps. A couple of passengers got out, but neither of them could be Adam's guest. He recognized the first person out of the plane, Jim Sargent's girl, Molly, back from school for the summer. The second was a businessman carrying a briefcase and two tennis rackets, probably coming up to the Cape for a long weekend.

A few moments passed and, through the plane's windows, Zach could see that only one passenger remained. At last she came through the door and down the steps. As he watched her from across the field, she stopped and shifted her bag on her shoulder. There was a sudden break in the cloud cover, and a shaft of light fell on her as she lifted her arm and brushed her hair back from her eyes.

Zach Eliot was stopped dead in his tracks.

He had the extraordinary sensation that the sunshine had come with her, breaking across the field just as she'd stepped from the plane, bathing the tarmac and the trees and the terminal building, and yes, Zach himself, with its warmth. As though it was for his benefit alone, the wind lifted her hair, and she brought up a hand to hold the strands away from her face, displaying, with that simple gesture, a lithe femininity that sent a tightening quiver through Zach's body. She was looking away from him, toward the trees that surrounded the field, and she seemed to be savoring the light and the sweet summer scents that filled the air.

The late afternoon sun, glowing behind her, lit the thick waves of her honey-gold hair, and the light breeze moved it gently away from her shoulders. In her slim figure, clad in white pants and jacket, poised against the breeze, with one arm raised, Zach saw gentle grace and quick energy combined in one lovely form.

He was totally stunned. It wrenched his gut to admit it, but damn it, Adam Talmadge had found himself an absolute knockout. With an effort, Zach forced himself into motion. He straightened up and walked across the field to meet her.

Allie looked around the airfield, made a quick study of her new surroundings, and understood immediately why artists liked to work

here. The light across the field was flat and clear, as if it came up from the ground instead of down from the sky. She liked the way it lit up the undersides of the low trees that surrounded the field. She liked the way the wind blew in from the ocean and lifted the hair away from her face.

And she had seen something else she liked right away. He was tall and slim and had a comfortable way of leaning against the wall of the terminal building. Allie had sketched hundreds of gorgeous male bodies in her art classes and her professional eye saw immediately that the body inside those tight jeans and denim work shirt was as lean and hard and healthy as any of them. He had strong hard-working muscles and a kind of easy, masculine grace that, even at a distance, had a surprisingly stirring effect on her.

He was walking across the field now, and she had a chance to get a good look at him in the bright sunlight. *Now, that*, she said to herself, *is an astoundingly good-looking man!* She let her eyes run over his body as he walked toward her, liking the look of his legs in the smooth jeans, the easy strength of his well-formed forearms, exposed by the rolled-up sleeves of his work shirt. With the experienced eye of a first-rate portrait artist, Allie did a quick inventory of his face. He had blue eyes set deep under strong black eyebrows, and black hair, cut short, trimmed close at the temples, where the gray was beginning to show. His mouth was wide and full, humorous; between deep furrows in a face so darkly tanned she knew he must spend most of his time outdoors.

She was especially attracted to that mouth. It was a mouth that would be quick to smile, quick to laugh. She recognized strength and poise reflected there. But there was something else, something she could not clearly identify. It was Allie's business to be especially sensitive to the emotions that were revealed—or concealed—by faces, and in this one there was evidence of a deep sorrow. But she saw also the self-control in this handsome, mature face, and she knew he'd be slow to reveal to anyone what lay behind that sorrow.

Her examination of him was brought to a sudden halt. To her surprise, he stopped in front of her and spoke her name: "Miss Randall?"

"Yes, I'm Allie Randall." How did he know her name? Then, abruptly, she realized that this very good-looking, sexy man must be

the one Adam had said would meet her. She'd been expecting a much older man. Certainly no one who looked like this! "You must be Mr. Eliot. Mr. Talmadge told me you'd be meeting my plane. I do appreciate your picking me up."

His response puzzled her. Some men had a way of undressing a woman with their eyes. Allie knew what that felt like and she knew how to handle it. This was different. This man was almost caressing her with his gaze, and yet, at the same time there was something angry in his expression. And his words, though polite, were just barely so, his tone unnecessarily brusque.

"No problem, Miss Randall," he said curtly. He took Allie's carry-on bag out of her hand and, with a quick gesture, slung it over his shoulder. "As soon as your things are off the plane, I'll get them out to the truck. I'll be able to drive you to the house but I can't take any more time to show you around." The irritation in his voice was unmistakable. "The harbor master's waiting for me down at the dock."

What's the matter with the man? She wondered. *And what's the matter with me? If I'd known he was going to be so rude, I wouldn't have given that handsome face a second look, much less such a thoughtful analysis. A "deep sorrow," indeed!* Allie could feel her own defensiveness spring up protectively around her. She'd barely arrived on Cape Cod, and already the natives were hostile.

"I realize you must have a very busy schedule, Mr. Eliot," she said, as coolly as she could.

"Well, as a matter of fact, ma'am, at this time of the year, what with setting the moorings in the harbor and getting the boats in the water and all, we do get a little pressed for time." His tone matched hers for coolness. They both waited silently while her luggage was unloaded from the plane's wing lockers and set down next to where they were standing at the terminal door.

"It's all mine," Allie said, pointing to the suitcase and the several boxes of art supplies and easels. "I'm going to be working while I'm here."

"Working for Mr. Talmadge?" He bent to pick up her suitcase and Allie tried to keep her gaze away from the strong muscles of his back and arms, apparent even through the soft denim shirt.

"In a way. I'll be doing some work in connection with a project

he's interested in." The words were barely out of her mouth when she remembered; Adam had said not to talk about it.

She was startled by the intense look he gave her, peering darkly at her from under those black brows, as though something she'd said had angered him. "Adam's project, hm?" He paused momentarily, and then said, "I'll show you where the truck is out in front, and then I'll come back and get the rest of your things."

She followed him through the little terminal building, aware that, although she'd been infuriated by this irritating man, she felt a powerful impulse as she walked behind him to reach out and touch his back, to stroke that shoulder, to run her fingers down that strong arm and along the tanned skin that was exposed by the rolled-up sleeve.

If I were a sculptor, what a great model he'd be!

Embarrassed by her sudden, confused feelings, she stuffed her hands into the pockets of her jacket.

Zach opened the door of the terminal and walked over to a heavy-duty green Ford pick-up that was parked at the curb. He dropped her suitcase into the bed of the truck and then opened the door for her. Allie's breath caught momentarily as she took his hand, needing his help to step up to the passenger seat. His grip was firm and the touch of his rough skin, warm against the palm of her hand, sent a hot current running through her. She could feel the flush rising in her cheeks and, as she sat back on the seat, she turned her face away from him, afraid that he'd see her reaction. But he had already left, gone back to the field to get her boxes.

Allie needed a minute to regain her composure. She took a couple of deep breaths, letting the breeze that was blowing in from the ocean cool her off, bringing back her usual self-control. And while she waited for Zach to return with the rest of her things, she studied the interior of his truck, comparing it with the elegant, dark gray leather interior of Adam Talmadge's sleek town car. On the seat next to her, there was a large flashlight and a short coil of rope. A couple of screwdrivers and a long wrench had been tossed on top of the dashboard, along with a yellow paperback volume that had *Eldridge Tide and Pilot Book* printed on its cover. She rifled through the book, but its contents, full of tables and charts, were a mystery to her, and she returned it to the dashboard.

She ran her hand lightly over the screwdriver, the wrench, the tide book.

So that's Zachariah Eliot. Not at all what I expected. Much younger, of course, and extraordinarily, ruggedly handsome. With that amazing, craggy face, like something out of an old magazine ad.

But something's making him mad, and it seems to be me.